RHYME, RIDDLE, AND ROMANCE

FAERIES OF DOOR COUNTY

TONI CABELL

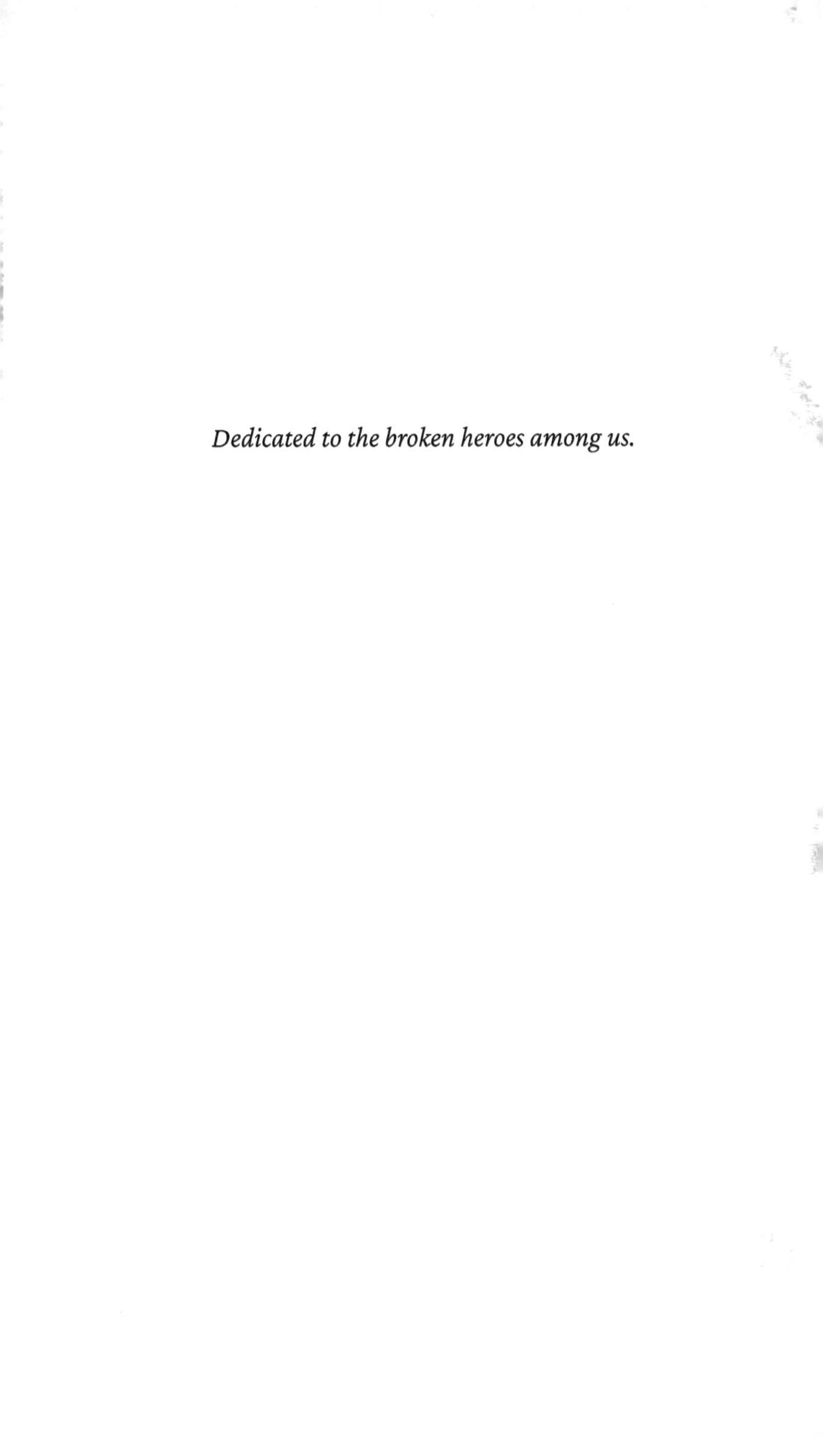

Dedicated to the broken heroes among us.

PREFACE

FAERIES OF DOOR COUNTY TIMELINE

Each book in the Faeries of Door County series is a standalone romance set in the same paranormal village of Riddle Hill, which means you can read them in any order. If you're new to the series and prefer to read in chronological order, then you're in the right place; *Rhyme, Riddle, and Romance* occurs the summer before the events of *Half a Faerie* and *Return to Mooncrest Inn*, which were published first.

Returning fans of the series, on the other hand, may be surprised to discover that rock star Will Rossi hasn't met Cassia Spellman yet, and Mona Lisa DeMaris hasn't thought about Jake Spellman in years (that's a lie, but Mona is still working as a cruise director in the Mediterranean).

Please don't blame the author; it's all Dragonfly Spellman's fault. The ancient faerie auntie has finally gone the way of her ancestors, but not before playing matchmaker one final time by sending Teddy Barker to the Rhyme 'N Riddle Bakeshop, where he meets his new boss, Sophie Spellman Brownlee.

Finally, a word about potential triggers. While this is a humorous, clean, and cozy paranormal romance, Rafe MacTire is the unrepentant villain of this tale; he is stalkerish, handsy, and a bully. Please be kind to yourself if you have any concerns about this content.

CHAPTER 1
DRAGONFLY SPELLMAN'S
LAST WILL AND TESTAMENT

SOPHIE

Friday, June 22

I unfurl my copper-and-green faerie wings, extending them as far as they'll reach, six feet, three inches on either side. Although a twelve-and-a-half foot wingspan is considered wide for a faerie woman, I'm not complaining. I can wrap my whole family in a feathery warm embrace, and they can't easily escape. Even my cousin Cassia, whose wings haven't manifested because she's half human and a complete bundle of nerves, just rolls her eyes when my feathers accidentally smack her in the face. She's my best friend, and most of the time I love her to pieces, except when she disagrees with me.

"Are you *sure* you don't want to make some discreet inquiries?" asks Cassia for the third time. She's on her knees scrubbing out the second-hand display cases I purchased from Vlad Lazar, who's refurbishing his gourmet grocery store down the street. That sweetie of a vampire practically gave them away to me, along with several of his killer cake recipes.

I arch my back and glance around the bakery-in-progress, courtesy of my recent inheritance. The garish red wallpaper is hanging down in strips, which Cassia and I have been slowly removing, leaving behind divots in the walls. The old oak floor is pockmarked, most of its finish worn away, and the street-facing windows are clouded and dirty. Only the tin ceiling has survived the ravages of age unscathed.

But when I close my eyes, I can clearly visualize the new Rhyme 'N Riddle Bakeshop: emerald green walls with ivory trim, several small, wrought-iron tables and chairs squeezed in front of the plate glass windows, and a row of gleaming display cases filled with mouth-watering desserts. For the walls, I'm thinking of hanging artsy posters like you might see in a New York bistro.

I know it's going to be just perfect.

What you *won't* see on these walls are any of my unalive ancestors, leaning out of their picture frames and offering dreary advice. My mother doesn't seem to mind, but frankly, they drive me almost as crazy as the gargoyles who blow raspberries every time I enter Mom's café across the street. Absolutely no mostly ghostly faerie ancestors will haunt my bakery, thank you very much.

Cassia is still waiting for a reply. I push a chunk of wavy brown hair out of my eyes and give my wings an emphatic little flap. "I have no intention of making any inquiries—discreet or otherwise. Owning ninety percent of the Rhyme 'N Riddle Bakeshop is just fine by me. I'm sure Auntie Dragonfly knew what she was doing when she insisted on bequeathing ten percent to Leslie T. Barker."

Cassia pushes herself off the floor, her soapy rag making little pitter-patters as it drips on the wood. "Auntie Dragonfly thought she was living in a villa off the coast of France for the past decade, instead of a musty old mansion in Michigan."

I burst out laughing. "It was pretty funny visiting her, especially when she demanded we speak only in French around her."

"My point exactly! Poor Auntie Dragonfly was losing almost as many marbles as wing feathers toward the end."

"I know you're only trying to look out for me. But I'm not worried about the mysterious ten-percent owner of my new bakery."

Cassia sniffs uncertainly. "If you say so."

I arch an eyebrow at my anxious cousin, who's three months older than me but acts like an overprotective auntie herself most days. She sighs but drops the subject.

If I'm being completely honest, I'll admit to being curious about my mysterious business partner and a teensy bit... concerned.

According to my great-aunt's will, I must use my inheritance to pursue my dream—opening a bakery in Riddle Hill, the only supernatural town in Wisconsin—and I must employ Leslie T. Barker at the bakery for one year. Further, I must provide Leslie with room and board, which isn't as onerous as it sounds. When I bought the shop, I also purchased the two-bedroom cottage that sits behind it.

After the year is up, I have the option of buying Leslie's ten percent ownership stake and asking her to make her own housing arrangements. The legal language, which makes my head hurt, also makes it abundantly clear I can't fire Leslie for twelve months. But if Leslie decides she doesn't want to work at the bakery and live behind the shop with me, she can walk away at any time, and then I'll have one year to buy her out.

That doesn't sound too awful to me. I can put up with anyone for twelve months. Besides, how unreliable can Leslie be? She was Auntie Dragonfly's companion for the past few years, although we've never actually met. Whenever I went to Michigan for the weekend, Leslie used the opportunity to visit her sister.

I retract my wings into the hidden slits in the back of my t-shirt and kneel down on the floor next to Cassia, who hands me a damp rag. She taps her phone, and we start singing along to the latest Roxie and Rossi album as we work. When we finish cleaning the display cases, we decide to tackle the wallpaper stripping again.

Ugh. I'd like to give a piece of my mind to whoever invented wallpaper. It may look nice when it's fresh and new, but removing it later is like peeling an onion one layer at a time with your fingernails.

I toss the scraping tool onto the floor in disgust. "At this rate we're never going to finish in time. I'm using magic!" The bakeshop's grand opening is a few weeks away, and there's so much to do I might start hyperventilating if I give it too much thought.

Cassia points at the drywall behind me, which looks like someone dragged a garden rake across its gouged, pitted surface. "But that's what happened the last time you tried! Aunt Phoebe specifically told you not to use magic again on these walls… they're not sturdy enough… and your magic isn't…"

"Stable enough," I grumble. "I know what Mom said, but I disagree. All my magic needs is a smidge more finesse. Now stand back."

Cassia scurries behind me as if she's afraid I'm going to bring the wall down on her head. Unfurling my wings with a powerful flap, I raise my hands and concentrate all my faerie magic on stripping the icky burgundy paper from the opposite wall. I close my eyes, feeling the power course through me, my wings vibrating with the sudden surge of energy.

I don't have a specific incantation in mind, and now I kind of wish I'd checked my old *Faerie Magick* textbook from high school. I'm pretty good at taking basic charms and adding useful little twists and modifications. And if I were a more studious faerie, I'd probably know half a dozen spells by heart that I could repurpose in the moment. I'd be more like my faerie parents instead of like… well, me.

It's too late now; I need to push on.

Cassia gasps, probably because she can see my magic swirling around me, which is a pretty cool gift, courtesy of her faerie father. She's the only person in our large extended family who actually *sees magic*, but I have no doubt she'd rather be able to cast spells like me. Sometimes I feel guilty because I manifested my faerie gifts when we were kids, and Cassia has given up all hope of ever becoming a proper faerie. But I keep telling her it's never too late. I just hope for her sake I'm right.

"Sophie!" screeches Cassia, yanking me back. "Look out!"

"Wah?" I murmur, my eyes still closed in concentration as I envisage the crimson paper peeling away in neat strips.

"The wall! It's... It's..."

My eyelids snap open, my shriek matching my cousin's. "O-oh no-o!"

Not only is the wallpaper shredding itself into grubby confetti—*so is the wall*. Beginning at the top where the wall and ceiling meet and then cascading down to the floor, small bits of wallboard are disintegrating before our eyes and crumbling in a grimy heap at our feet. Soon we're both coughing as plumes of dust waft upward, tickling our throats and coating us in a fine layer of grayish-white powder.

I wait until the dust settles—a phrase I've never used literally before—and then wipe the grit from my eyes with the hem of my tee. While the wall to the left of the display cases has disappeared, I'm relieved to see the wood studs are still rooted in place. "At least I didn't break the building," I murmur through dry lips, retracting my dust-covered wings, which will need a thorough washing once I'm home.

Cassia is sneezing and wheezing so much she can't catch her breath, so I grab her purse and sweater from the storage closet and tell her I'll meet up with her later. "And maybe don't mention this fiasco to anyone in the meantime… please?" Nodding, she chokes out a shaky goodbye before fleeing from my latest magical misfire.

My secret is safe with Cassia, but it won't be long before my parents find out. Mom and Dad own the Sit for a Spell Café across the road, on the opposite side of Main Street. The only reason they're not already over here lecturing me on the misapplication of magic is due to the bakery's front windows, which are so filthy no one can see into my shop.

Rather than try a cleaning spell that might go awry, I grab the push broom and attempt to corral the mess, but all that does is raise more dust. Scowling, I pause and consider whether to throw in the towel and hire a professional contractor with what remains of my rapidly dwindling inheritance.

A pleasant little tinkling sounds from the bell above the shop's door, drawing my attention away from the gaping hole on the left side of the bakery. The shop is obviously closed, but since I forgot to lock the door after Cassia left, I paste on a smile before turning to greet the prospective customer.

"How may I help—" The words fade on my lips. I back up involuntarily, stomping into the pile of broken wallboard I just swept, staring slack-jawed at the gorgeous Nordic god standing in the doorway.

A weird thought flits through my overactive brain: Am I hallucinating? Or did my magic somehow conjure this giant, muscular Norseman in his periwinkle button-down shirt and pressed khakis? The big, blue-eyed blond man clears his throat uncertainly.

Alright, at least I know he's real. But that means... wow.

I'm struggling to process why this hot Viking-type with flowing blond locks, chiseled, clean-shaven jaw, and biceps the size of tree trunks has entered my not-yet-open bakery. He has an expectant look on his handsome face, and the corners of his mouth are tipping up ever so slightly, like he wants to smile but is restraining the impulse. As I peer into his sea-blue eyes I notice flecks of gold around the irises, which are darkening all of a sudden; his posture is friendly but slightly guarded. He's watching me carefully without trying to appear he's doing so.

Snap! Suddenly I'm on guard too, because now I know *what* he is.

This man is neither a lost human tourist nor a misplaced Scandinavian model—he's a werewolf! Of course, only another super like me would recognize his true form, since his appearance is one-hundred-percent hunky male at the moment. But during a full moon, when his inner wolf emerges, woe to any tourist who happens to be taking a late-night stroll. Not that werewolves are dangerous, but the average human would still have a coronary if they came face to face with one.

I sigh inwardly. I know every werewolf in my cousin Jake's pack, and this guy isn't one of them, which makes him a stranger and possibly a lone wolf. And lone wolves nearly always spell trouble.

The werewolf nods at my dirt-and-dust-strewn appearance. "Are you alright? Do you need to see a healer perhaps?"

I rake a hand through my long brown tangles, bits of wallpaper drifting to the floor. "Um, no. Um, yes. I mean yes, I'm alright, and no, I don't need to see a healer."

"Are you sure? You have a cut on your arm." He takes a few steps toward me, but I don't know this guy, and the way he's gazing at me makes me feel all nervous and fluttery.

Raising my hands, I sputter, "Stop right there. I... I'm fine."

He immediately stops in his tracks, but the way he continues staring at me is really freaking me out. It's like he's never seen a grimy faerie before.

"Look, as you can see, we're not open." I wave a hand around the imploded interior. "And I have a lot of work to do before we're able to open. So if you don't mind coming back during the Riddle Hill Summer Fest, I can promise a much more welcoming experience." I say the last part cheerily, as if I'm taping a promo reel for my bakery's SuperSuite page.

Mr. Tall, Blond, and Drop-Dead Gorgeous arches one perfect eyebrow at me. "I realize I'm a few days early, but by the looks of it, I think you could use my help now."

It dawns on me I'm all alone with a strange man who's obviously confused and possibly dangerous. I glance around, wondering what I could use as a weapon if he tries anything, since my defensive magic is non-existent. Keeping my eyes firmly trained on the were-wolf, I bend down to retrieve my broom from the floor. Gripping the handle firmly, I ask, "What do you mean, you're a few days early?"

"I suppose introductions would be helpful here." He

chuckles nervously. "Is it safe to assume you are Sophie Spellman Brownlee, ninety-percent owner of the Rhyme 'N Riddle Bakeshop?"

My mouth starts to gape open again, but I clamp it shut. Is this one of the attorneys overseeing Auntie Dragonfly's estate? I attempt to brush the dirt off my t-shirt and jeans, leaving behind more dark smudges everywhere my grubby fingers touch. It's useless; I look like a walking demolition experiment gone awry.

"Yes, that's correct."

The sculpted features of his face soften as he beams down at me. When the werewolf smiles, his teeth are pearly white. "Splendid!"

But I still don't know *his* name. "And you are?"

"Ah yes, of course." The man nods, clears his throat, and then clears it a second time. "I'm your new employee."

"But I haven't hired anyone yet."

"It's all in the will," he says, suddenly very serious. "Miss Dragonfly made sure of it."

I narrow my eyes at him, wondering whether I should have studied Auntie's will in more detail. *What am I missing?* "What's in the will?"

"The employment clause, of course!"

Employment clause? The only person I need to employ is Leslie T. Barker, ten percent owner of my bakery. Leslie sent me an email last week, informing me she'd be arriving in Riddle Hill the day after tomorrow.

Unless... no way.

It's not possible... is it?

But then I notice how this curious werewolf is gazing

at me, his blond head tilted slightly to the side, like a very large dog waiting for his owner to catch on it's dinner time.

"What a minute... you're not... your name isn't... you can't be..." I'm stammering, unable to string together a coherent sentence. Idly I wonder whether I'm suffering from a magical hangover, which can happen after a faerie expends a large surge of spelled energy.

The werewolf breaks into a smile so dazzling I take one step back, sending another curl of dust into the air.

"I'm Leslie T. Barker. Although everyone calls me Teddy."

CHAPTER 2

APPENDIX C

TEDDY

Friday, June 22

"But... but... your name is *Leslie*," pouts the faerie, who's so filthy I doubt I'll be able to recognize her after she cleans up. Every square inch of the woman, from the top of her head to the bottom of her sneakers, is coated in a fine layer of gray construction dust. Small bits of paper and wallboard litter her hair and shoulders, and her grimy face looks almost macabre in the late-afternoon light, more ghoulish than girlish.

According to Miss Dragonfly, my late patroness, Sophie Spellman Brownlee is a gifted kitchen faerie with a special affinity for baking desserts. She might make fabulous cakes and cookies, but I'm doubtful she's capable of running a shop, which doesn't bode well for either of us. I don't intend to work for nothing, and this woman fills me with... something I can't quite identify. But it's definitely not confidence in her business skills.

No, as soon as I stepped into the bakery and laid eyes on the frowsy faerie, an odd sort of fizzing sensation bubbled deep my gut, an uncomfortable spasm that felt like part warning pangs and part hunger pains. However I'm not hungry, and this grubby girl poses no threat to me... although, her obvious incompetence does imperil my meager bank account.

I'm beginning to worry; it seems Miss Dragonfly's grand scheme to give me a fresh start might be in jeopardy of failing before liftoff. My ownership stake needs to be worth more than the parchment it's printed on, which right now seems highly unlikely.

Clearing my throat, I provide my standard answer when people question my name and identity. Sometimes I wish Johnny Cash had written a song about a boy named Leslie instead of Sue. "My mom is from a werewolf clan in the Scottish Highlands, where Leslie is a popular name for both girls and boys."

The woman stammers, "I see." Then she emits a strangled gasp. I wait patiently as the full ramifications of our arrangement, courtesy of Miss Dragonfly's will, finally dawn on her. "Um... ah... this isn't going to work."

"Why is that?" I growl, straightening my spine and glowering down at her.

To her credit, she doesn't retreat. Instead, the faerie waggles her broom at me and says through gritted teeth, "Because you're a boy, and I'm a girl. I have no intention of sharing my living quarters with the opposite sex, regardless of Auntie's will!"

I fold my arms across my chest, not sure whether to feel consoled that I don't have to work with this woman… or disappointed. My stomach fizzes again, probably in relief. "That's perfectly fine with me. We can place a call to Miss Dragonfly's attorney, informing him of your decision. I'll give you three days to vacate the premises."

"What?" she screeches, her voice so high pitched my inner wolf cringes in annoyance.

"Do you need more time to clear out? I suppose I could see my way to giving you five days, but that's my final offer." I have a feeling this frumpy faerie didn't read Miss Dragonfly's will as thoroughly as I did, and it looks like I'm right. Despite the grime covering her face, I can see her cheeks and neck reddening in anger.

"I'm not going anywhere!" she spits. "I'm ninety-percent owner… and you're… you're…"

"Ten-percent owner. Yes, that's true, so long as you accept the terms of Miss Dragonfly's will. But you just told me this isn't going to work. I'm merely citing the forfeiture clause in Appendix C."

"Forfeiture clause? Appendix C?" Her gray eyes are now blazing with fury. I steel myself against a potential magical outburst.

Miss Dragonfly only used her faerie magic twice in anger during the three years I was her companion. The first time, she demolished a vase of roses sent to her by an admirer. It took me hours to clean up all the shards and petals. The second time she blew up her motor bike because it had broken down on the highway. I'd suffered a minor injury, but Miss Dragonfly was extremely protective of her staff.

"Perhaps you would like to re-read Appendix C? I have the original will in my car parked out front."

"Show me," demands the faerie, flinging aside her broom.

I shake my head. "Not while you're covered in all that debris. I'll not have you smearing an important legal document. You need to bathe and change first."

"You are the rudest man I've ever had the misfortune of encountering!" She huffs, stomping her foot on the floor and forcing another spiral of gray powder into the air.

I cough, plaster a neutral expression on my face, and decide to wait her out. Even a woman as tempestuous as this faerie should soon realize I'm right.

After a minute of pouts and scowls, she finally lifts her shoulders in a half shrug. "Fine. Give me an hour, and then come to the cottage around back."

"Very well. In the meantime, would you like me to pick up something for dinner?"

"Dinner?" She seems to realize it's nearly five o'clock. "Um, that won't be necessary. I have... plans for later this evening."

She seems almost hesitant to admit she has plans, which I find curious. But it's none of my business. I nod curtly. "Then I'll see you at six."

I climb into Miss Dragonfly's low-mileage, bronze-and-beige, 2009 Cadillac DTS, which she sold to me for a dollar a few months before she passed. Other than the truck-stop hot dog I consumed five hours ago, I haven't eaten all day. And while I'm not hungry—a werewolf needs to control all his urges, including his appetite—I do need sustenance before another encounter with the bossy faerie.

The café across the street doesn't serve dinner, and I didn't spot any restaurants on the way into town, so I decide to explore farther north. I pass up the boutique grocery store because I need a real meal, and the supper club because I don't have that much time, finally parking near a tavern with a porthole-style door.

The Howling Shores Pub obviously caters to shifters. Good, perhaps I can learn more about the local pack and get an introduction to the alpha. I pull open the heavy door and step inside, taking a moment for my eyes to adjust to the gloom as I inhale the twin scents of yeasty beer and funky fur. The place is awash in shore-themed trinkets and trim, with nets holding shells and starfish dangling from the ceiling and lots of pictures of tall ships and stormy seas on the walls.

I head over to an empty stool at the bar, where a large man with a scruffy black beard rattles off the daily specials, all of which involve beef, pork, or chicken, and pours me root beer from a local brewery. I'll need all my wits when I return to Sophie Spellman Brownlee's cottage to complete our negotiations, so I eschew anything stronger, a habit I picked up in college after a particularly embarrassing incident involving a fraternity party, barbecued ribs, and warm beer.

All faeries are tricksters at heart; even Miss Dragonfly would lecture me on the perils of dealing with faeries. That's why she hired the best supernatural estate-planning firm in the country to handle her affairs. She explained everything to me in advance. Miss Dragonfly wanted to provide for her two great-nieces, Sophie and her cousin, Cassia Spellman, a single mom with a greedy ex-husband.

Miss Dragonfly established an education trust fund for Cassia's young daughter that is so ironclad her faerie father won't be able to access a dime. Then she left the remainder of her estate, minus ten percent, to Sophie so she could establish a bakery. Miss Dragonfly was quite meticulous about the conditions set forth in her will for two reasons.

First, she told me Sophie is a kindhearted but impetuous faerie who could make serious mistakes if she didn't have someone looking over her shoulder. Given what I just witnessed inside the bakeshop, I'd have to agree.

Second, Miss Dragonfly wanted to provide me with the means to start over; she knew my options were sketchy at best. She'd discovered me, unconscious and barely alive, on her grounds three years ago and nursed me back to health. I wouldn't be here today if it weren't for Dragonfly Spellman—and I'll do everything in my power to see that her final wishes are carried out.

The bartender delivers my eight-ounce burger, which comes with blue cheese crumbles, caramelized onions, two bacon strips, and seasoned curly fries on the side, pours me another root beer, and cocks his head. He inquires, in a not unfriendly way, about my plans. "Just passing through?"

Typical werewolf behavior; so protective of their territory and so distrustful of loners like me. While it's smart to be cautious around lone wolves as a general rule, I'm about as harmless as a ghost. I take a bite of my burger, chew slowly, and then meet Black Beard's gaze. "Not exactly. I intend to relocate here."

"Humph," he replies, adding, "You a loner?" All pack-mates carry a whiff of their leader, but my old alpha's scent faded long ago. I've been packless for three years, which means I'll have to work harder than most loners to prove my worth and sincerity.

"Not by choice," I say around a curly fry I've just popped into my mouth. "It's a long story."

"You looking for an intro to our alpha?"

I wipe my mouth on a napkin and look him in the eye, hoping he sees what I want him to see: my earnestness. I give him a firm nod. "Yes. Can you arrange it?"

The man grunts. "Pack meets upstairs every Sunday night at seven. I'll let him know you'll be stopping by for a sniff and a tussle."

He must see the wariness in my eyes because he adds, "Nothing a big fella like you can't handle. Name's Wes Forrester."

I extend my hand, and we shake. "I'm Teddy Barker. And thanks."

After I finish my meal and pay Wes, I realize I still don't know the name of the local alpha. "Who's the pack alpha, by the way?"

As Wes wipes the crumbs from the counter he replies, "Jake Grayclaw Spellman."

"Spellman?" I yip in surprise.

Wes glances at me, his black eyebrows drawn together. "Yeah. What's it to you?"

"All the Spellmans I know are faeries."

He chuckles. "Don't let the name confuse you. Jake's werewolf father died when he was an infant. His human mother remarried a faerie who adopted Jake and gave him his surname."

"Interesting. Well, see you around," I say with a nonchalance that belies my excitement. Perhaps Jake Grayclaw Spellman will be more sympathetic than most pack alphas to my loner status. He might even overlook the fact I've been living with an ancient faerie for the past three years, avoiding pack life entirely.

Who knows? Perhaps Jake Spellman's faerie stepfather was related to Miss Dragonfly.

As I pull open the door to my car, I take a fortifying breath. Regardless of the number of Spellmans populating this small community, there's only one Spellman I need to deal with at the moment: a furious spitfire of a faerie who's looking for a way to kick me to the curb.

Sorry, Miss Sophie Spellman Brownlee. The odds of you winning are zilch. But it'll be fun to see you try.

CHAPTER 3
SHORE SHACK

TEDDY

LATER, JUNE 22

I follow the narrow, weed-strewn path around the side of the bakeshop, hoping its unkempt appearance isn't a harbinger of what I'll find out back. Surely my new faerie employer takes better care of her personal residence. The cottage must be in better condition... right?

Wrong.

Mongrels and moonbeams! It's not a cottage at all... It's a dilapidated little shore shack. The formerly white wooden siding is so weathered it's turned a dingy gray, most of its paint peeled away, the battered front door is sagging on its hinges, and every window is crusted with grime.

I'm a fastidious man, which I realize is a bit unusual for my species. My old pack alpha used to say I should have been born a vampire instead of a werewolf. He was teasing me of course; he understood me better than my own parents. A wave of sadness washes over me at the memory of Jarrod and the fight that took his life—and nearly ended mine.

I shake off my melancholy and step up to the door. Unable to locate either a door bell or a knocker, I use the side of my fist to pound on the flaking green paint. I pause, hear nothing inside, no swish of fabric or footsteps on floorboards, and resume my assault on the door.

A female voice finally shouts, "Geesh... I'm coming! Hold your horses!"

My eyebrows quirk upward at the quaint expression, reminding me of Miss Dragonfly. I heave a sigh, ignoring the surge of nostalgia threatening to sink my spirits yet again. I have no choice but to forge ahead; I must find a way to work with slovenly Sophie.

But when she pulls open the door and steps aside so I can enter, my breath hitches and my feet refuse to move. The faerie standing before me *can't possibly* be the same person I encountered in the shop.

This faerie is wearing a coppery silk blouse that shows off her flawless complexion, black jeans that hug her curvy hips, and ankle boots with four-inch heels that boost her to nearly my height. Her lustrous brown hair falls in long, loose curls past her shoulders, and her gray eyes have flecks of blue, almost like the lake when a cloud passes over the sun. I gaze unabashedly at her glossy lips, which are painted the color of burnished bronze.

And then there's her scent, which I didn't notice earlier in the bakery, probably because it was masked by all the construction dust clogging my nostrils. But now the mossy aroma of damp grass after a gentle rain wafts toward me; I smile, inhaling the greening scents of spring, my favorite season.

Sophie Spellman Brownlee is a vision of such loveliness and perfection that I'm struck speechless—until she purses her pillowy lips, draws her slanted faerie eyebrows into a mighty scowl, and hollers, "Well, what are you waiting for? Come inside so we can get this over with."

I'm so startled by the contrast between her natural beauty and her snippy mouth that I take a step back. Then I realize it may appear I'm retreating, so I square my shoulders and cross the threshold, entering the monstrous mess this faerie calls home.

I pause, wincing at the disorder, uncertain where we'll find an unoccupied spot to review Miss Dragonfly's will.

Half-open boxes are stacked haphazardly around the living room; torn newspapers and bubble wrap lie scattered across every available surface, and the scarred floorboards are grimy underfoot. To my left sits a lumpy sofa covered in a bilious brown throw. Two oversized chairs with frayed slipcovers, one green and the other gold, are shoved against the far wall.

"Follow me," calls Sophie over her shoulder. "We'll use the kitchen." I notice her wings are partially protruding from the specially-designed slits in the back of her silk blouse.

Trailing behind her, I'm momentarily distracted by the sway of her hips until I step on something soft and cushy. An indignant screech causes me to jump as a flurry of white fur streaks past. Sophie chases after the creature and returns moments later, cooing at the fuzzy bundle in her arms. "Poor baby. Leslie is clumsy and didn't mean to step on you."

"The name's Teddy. And what is that? Some sort of *rodent?*"

Sophie's gray eyes darken. "Shh, you're insulting her!" She coos some more endearments at the ratty creature with the voluminous tail... er make that plural. The rat has too many tails to count.

"This is Zosia, my nine-tailed fox. She's still a kit and doesn't know to hide from big, bad wolves yet."

I ignore her jab. "I'm sorry, I didn't mean to step on... er... one of her tails. What's she doing here?"

"She lives here."

"Not with me she doesn't," I say firmly. "No pets."

"Who says you live here?"

"Miss Dragonfly's last will and testament says so." I square my jaw. "Look, let's get on with the review of Appendix C. Didn't you say you had dinner plans?"

Sophie glares daggers at me. "As if *you* could make *me* forget I have a date tonight!"

For some inexplicable reason, I find myself almost jealous that she's going out with someone else tonight. A ridiculous notion, since I find her far too showy, snappy, and sloppy for my taste. Sophie is the embodiment of everything I abhor. Well, except for the way she smells... and looks; she could stop traffic in that outfit.

Sophie kisses the top of the little fox's head, puts her down, and leads me through a set of swinging double doors into the kitchen. The room reeks of Pine Sol—at least the cracked linoleum floor and avocado green appliances appear recently scrubbed—but the kitchen is just as cramped and cluttered as the main room. Pots and pans and dishes and pantry items are stacked on the counters and crowded into cupboards; there isn't an inch of unoccupied counter space anywhere, and half the cabinet doors are slightly ajar, obviously overflowing with contents.

I pinch the bridge of my nose, trying to stave off the migraine forming behind my eyes at the sheer chaos that is Sophie Spellman Brownlee. She seems to realize we need at least fourteen square inches of clear space to review Miss Dragonfly's will, because she grabs an armful of cookbooks from her Formica-topped table and stacks them *on top of the stove.*

"Er… that's not safe," I say, wondering what other hazards are hidden within these claustrophobic walls. I'm somewhat of a fanatic when it comes to fire safety; I have a fire science degree and long for an opportunity to put my knowledge to good use.

"What do you take me for? Some feather-brained faerie?" Sophie grumps, pulls up a chair at the table, and waves me over.

"If you know it's an unsafe practice, then why do you do it?"

"Really? Are we going to waste precious time discussing my decluttering skills, or are we going to look at this will?"

"No offense," I reply stiffly, taking my seat next to her. "But you don't appear to have any decluttering skills. You merely move stacks of stuff around, like those rail cars that crisscross the country hauling expired waste from coast to coast."

Sophie shakes her head and huffs, "If you're not careful, you're going to insult the wrong person in Riddle Hill, someone far less easygoing than me. And then you'll be lucky if all you're fending off are fangs and claws." At my quizzical expression, she adds, "Visit the Sit for a Spell Café and take a look at the gargoyles beneath the countertop. That's what happens when you cross a faerie!"

"I don't understand."

"They weren't always made of stone."

My eyes narrow into twin slits. "Are you threatening me?"

Sophie shrugs. "If the boot fits… "

She's intentionally trying to goad me, and I refuse to take the bait. Instead I paste a neutral expression on my face, determined to reach detente with this infuriating faerie so I can unpack my car and get some much-needed rest. "I've been on the road since eight this morning. I have no energy for a verbal tussling match; let's just get on with it."

I withdraw Miss Dragonfly's will from its leather portfolio, turn to the appendix in question, and show Sophie the relevant paragraph. She snatches the document from my hands and begins to read. I watch her through half-lowered lids, waiting until her eyes widen, and she hisses, "This is ridiculous! It's bad enough I'd forfeit my bakery if I don't employ you for a year. But if I refuse to give you room and board, it amounts to the same thing!"

"True, but Miss Dragonfly adds protections for you as well. If you deem my work ethic unsatisfactory—for example, if I fail to show up for work without a valid excuse—then you may send me packing and buy out my shares at the end of the year." Shrugging, I add, "However, I think you'll quickly find my work ethic is outstanding, and you'll have no reason to activate the forfeiture clause. In my three years of employment with Miss Dragonfly, I never missed a day."

"Unbelievable." Sophie slaps her hand on the table. "I assumed all along you were female and had a tolerable personality—but Auntie knew the truth, and she still drafted this will! What was she thinking?"

I can't help myself; my sister Bella always says I'm too curious by half. "What's wrong with my personality?"

Sophie glares at me. "You've done nothing but look down your nose at me since you arrived at the shop. You insisted I had to bathe and change before discussing the will, and you've been wincing and grimacing ever since you entered my home. You called poor little Zosia a rat and compared my decluttering skills to managing radioactive waste. Seriously, how did you survive into your twenties without one of your packmates taking you out?"

My mouth turns sharply downward as I pin her with a wolfish glower. Sophie's estimate of my issues with pack life hits a little too close to home. Not that my "personality" was the problem; no, it was my loyalty to my alpha that nearly got me killed. But Sophie doesn't need to know that. I rise from the chair and tower over the outspoken faerie I have to live and work with for the next twelve months.

I refuse to dignify her question with an answer. Instead I ask, "Is this a roundabout way of telling me you wish to forfeit?"

Sophie hurtles out of her chair like it's on fire and jabs her finger into my chest, which sends a frisson of tingles around my torso, down my spine, and into my gut. Peering down at her shiny brown hair, I inhale her delicious scent, and suddenly, I'm struggling to swallow. I notice Sophie seems immobilized; her forefinger is still pressed into my chest, but she's not saying or doing anything.

I have this inexplicable desire to wrap my arms around this maddening faerie and draw her close for a kiss. Her scent, her curves, her lips seem to beckon me... Whoa! I blink away the thought, wondering if Sophie is part siren.

I cough to clear my throat, and she whips her head up at me, dropping her hand. Her pupils are dilated, but her voice is as loud and brash as ever. "I am not forfeiting, Leslie T. Barker!"

"The name's Teddy," I remind her, slipping the will back into its carrying case. "In that case, would you please show me to my room? I need to unpack." I'm desperate for some alone time, preferably in a quiet, uncluttered room so I can process what just happened when Sophie stabbed me with her finger.

Sophie's plush lips form an *O*. "But, but... you're staying?"

"I believe I've already established that fact."

"How am I going to explain you to my prospective boyfriend?"

A tiny pang forms beneath my rib cage at the mention of a boyfriend. I give myself a good mental shake. Although this ridiculous faerie causes an occasional fizzle in my belly or tingle down my spine, there's a perfectly rational explanation that has nothing to do with the fact she's stunning—even more so when she's angry.

I'd have the same reaction to any reasonably attractive woman who paid me a little attention. I'm a twenty-four-year-old man who hasn't been on a date since college, and who's been living with an ancient faerie for the past three years. Other than periodic visits to my sister Bella, I've eschewed all social engagements.

The simple truth is I'm starved for affection.

Sophie appears to be waiting for my answer. "Tell your boyfriend the truth."

"Prospective boyfriend," Sophie corrects me. "I haven't met him yet."

"Huh?" I know I'm weary, but Sophie isn't making any sense.

Sophie waves her hand in the air. "I'm speaking hypothetically."

"Well then," I reply, secretly relieved by Sophie's non-existent love interest. One less complication at the moment. "Tell your hypothetical, prospective boyfriend that I'm your business partner."

"Oh please," Sophie snorts. "No one is going to believe that."

"Why not?"

"You're too good looking."

"Oh I see." I smirk, some of the heaviness in my chest lightening at the compliment.

"Don't let it go to your head. You're not the only pretty face in Riddle Hill," Sophie grumps.

I bite the inside of my cheek to keep from chuckling. "I look forward to meeting the other pretty faces in town. Perhaps we could start a club."

"Spare me your dog-eared werewolf humor." Sophie shakes her head. "Come on, let me show you to your room."

"Just a sec." I remove the stack of cookbooks from the stove and pile them back onto the table.

Sophie gives me an eye roll before heading through the double doors. I pat the ugly green refrigerator on my way out like it's an old chum, welcoming me home.

CHAPTER 4
FORCED PROXIMITY

SOPHIE

Later, June 22

I stalk through the living room, make a beeline for the short hallway to the right, and fling open the door to Leslie's—er, Teddy's—room, which unfortunately is a bit of a mess at the moment. There's a mattress on the floor because the bed hasn't arrived yet, a dusty antique dresser from my grandmother's attic, a second-hand club chair that I plan to reupholster, several old lamps in dire need of rewiring, a large pile of my dirty laundry, and boxes stacked everywhere in between.

I glance over at the werewolf, who's standing by my side; his posture has gone rigid, and he seems kind of in shock. What did he expect? The man arrived two days early, so he'll just have to deal with it. Then I notice his fingernails have sharpened into claws, and the backs of his hands are covered in sleek blond fur.

Sweet moonglow! The last thing I need is my auntie's

former companion wolfing out. When I poke Teddy in the arm, he jumps a foot. "Geesh, get a grip on your wolf! What's wrong with you anyway?"

He waves the leather portfolio containing Auntie's will around in the air. "Isn't it obvious what's wrong?" he cries. "This is one hundred percent unacceptable! You... you've been using my bedroom as a storage facility for old junk... and your dirty socks... And—" he stomps over to Zosia's litter box and shakes his finger at it "—That. Is. Excrement. In my bedroom!"

"I was planning to move that to the bathroom."

"I hope you mean *your* bathroom," he growls.

"Um, no-oh... I mean *the* bathroom. We're sharing, but don't worry, there's plenty of room for Zosia's litter box."

Teddy cringes. "No! Out of the question! I don't want to see fox dung when I use the facilities. Keep it in your room, out of sight."

This is the weirdest werewolf I've ever met. My cousin Jake's packmates are sweet, grungy types who couldn't care less about litter boxes and a little mess. It's like Teddy has some sort of a cleanliness disorder. "Fine. I'll take care of it when I'm back from my date."

He's shaking his head and backing away, like the whole room has cooties or something. "Oh no, that won't do. You need to move it right away."

"But look at me! I'm all dressed up. I can't possibly do it now."

Teddy peers down at me, his sea-blue eyes steely. Then he heaves a dramatic sigh, as if I've just asked him to make some enormous sacrifice on behalf of all supernaturals everywhere. "Just this once I'll move the disgusting fox box. But don't expect me to have anything to do with that ball of white fuzz. Here—"

Teddy hands me the zippered leather case containing Auntie's will and walks stiff-legged into the bedroom. He stoops down with a grimace to retrieve the litter box and then carries it at arms-length down the hallway. As he waits for me to open the door to my room, I notice small beads of sweat dotting his upper lip and forehead. But at least his hands are back to normal again.

Teddy gingerly deposits the box where I indicate and then asks to use the bathroom. I'm a smidge worried he might lose control of his wolf, possibly damaging my home in the process, so I decide to stick around another five minutes.

I put Auntie's will back in the kitchen, freshen up Zosia's water bowl, and reapply my lip gloss, but I can't wait much longer. I'm just grabbing my purse when I hear a crash in the bathroom, followed by Teddy shouting.

Oh no! I completely forgot about—

Teddy throws open the door, which slams into the wall so hard the doorknob leaves a dent. "Sophie!" he hollers. "There's a giant snake in your tub! We need to call an exterminator right now."

I don't think Teddy Barker would appreciate me laughing in his face, so I promptly swallow the giggles forming in the back of my throat. "No one is going to come out tonight for a non-emergency call."

Teddy's eyes pop wider. "That... thing in there is a

definite emergency. Maybe we just need to call animal control."

"Relax," I reply calmly. This werewolf is such a big baby. "That's not a snake, it's an eel. My dad just dropped it off; he'll swing by tomorrow to pick it up and cook it for a wedding he's catering. I guess the groom's family loves fried eel."

"You keep eels in your tub? Foxes in your bedroom? What next, a vampire in your garage?" Teddy drops into one of the chairs in the living room, leans his head back, and closes his eyes; his complexion is nearly the same shade as the green slipcover.

I'm already late, but this werewolf looks... almost defeated, like all the fight's gone out of him. "Would you like some herbal tea before I go? I've got lemon-ginger, chamomile, and peppermint."

Teddy blinks open his blue eyes. "Don't you have a date tonight?"

I fiddle with my purse strap, not meeting his gaze. "It's not an actual date, but a meetup with a few friends, one of whom is bringing an extra guy she thinks I might like."

"I see." Teddy's mouth lifts slightly on one side, creating a tiny dimple in his right cheek.

"Then you best be going." Teddy nods toward the door. "I don't want to delay you. Besides, I'm perfectly capable of microwaving a cup of water and dropping in a tea bag."

"Um... we don't have a microwave. You'll need to put on a kettle."

"No microwave?" Teddy heaves another one of his

dramatic, woe-is-me sighs. "Look, I think we could both use a little... space... right now. Why don't you go meet your friends and let me recover."

"Recover from what?"

"From this." He throws his arms open wide, indicating the whole room or cottage or whatever. "From my Sophie Spellman Brownlee full-immersion experience."

My mouth gapes open. I'm giving this yahoo a job, room, and board for a solid year, and all he can do is insult me? "Yeah, well, you're not much of a package deal yourself, werewolf!"

I storm out of the cottage, slamming the door behind me. As I pause on the front stoop and inhale a steadying breath, I hear Teddy muttering through the poorly insulated walls, "Miss Dragonfly, *what* were you thinking?"

"Yes Auntie," I whisper. "What indeed?"

CHAPTER 5
MY ACHING HEAD

TEDDY

LATER, JUNE 22

My migraine tablets are packed, along with the rest of my meager belongings, in the trunk of Miss Dragonfly's old Cadillac parked out front. But before I can unload my luggage, I need to organize and clean my room. I don't mind the mattress on the floor—I've slept in far worse—or the dusty dresser and ugly chair, but everything else has to go.

I rub my throbbing temples and decide to close my eyes. Perhaps a short nap will revive my spirits, although I don't see how. I'm going to be suffering from headaches for the next three hundred and sixty-five days, courtesy of my new faerie boss. Sophie is a walking contradiction, a woman of such curvaceous loveliness and expressive eyes and luscious springtime scent that she brings a smile to my lips—until she pops her fists on her hips, opens her pouty mouth, and hollers something nonsensical at me.

Why bring up a hypothetical, prospective boyfriend she hasn't even met yet? It's ridiculous. But then so are her deplorable organizational skills and wayward magic. I knew as soon as I stepped into her shop that Sophie had magically blown up the missing wall. I can only hope Sophie bakes better than she cleans and casts spells.

I must have dozed off, because suddenly a warm sensation in my lap brings me back to full wakefulness. My eyes snap open as I take in the white furry mass sprawled across my legs. "No, no, no," I growl. "Get down now. Off."

Zosia opens one silver eye, lets out a little "*Meep*," and snuggles in deeper.

"Zosia," I say in my most commanding voice. "Down. Now."

Zosia must realize I'm serious. She reluctantly hops down, but not before one of her tails bops me in the face. Disgusting! Where has that tail been?

I push myself out of the chair with a grunt; my head still hurts, but at least it's not pounding. Time for me to get to work on this monstrous dump Sophie calls home. But first, I need to address Zosia, who is licking one of her front paws.

"I'm not a pet person."

Zosia gives me an indignant glare and another, "*Meep*."

"But you were here first, so I'm going to make an exception."

Zosia turns around, raises all nine tails in the air, and

shows me her derriere. Great, just wonderful. Honestly, I don't think a werewolf can sink any lower.

I've just been mooned by a baby fox. And she knows I'm such a softie I'm not going to do anything about it. "Alright, now that we understand each other, I'm going to get to work. I don't want to scare you, but I work much faster in my werewolf form."

Zosia tilts her head to the side, all her tails flicking in the air behind her with a, "*Wump*," which I think is her way of saying *whatever*.

Before I shift I need to undress; there's no point in tearing my new khakis and button-down shirt. I'm a modest man, so I take a quick glance around to see whether Sophie bothered to close the ugly harvest gold draperies in the living room. Of course not; she's as careless with her privacy as she is with her belongings.

I pull the cords on the tatty drapes, sneezing at the dust motes wafting upward. My hand comes away grimy after I've finished the task, so I wash up in the kitchen sink; I'll be avoiding the eel-occupied bathroom unless absolutely necessary.

I prefer to wear a pair of loose-fitting sweats before shifting, but since they're packed along with everything else, I need to strip down to my boxer shorts instead. I pull off my shoes and socks, and then peel off my shirt, slacks, and undershirt, neatly folding each article of clothing before placing the stack on the green chair.

Zosia has moved onto her other paw, which she licks lazily as she watches me through her silver eyes. "I'm going to shift now, but there's no need to be frightened. I retain full control over my reactions and faculties, so you'll be entirely safe with me."

Zosia yawns, obviously not concerned, forcing a chuckle from my lips. As I transform, I concentrate on each stage to ensure it's smooth and measured. I abhor werewolf dramatics; all that howling and whining during a shift is entirely unnecessary if you're disciplined about it.

Holding my hands in front of me, I watch as blond fur blooms along the backs and my fingernails sharpen into claws. A fraction of a second later, long incisors break through my gums, replacing my front teeth, and then my furry tail emerges, requiring a quick adjustment to my boxers before they rip. I allow a small grunt to escape my lips as my human facial features meld into my wolfish snout and brow.

Next my forearms and chest expand, followed by my thighs and calves, blond fur spreading rapidly over bulked-up muscles and bulging veins. Lastly, my feet curl slightly against the floorboards, my claws scraping the wood as they lengthen. I take a few shaky breaths, the only indication of the effort required to control my shift without a single yowl.

Zosia stops licking her paws and tips her chin at me as if acknowledging my changed state; not quite submissive but no longer dismissive either.

"Am. Clean-ning. No-oww," I yip. To the untrained ear, wolf-speak sounds garbled and can be difficult to understand. I speak as little as possible in my werewolf form, preferring to communicate through actions; words sound so inelegant when verbalized through my furry snout.

"*Wump.*" Zosia trots over to the gold chair and leaps up, curling into a ball before closing her eyes. Apparently it's past her bedtime.

I give a growly chuckle and then get down to work.

First, I need to sort out the crowded living room; it's the only way I'll be able to clear away enough space to transfer the unwanted boxes and other paraphernalia out of my bedroom. I begin by picking up every loose piece of newsprint and paper lying about and stuffing them into the recycling bin in the kitchen. Next, I find some large, black trash bags and start filling them with loose bubble wrap, food wrappers, a broken vase, a single mitten too small for Sophie's hand, and anything else that I deem unsalvageable. I stack the bags by the door; once I've shifted back into my man form, I'll haul everything to the garbage bins outside.

I move the boxes, broken lamps, and remaining unwanted junk out of my room, rearranging everything in neat rows in the living area. I pull down the bedroom curtains too, which are so old and filthy they'd not survive a trip to the laundromat. I realize that a passerby might be able to peer inside the window and see my werewolf form, but I feel it's a small risk at this hour. Besides, I won't be able to rest until my personal quarters are clean and orderly.

The mattress and box spring on the floor are new and still covered in plastic; I hoist them up, temporarily moving them out of the way. Next, I find a broom, mop, pail, and other cleaning supplies in the hall closet. Humming under my breath, I scrub my bedroom until not a speck of dirt remains. Then I move the dresser, chair, and mattress around until I'm satisfied I've achieved Feng Shui. Finally, I locate a set of sheets in one of the cupboards in the kitchen, which of course makes no sense, but then again, neither does anything else Sophie does. I make my bed, tucking and tugging the sheets until they are so taut I could bounce a quarter off them.

Smiling, I pat the antique dresser I've just polished and step into the hallway, intending to shift back before Sophie returns home. A rustling at the front door tells me I'm too late. I dash into the living room to retrieve my clothes, hoping I have enough time to retreat to my bedroom before she opens the door. We've already gotten off to a bad start, and the last thing she needs to see is a werewolf in boxers.

But Zosia suddenly streaks past me and dives under Sophie's bed. The fur along the ridge of my back rises in response; Zosia shouldn't be running away from Sophie. My gut tells me something is definitely wrong, but I'm clueless about what—or who—is scaring Zosia. I drop my clothes onto my mattress and stalk purposefully toward the door. If someone is attempting a break-in, they're going to have a big, furry surprise.

Suddenly the door bursts open, and two cops with guns drawn dash through. "Assume the position!" barks one of them, a towering man with light brown hair and a trim beard; his werewolf hovers just beneath his man form.

The other cop is shorter, with spiky black hair, but

just as muscular; he's glamoured his faerie features to appear human. Waving a gun at me, he shouts, "You heard him. Assume the position!"

"Huh?" I grunt. "Wha-what?" I have no idea what position they're talking about.

The werewolf cop must realize my confusion, because he snarls an explanation. "Hands up, turn around, and lean against the back wall." I follow instructions, my insides shaking, and then he adds, "Now spread your legs, and don't move!"

"B-but. W-why?"

"We'll ask the questions," snaps the faerie as his partner places an iron manacle around my right wrist. The cop forces my right arm behind my back and then my left, clicking the other manacle into place. Anger flares within me, but I control my wolf. There's no point in resisting arrest; this is all some terrible misunderstanding. I've done nothing wrong, and the best course of action is cooperation.

"Who the blazes are you?" growls another voice from somewhere behind me. The werewolf cop spins me around, gripping my upper arm with one hand, his gun poised in the other.

The third man's eyes glower at me, the gold around his amber irises flaring; another werewolf, and a huge one, bigger even than Jarrod, my old alpha. "Answer the question!" he barks.

"Name. Is. Ted-dy. Bark-er," I yip through my muzzle.

"Never heard of you." He glances at the two cops. "He's clearly trespassing and—and practically indecent —arrest him!"

"Wait—" I start to object.

"Shut it, wolf," snaps the faerie cop.

My pulse races, and my breathing grows raspy. Now I'm just plain scared. Supers operate on a different set of laws than humans; stricter, harsher, and swifter. I'm hauled outside and shoved into the back of a police van, heading to jail in the supernatural village I'd hoped would give me a fresh start.

Even worse, there's only one person I know in Riddle Hill—and Sophie Spellman Brownlee would be only too happy if I simply... disappeared.

CHAPTER 6
COLLECT CALL

SOPHIE

Later, June 22

Pru Albright, my friend from culinary school, checks her phone. "The guys will be here any minute." Her fangs catch slightly on her bottom lip, the only visible sign she's a vampire. Pru quickly tucks them inside her mouth, ensuring any non-super in the vicinity would think she's just a cute redhead with green eyes and a smattering of freckles in designer jeans.

"I wonder why they're running so late," says Cassia, stunning as always, her long blonde hair cascading down her back. She's wearing a short purple dress that I know is a size two, because I was with her when she bought it. My curvier size ten means we can never swap clothes; it's a good thing she's my bestie and I love her, because otherwise I'd hate her.

When we were teens I struggled with jealousy because the hottest guy in high school—and my secret crush—pursued Cassia until she finally agreed to date him. Eventually she married him, but her new husband turned out to be as selfish as he was handsome. I'd dodged a bullet named Derek Taylor, but poor Cassia wound up with a broken heart. My cousin now works two jobs to make ends meet after Derek dumped her and their daughter so he could go to Hollywood. Last I heard, he's an extra on a couple of dog food commercials.

Everyone in our family helps Cassia and her daughter as much as we can, trying to make up for all the hurt Derek has caused them. My mom is babysitting Olivia tonight so Cassia can have a rare night out with Pru and me.

I turn to Pru with a wry smile. "So tell me about this guy you think is my type." We're waiting outside on the dock for a table to open up at Pru's favorite water-front restaurant in Sturgeon Bay, a non-super town about thirty minutes south of Riddle Hill. The crescent moon casts a blurry reflection in the harbor below us.

We're still fully glamoured even though night has fallen; it's the law. Don't show your fangs, fur, wings, or tails in front of non-supers. Ever.

Secrecy keeps supers safe.

Pru smirks. "If I weren't already in love with Vreeland, I'd snap Rafe up in a heartbeat."

"Please elaborate!" I arch an eyebrow and grin.

"Rafe's a tall, dashing werewolf with bodybuilder muscles and hair black as ink. He's a personal trainer, the hunky kind that rich ladies hire so they can ogle him while they're working out. He's also the silent type, so you'll need to chat him up to learn about his personal life."

"How did Vreeland and Rafe meet?" asks Cassia.

"They work out at the same fitness club."

Cassia frowns, chewing her bottom lip. "That's a bit unusual, don't you think? Werewolves and vampires rarely frequent the same clubs."

Pru shrugs. "Rafe moved to Sturgeon Bay in late spring. Vreeland says he's planning on joining a pack in the vicinity but hasn't gotten around to it yet. For now, he's hanging out with the vamps."

Cassia catches my eye and gives me one of her "stranger danger" warning gazes. Every super knows that lone wolves are often bad news, and any wolves hoping to relocate are supposed to check in with the local alpha within a few days... not weeks or months. I realize Cassia means well, and she's been through the ringer with her ex, but I don't need her mothering me. I get more than enough of that from my actual mother.

I'm sure Rafe has his reasons for biding his time, and I'm not going to let that faze me. "Rafe sounds cool... and maybe a bit deadly."

Pru and I chortle, but Cassia looks away uneasily. I wish she'd lighten up; it's not like I'm going to marry the guy. I simply want to date someone I find attractive, and if he's got a little edge to him, so what?

"Who's deadly?" asks a low, gravelly voice from behind me. "Do I need to sharpen my claws?"

I turn toward the newcomer and wind up taking a step back. Since he's arrived with Vreeland and Julien, my vampire guy friends, and I can see the wolf hovering beneath the gold flecks of his brown eyes, I assume this is Rafe. Dressed all in black, he's every bit as muscular and dashing as Pru said, with his tousled dark hair and square, stubbled jaw. A jagged pink scar mars one pale cheek, and I get the distinct impression Rafe solves his problems with his fists, which doesn't bother me the way it would bother Cassia. I prefer action over words anyway, even if that sometimes gets me into trouble.

This guy's giving off bad-boy vibes from here to Milwaukee, but I'm not worried. My magic may not always behave, but I'm a strong faerie and can take care of myself.

As Rafe waits for my reply, he casts his eyes over me and smirks. My heart speeds up at the way his gaze sharpens, as if he's ravenous... *for little ole me*. Okay, a teensy warning bell just tinkled inside my head. I'm going to have to slow this werewolf's roll; Rafe needs to know who's in charge, and it's definitely not him.

"I'm deadly," I reply, folding my arms across my chest. "So don't cross me, wolf."

That earns a guffaw from Rafe. He grins down at me. "So I've been warned."

"Oh really." I glance over at Pru, who gives me a wink; apparently she's told Rafe something about me. I just hope she didn't overshare. She's leaning against Vreeland Silva, her fiancé, a cute vampire with long brown hair and eyes that twinkle with humor. Pru has good-natured Vreeland wrapped around her gel-tipped pinky.

Vreeland sweeps his free arm in the air, making the

introductions. "Rafaellus MacTire, this is Sophie Spellman Brownlee and her cousin, Cassia Spellman."

Rafe smiles first at Cassia and then at me, his eyes lingering on my face before slowly scanning the rest of me. He's taking his time checking me out, and I'm turning pink from the extra attention.

Cassia holds up the blinking pager. "Looks like our table's ready." She falls into step beside Julien Drakus, whose dark good looks are every bit as appealing as Rafe's. He and Cassia are good friends but nothing more; Julien is the only photographer Cassia will hire when she's planning a wedding, her side gig when she's not working at my parents' restaurant. As a top-notch super-natural photographer, Julien returns the favor, sending plenty of business Cassia's way. They also share a similar personal history that's solidified their friendship; Julien's supermodel ex-wife left him and their young son a couple years ago.

Rafe saunters alongside me, his muscled arm brushing against mine. "I hear you'll be opening a bakery soon in Riddle Hill. How's it going?"

"Oh… things are a bit messy right now. The shop's interior is still under construction." An understatement, but technically true. Wrinkling my nose, I recall Leslie T. Barker. "Unfortunately I'm also dealing with a rather thorny legal issue."

"A legal issue?" Rafe grins, his teeth flashing white as we take our seats. "And here I thought you were an honest faerie." His tone is light, but I sense a steely toughness beneath his smooth exterior that leaves me feeling slightly breathless and unsettled.

Averting my eyes, I scan the menu the server handed me, unwilling to let Rafe see he's unnerving me. No one rattles Sophie Spellman Brownlee, the most fearsome faerie to barely graduate from Riddle Hill High. More than a decade later, my pranks have become the stuff of legend, although in retrospect, I'll admit I went too far with my last stunt. I wouldn't have graduated if my parents hadn't paid for the damages to our science lab and offered free meals to anyone whose clothes were ruined by my exploding lime-green super goo.

"I'm an honest businesswoman," I reply coolly, closing the menu.

"Of course you are." Rafe gives a growly chuckle.

I glare at him, but his eyes are twinkling with humor; he's obviously teasing. Leaning against the back of the chair, I can see I have an audience. Everyone around the table, even my cousin, is waiting for me to explain. "My elderly auntie left me an inheritance along with one very unpleasant employee."

Cassia quirks an eyebrow. I give her a little head shake; I know she'll pepper me with questions later, but for now she'll remain discreetly silent.

"Ah." Rafe replies knowingly. "If your employee's bothering you, I'll be happy to show 'em who's the boss."

An image of Rafe and Teddy locked in gruesome werewolf combat pops into my head. I don't think Teddy, the infuriating cleanliness freak, would survive the encounter. My throat goes dry; I may not like Teddy, but I certainly don't wish him bodily harm.

Waving my hand, I say breezily. "No need; it's nothing I can't handle."

"Well if you change your mind, let me know." Rafe smirks. "I'll gladly manhandle anyone who gets in your way."

Cassia scowls at Rafe's somewhat menacing statement, but it's obvious he's flirting. Enjoying this little game with Rafe, I shrug. "I'll keep that in mind."

The dinner conversation focuses mostly on Pru and Vreeland's August wedding, which Cassia is planning and Julien is photographing, and the upcoming bridal shower that Cassia has offered to coordinate on my behalf because I have zero organizational skills. As Pru's maid of honor, I'm still in charge of the bachelorette party, but I'm leaning heavily on Cassia for advice; I'm not proud when it comes to asking for help and would even consider asking Teddy Barker, if he weren't so self-righteous. About the only person at the table without a role in the wedding is Rafe, who listens politely. His eyes drift over in my direction every so often, causing my palms to grow sweaty with nerves.

After dinner, everyone lingers over decaf cappuccinos and dessert. Rafe and I decide to split a slice of lemon cake. "I'd like to see you again, Sophie," he murmurs, lifting the last bite to his mouth.

"I'd like that too," I say with a smile, despite a flutter of misgivings deep in my gut, which I blame on the stranger-danger glares Cassia keeps casting my way.

Rafe asks for my number and promptly sends me his contact info. Since I always turn down the volume when I'm having dinner, I pull out my mobile to confirm Rafe's text came through. But what pops up causes me to inhale sharply.

"Anything wrong?" asks Rafe.

Cassia overhears him and glances at me, a small line creasing her brow. "What's up?"

"I... I'm not sure," I sputter. "I've received a couple of collect calls in the past hour, plus two voicemails—one of which is from your brother."

"Jake left a message?" Cassia's shoulders hunch as she retrieves her phone, probably worried in case it concerns her daughter. Scanning the screen, she releases the breath she's been holding, visibly more relaxed. "He hasn't called me."

"Collect calls... Who does that anymore?" Pru wonders aloud.

Rafe shrugs. "Inmates need to make collect calls from jail."

A twisty feeling settles in the pit of my stomach. My family and friends are all a law-abiding bunch; I can't imagine any of them calling me from a jail cell. But... I've recently acquired a ridiculous new acquaintance. Has blasted Teddy Barker gotten himself arrested?

Nah. Impossible. Teddy is so squeaky clean I doubt he drives above the speed limit.

I rise from the table. "I'm sorry everyone, but I'd better be going. Something's obviously up, possibly with the bakery."

Rafe stands as well, pulling out my chair. "I hope everything's alright."

Cassia waves goodbye to our friends and joins me. We head to my car so we can listen to the messages in private.

The first is from Jake. "Hey Soph. I don't mean to

startle you, but one of your neighbors reported a burglary in progress at your place. I was chatting with Marv and Sam outside the police station, and when I heard the call come in and your address, I followed them in my car." My cousin Jake is the mayor of Riddle Hill, and the fire chief, and alpha of the local pack. If he wants to join the police on one of their calls, no one argues. "We apprehended a strange werewolf in your cottage who claims he's your employee and... ah... your roommate. He was wearing nothing but boxers when we found him. I honestly think he may have some screws loose. Alright, call me when you get this message."

I pound my forehead against the steering wheel and mutter, "I don't believe this."

Cassia shudders. "What a creep, to be lurking inside your cottage in his underwear!"

I don't bother explaining about Teddy Barker just yet. I scroll to the voicemail left by someone at the *SIU*, which I'm guessing is the Supernatural Incarceration Unit at the Riddle Hill police station, and hit playback. There's a lot of static, and then I hear Teddy's muffled voice; I have to raise the volume because he's speaking so softly. He doesn't sound nearly as sure of himself as he did earlier this afternoon, when he was shoving Auntie Dragonfly's will in my face.

"Hi, um... it's Teddy. I hope you're having a good dinner and that you get this message... The thing is.... um, I got arrested. I swear I did nothing wrong. I was minding my own business, cleaning my room, and suddenly two cops charged into your home and arrested me. Can you, er... can you please come bail me out and give me a lift back to the cottage? I promise to pay you back." Teddy's voice hitches. "I'm sorry. Really, truly sorry. But I don't have anyone else I can call. I'll make it up to you. I promise."

Groaning, I close my eyes and lean my head against the car seat. Twelve months. Three hundred and sixty-five days. A whole year of dealing with Teddy Freaking Barker.

Cassia stares at me as I hang up the phone. "What's happening? Who was that?"

"Do you remember the summer we turned ten and stayed with Auntie Dragonfly for two whole weeks?" I wait for her to give me a hesitant nod before continuing. "And I accidentally broke Auntie's Royal Vienna iridescent porcelain vase?"

Cassia's eyes widen. "Ye-es. She'd warned you not to run through the gallery."

"And Auntie was so mad she said I'd have to pay for it?"

"I remember. It was worth over forty thousand dollars, and you burst into tears when she handed you the bill."

Rubbing my temples, I mumble through my clenched jaw, "Auntie Dragonfly has found a way to make me pay —over and over and over."

"What are you talking about?" prods Cassia, sounding exasperated with my rambling.

"Leslie T. Barker is Auntie's final revenge."

CHAPTER 7
SUPERNATURAL INCARCERATION UNIT

TEDDY

Very Late, June 22

The werewolf cop, whom everyone calls Marv, straps me into a deep bucket seat in the back of the van. As I sink down into the foam-like cushions, their edges curl over my arms and legs, locking me firmly in place; even my head is swathed in the pillowy material. I'm unable to move, bound by a magically-altered car seat that's designed to secure dangerous supernatural criminals, not someone like me, an innocent werewolf caught with my pants down, so to speak.

Even worse, we're careening around sharp curves as we speed toward the police station, the faerie cop named Sam driving like a demon with a death wish. I have a sensitive stomach, which grows increasingly queasy each time Sam jams on the brakes.

Mumbling through my wolfish snout, I plead, "Sloower. Pleeze." But the cops don't seem to hear me until I moan, "Pleeze. I'm gonna be-ee sick-k!"

Marv turns around, takes one look at me, and shouts, "Pull over, Sam! And roll down the windows; it looks like he needs some fresh air."

Sam brakes, rolling to a stop so sudden the van rocks back and forth, and I grind my teeth together to keep the contents of my stomach where they belong. He opens all the windows, sending a gust of cool air into the van. "How. Much. Far-r-ther?" I gasp.

The dark-haired faerie turns around to look at me, his brown eyes softening. "Three blocks. I'll take it real slow."

"Tha-anks," I sputter.

Sam drives the rest of the way at a reduced speed with the windows down. Once we arrive, Marv hauls me out of the van and through the police station's rear door; I figure it's the entrance they use for supers so the humans don't get spooked. He unshackles my wrists and takes me into the showers, where he turns on the spigot. The blast of cold water is a welcome relief after that drive.

Marv waits until I'm thoroughly soaked before turning off the faucet, tossing me a towel, and ordering me to shift on the spot, which I do, shivering as goose-bumps prickle my flesh. He turns me over to a stern-faced vampire with long, yellowish fangs, who hands me an orange jumpsuit and dry underwear. After I change, the guard escorts me to a vacant holding cell that smells of ammonia, closing the door behind him with a sharp clang. Then he flips a switch, plunging my cell into darkness.

"Wait!" I cry out, not caring that my voice cracks. I'm definitely scared, and I don't like being alone in the dark. "Don't I get to make a call?"

"Once Marv and Sam get you processed, you'll be able to make your call."

After the vampire leaves, I slump onto the thin cot, dropping my head in my hands with a low moan.

How will Sophie react to my arrest? Will she bail me out? Or will she leave me here until... what? There's some sort of hearing?

Then another thought, even scarier than Riddle Hill's supernatural justice system, rears its head. Can Sophie fire me outright? I know there's a clause in Miss Dragonfly's will permitting Sophie to sever ties if I violate the law.

But how can mopping floors in my boxers constitute criminal activity? Did I inadvertently break some local law by shifting inside a faerie's domicile?

I continue to wrack my brain, trying but failing to come up with a rational explanation for my arrest, until it dawns on me someone must have witnessed my werewolf form after I'd taken down the curtains in my bedroom. I slap my forehead with the palm of my hand, angry with myself for being so careless in Riddle Hill, a town that attracts large numbers of tourists—both supers and non-supers—especially this time of year.

Aargh! I probably broke several village ordinances. I'm bemoaning my own stupidity when the toothy vampire guard finally reappears. He escorts me into a small, mint-green room with an oval table and three chairs. "Have a seat. Can I get you any coffee?"

I shake my head. "No thanks." After he leaves, I notice the large mirror spanning the back wall: probably two-way glass. Is someone on the other side watching me? How many violations can the Riddle Hill cops charge me with? That last thought makes my gut twist even tighter, and I take some deep breaths to calm my jittery insides.

Marv and Sam enter the room, shutting the door firmly behind them. They sit across from me and stare hard. I drop my eyes submissively; I'm in no position to vent or show anger. And frankly, I abhor fighting unless it's an absolute last resort.

Rubbing my sweaty palms down the pants of my jumpsuit, I take a stabilizing breath, forcing my racing heart to slow down. I need to remain calm. Steady. In control... or as much control I can muster while I'm a guest of the Riddle Hill Supernatural Incarceration Unit.

Sam tosses my Michigan driver's license onto the table. "Leslie T. Barker. I take it the *T*'s for Teddy?"

"Technically it's Theodore," I reply politely.

Marv rubs the bristles on his chin. "So tell me, Leslie Theodore 'Teddy' Barker, what possessed you to break into that cottage, strip down to your undershorts, shift into your werewolf form, and then dance in front of the windows for every non-super in Riddle Hill to witness?"

Shaking my head, I stammer, "I-I didn't break in; I was invited inside. I wasn't dancing but... but working, er... cleaning actually, and I always shift before doing any sort of physical labor. You're a werewolf... surely you know what happens when you shift in tight-fitting clothes."

Sam rolls his brown eyes, like he can't possibly believe I'm telling the truth, while Marv shrugs his beefy shoulders. "And that's the story you're sticking with?"

"That's the truth." I fold my arms across my chest. "When can I make my call?"

Marv nods at Sam, who places a large, black phone on the table. "Go on. Make your call."

I wait for them to give me even a modicum of privacy but realize they're not budging from their chairs. Huffing a sigh, I take the phone and turn my chair so I face away from them. I dial Sophie's number, which I'd memorized weeks ago, when I first learned about the bakery and that she'd be my new boss. It rings six times but she doesn't answer. Grimacing, I swivel back around. "The call went to voicemail."

"Try again, and this time leave a message." Sam nods at the phone in my hand. "And then we have some more questions for you."

Swallowing hard, I turn away for the second time and leave Sophie a voicemail that I can only pray she picks up. When I'm finished, I lay the phone on the table. "Okay, I left her a message."

"Her?" Marv quirks his brow. "Who'd you call?"

"Sophie Spellman Brownlee."

The door to the room opens, revealing a big, burly man with thick brown hair and beard, and a curious expression in his amber-gold eyes; it's the werewolf who ordered my arrest. He walks into the room, nods at the two cops, and says, "I'd like to ask the suspect a few questions, if you don't mind."

They leave, although a look passes between the three of them, and I'm certain they're scurrying around to the other side of the mirror so they can observe me sweating in my hard plastic chair. And that's exactly what I'm doing... perspiring profusely... because this man is giving off undeniable alpha wolf vibes.

When he drops into the seat opposite me, the plastic chair is swallowed up by his bulk. This werewolf is a solid wall of muscle; he's someone I'd like fighting *for* me, not against. He introduces himself, confirming my suspicions. "My name's Jake Grayclaw Spellman, and Sophie is my cousin. So you could say I have a personal interest in the shifter who was discovered dancing around in his underwear inside my cousin's home."

Jake squints at me, but I remain silent until he's finished speaking; there's no point in provoking him further. "I'm also alpha of the Bay Howlers pack, and I don't take kindly to werewolves who get arrested in my territory, particularly ones who've not properly introduced themselves."

Mongrels and moonbeams!

I'm in Riddle Hill for less than a day, and I've already managed to antagonize my new boss, get arrested, and tick off the local alpha. Despite Miss Dragonfly's best intentions, I don't think I'll be getting my fresh start in Riddle Hill after all. Maybe I could move farther north; Toronto perhaps?

I decide to address his second objection right away, since that's the one that can bury me for good, if and when I get out of here. "I made inquiries at the local pub and spoke with Wes, your packmate. He invited me to the pack meeting on Sunday so I could present myself properly."

Jake narrows his amber eyes at me. "That so?"

"Yes sir." I nod.

"It's late," he grunts. "And I'm in no mood to entertain explanations from unfamiliar wolves arrested for breaking and entering. So let's cut to the chase: why are you in Riddle Hill, and how do you know Sophie?"

I fold my hands on the table in front of me and peer directly into his eyes; I want this alpha to know I'm sincere. "I worked for Miss Dragonfly Spellman, of Grand Shores, Michigan, for the past three years; I was her live-in companion, chauffeur, and personal secretary. When Miss Dragonfly passed, she apportioned a part of her estate to me."

I pause when I notice Jake's scowl deepening, but he waves a hand for me to continue. Taking a deep breath, I hurriedly explain, "Miss Dragonfly's will contained quite a few stipulations in order for me to inherit my portion, including moving to Riddle Hill and working for your cousin—in exchange for room, board, and the opportunity to own ten percent in one year's time."

"Ten percent of what?" replies Jake.

"The Rhyme 'N Riddle Bakeshop."

"Wait a minute." Jake runs a hand through his hair. "You're *that Leslie?* We all assumed Leslie was a girl."

I roll my eyes. "You'll have to take that up with my mother."

"You didn't actually break in, did you?" When I shake

my head, Jake asks, "But why were you dancing in your boxers? It may not be illegal, but frankly it's worrisome. In case you haven't noticed, I'm very protective of Sophie and the rest of my family."

"I wasn't dancing; I was cleaning. I work much faster in my werewolf form."

"And you clean in your undershorts?"

I huff out a sigh. "Normally I wear sweats, but all my stuff's still in the trunk of my car. I didn't want to unpack until I'd... er... organized and disinfected my room. Your cousin is..."

"A brilliant baker," says Jake, "and a tad messy."

"Y-yes."

Jake leans forward, the chair creaking beneath him. "I'm going to confirm your story, Mr. Barker. And if it checks out, we'll see about dropping the charges. But let me make one thing perfectly clear: if you so much as look the wrong way at Sophie, you'll have to answer to me. Understand?"

"Yes sir."

"And the next time we meet—assuming you really are *that Leslie*—I'll want to hear about your last pack and all the pertinent details."

I'm certain Jake has noticed the lack of an alpha-scent on me; he must realize I'm a loner. I mumble apologetically, "I don't have a pack, not any longer."

Jake's eyebrows bend inward. "For how long?"

"Three years... ever since Miss Dragonfly employed me." I hesitate. "It's a long story, perhaps best saved for another time."

Jake stands up, pushes in his chair, and pins me with

a steely glower that makes my tongue go immediately dry and stick to the roof of my mouth. I know he's trying to shake my resolve, but I refuse to flinch; I need to prove I'm a werewolf worthy of joining his pack. "Alright, Mr. Barker. I'll listen to your tale, but know this: if I smell anything fishy, I'll run you right out of Riddle Hill, regardless of Dragonfly Spellman's last will and testament."

Since I can't think of anything to say in my defense, I don't reply. Jake straightens, his scowl replaced by an assessing gaze. Then he asks, "Do you have any questions for me?"

"No sir." At this point, all I want is to shed my orange jumpsuit, leave the SIU, and tumble onto the mattress in my spic-and-span bedroom.

"Then I'll offer a word of advice, Mr. Barker," says Jake wearily. "While you're in my town, keep your clothes on and your nose clean."

CHAPTER 8
LONE WOLF

SOPHIE

Almost Midnight, June 22

"He appears legit... except for the fact he's not a member of any pack, which I'll need to explore further," says Jake, pushing the SIU police report across the table at me. We're in one of the small conference rooms at the Riddle Hill police station; it's nearly midnight, and I'm positively bushed. Teddy Barker's arrest is the very last thing I feel like dealing with at the moment. I'm half tempted to leave him in jail until the morning so I can go home and get some shut-eye, but then I recall his apologetic message... and the low rumble of his voice as he pleaded for my help... and I heave a sigh.

"It says here that his old pack disbanded three years ago when the alpha died." I tap the report and glance at Jake. "Is that normal? Why wouldn't another werewolf have assumed the alpha role?"

Jake shrugs. "It's not uncommon, particularly with a

small pack. The rest of the werewolves probably merged with another group."

"Then why wouldn't Teddy Barker have done the same thing—joined another pack?"

"That's what I aim to find out," says Jake. "You know how I feel about loners; they're generally self-absorbed and rarely loyal. I've yet to meet one I'd invite into my pack."

I shift uneasily on the hard chair as I think of Rafe MacTire, the bad-boy werewolf I had dinner with earlier this evening. I'm pretty sure Jake wouldn't like Rafe any better than he likes Teddy; best not to mention Rafe's loner status around him. "If you're trying to warn me that Teddy Barker can't be trusted, you have nothing to worry about."

Jake shakes his head. "That's the thing; I'm not getting typical loner vibes from him. I think Teddy Barker yearns to belong to a pack. He's coming to my pack meet Sunday night for a sniff and a tussle; I'll get a better sense of him then. But Teddy strikes me as lonely, so whatever's been keeping him from pack life must have been pretty traumatic."

I draw my brows together, feeling a twinge of remorse for how I've treated Teddy. Stifling a yawn, I say, "I'll keep that in mind."

Jake pats my hand. "Why don't you pull the car around front; Teddy can leave whenever you're ready."

"Thanks Jake... for everything." I grab my purse and head for the door.

"No problem. And Sophie—" Jake waits for me to turn back around "—If I'm wrong about him, or if he gives you any trouble, I'll run him out of town so fast he'll be glad his tail is still attached to his butt."

I grin at my overprotective cousin. "I think I can handle Leslie T. Barker, but I'll let you know if I need any assistance."

I pull up in front of the police station in my ancient, silver, Subaru Forester, which my dad bought from a used-car dealer when I turned sixteen. With two-hundred thousand miles on the odometer, and more dings and divots than the first tee at the public golf course, I'm grateful it's still running. Ten minutes later Teddy drops into the passenger seat, pulls the door shut, and gives me a small, shy nod. "I'm so sorry, Sophie; I made a stupid mistake. I've gotten used to shifting anytime I want—everyone on Miss Dragonfly's staff was a super—and the nearest neighbor was three miles away. It won't happen again; I promise."

"If it happens again, you'll be arrested and convicted; the elder council is very strict." I sound grumpier than I intend, so I soften my tone. "Marv let you off with a warning this time. You have to close all the curtains before you shift."

"Got it, boss." Ducking his head, he fiddles with his seatbelt.

As I watch Teddy buckle up, I'm suddenly distracted by the black tee he's wearing, which is so form-fitting I can see the ripple of his biceps beneath the stretchy fabric. Dropping my gaze, my eyes snag on a pair of muscular thighs encased in skin-tight, black leather.

"What in faerie-land are you wearing?" I sputter.

"Oh... um... " Teddy gives me an apologetic grin. "I

had to borrow these from lost and found, since the police wanted their jumpsuit returned, and I wasn't about to ask you for a fresh change of clothes, not on top of ruining your evening." He shrugs. "I gave them a good sniff; the shirt was recently laundered, and the pants are practically new."

Rolling my eyes, I pull out of the parking spot. "Well, they don't fit you properly. Please donate them or something."

"O-okay." Teddy glances down at his leather breeches. "Do you have a dress code at the bakery?"

"Once we open, we'll have aprons that we'll wear over our clothes; jeans and tees will be fine. Until then, wear stuff you don't mind getting dirty." Keeping my eyes firmly planted on the road ahead, I flap one hand in his direction. "Just nothing too... er... like that."

"Too... black?"

"And too... leathery." I huff. "We're a family-friendly bakery."

Teddy scrunches his brow. "No black leather. Check."

"And nothing too tight," I add.

"No *tight* black leather. Double-check." Then Teddy starts to chuckle.

"What's so funny?" I purse my lips, frowning.

"It just occurred to me that Miss Dragonfly would have told me I could wear these ridiculous leather pants whenever I wanted." He's laughing harder now. "She was a stylish, elderly faerie with an adventurous spirit. And you're... er..."

"I'm what?"

"... Oh, nothing."

"You can't just start to say something like that and then stop abruptly. Out with it, wolf."

Teddy gets himself back under control, mostly. "You're a beautiful young faerie with... um... with a frumpy spirit."

Did Teddy just call me beautiful? And at the same time insult me?

"Frumpy?" I practically spit as I park the Subaru in the driveway, stomp out of the car, and fling open my front door, fuming at Teddy Freaking Barker. How dare he compare me to Auntie Dragonfly and find me wanting?

"And grumpy," he adds mildly.

I flip on the lights in my cottage and turn back to glare at him, but his head is cocked to the side like a big, happy dog, and his eyes are sparkling with humor... and something else... something almost like tenderness. He's teasing me, and I'm not sure how I feel about it.

"So I'm a grumpy, frumpy faerie, eh?" I snort.

"And beautiful. Don't forget beautiful." Then Teddy smiles, and it's almost dazzling in its intensity.

That smile does something to my chest, something I'm not prepared to examine right now. Despite my irritation at this annoying werewolf, the corners of my mouth tilt upward.

"Sweet dreams, Sophie," he murmurs. "See you in the morning." Then Teddy heads into his bedroom and shuts the door quietly behind him.

What just happened? And why do I feel cuddly and warm all of a sudden, like I'm swaddled in a soft, fuzzy blanket?

Gah! I can't afford to lose my edge around Teddy, despite his good looks and charm. That werewolf poses a substantial threat to my dream of owning the bakery free and clear—without any encumbrances or meddling ten-percent partners.

"*Meep!*" Zosia welcomes me, weaving in and out of my legs.

I scoop up my baby fox and bury my face in her glistening white fur. I think back over my day and the two werewolves who've entered my life: fastidious, ridiculous Teddy, and dark, dangerous Rafe. One I definitely need to keep at arm's length, and the other... Well, I'd like to explore that possibility further.

What would dating Rafe be like? And would my werewolf cousin get on my case about it? Probably.

"Oh, Zosia," I whisper. "I have a feeling my life's about to get very muddled."

CHAPTER 9
WELCOME TO JUMANJI

SOPHIE

Early Saturday, June 23

"Hello?" I mumble into the phone. It's six-thirty; once the bakery is open, I'll be up at three, but for now I'm enjoying the extra hours of sleep.

"It's me," whispers Cassia, who's probably calling from my parents' café. "I overheard your mom talking to Granny Catbeam a few minutes ago. They know about the... ah... magical misfire, and they're not happy. They plan on paying you a visit this morning."

"Oh no." Clutching my head, I come fully awake. Dealing with my mom is bad enough, but Granny represents the faerie community on the Riddle Hill elder council. Catbeam Spellman is charged with keeping faeries and our magic in line. If she knows I lost control and blew out a wall, then I'm toast.

"I'm sorry, Sophie," murmurs Cassia.

"Thanks for the heads up," I grumble. "I'd better get

"

dressed." Hanging up the phone, I push myself out of bed and stumble toward the bathroom, bemoaning my fate.

Teddy's door opens just as I step into the hall. His shoulder-length hair is a tousled, blond mop, and he's yawning, oblivious to the fact he has an audience. He's wearing his rumpled beige slacks from yesterday and his blue shirt, which is unbuttoned, revealing a manly, muscular chest covered in fine, golden hair.

Why does Leslie T. Barker have to be so... hot? I have a sneaking suspicion that's half the reason Auntie Dragonfly employed Teddy; she enjoyed the view.

Teddy glances up, sees me standing in the hallway in my shortie pajamas, and rears back in surprise, like he's never seen a girl with long, bare legs.

Is he finding me as distracting as I'm finding him? I fold my arms and scowl, reminding myself there's another werewolf I want to get to know better... much better... than this big, Nordic nuisance.

"Oh, um... are you... er... why don't you go first," he finishes lamely.

"I'll be quick," I tell him brusquely, squashing my momentary attraction like a bug at a July picnic. Then I recall my dad's eel in the tub, and I feel like I ought to remind Teddy, given his overreaction yesterday. "But no showers until tonight."

"Huh?" He peels his gaze away from my legs long enough to look me in the eye.

"There's still that eel in the tub. You can't use the shower until tonight."

"Oh." Teddy nods slowly. "Right."

I think perhaps Teddy is still somewhat in shock

from his arrest last night, which probably spooked him; he strikes me as a pacifist at heart. Either that, or he needs some coffee first thing in the morning to fire up his brain cells. His pupils appear partially dilated.

After washing my face and brushing my teeth, I toss on a pair of cutoff jean shorts and a gray tee, shove my feet into my green Converse sneakers, and head into the kitchen to feed Zosia. I put on a pot of coffee and ponder my upcoming showdown with Mom and Granny Catbeam, who won't overlook my haphazard magic this time, which isn't fair. It's not my fault I didn't inherit their amazing gatekeeping magic, the most powerful faerie magic anywhere. No, I had to inherit my dad's kitchen magic, which is great for cooking and baking, but it's really a limiting factor when you want to do so much more.

I'm lost in thought about what sort of punishment Granny's going to mete out—because I have no doubt she's going to make sure I pay for my mistake somehow —when Teddy wanders into the kitchen looking prepared to lead a safari. He's wearing neatly pressed, knee-length khaki shorts; a tan, short-sleeved shirt with a breast pocket; a pair of thick, beige socks that reach almost to his knees; and steel-toed combat boots. Add a pith helmet and walking stick, and Teddy would be ready to explore Jumanji.

What does he think he's going to encounter in my bakeshop?

Since I criticized his black leather pants last night, I figure I should keep my mouth shut this morning, but it's hard not to giggle. I take a long swallow of my coffee as I struggle to get myself under control. Pointing to the pot, I sputter, "Help yourself."

Teddy gives me a curious glance, grabs a clean mug from the counter, and proceeds to scour it under hot water for thirty seconds. Geesh, this guy is a major germophobe. If this is his mother's influence, she must be a real piece of work. Then again, she named her son "Leslie," which just proves my point; Teddy probably never had a chance at being normal.

"What are your plans for today?" I ask.

He seems surprised by the question. "I'm your only employee, and your bakery is a mess. I'm here to help."

"Well, you might want to delay your arrival until after my mom and grandmother visit."

"Why?"

"I expect some faerie fireworks."

Teddy's eyebrows quirk upward. "Well in that case perhaps it would be helpful if I'm there for moral support."

I purse my lips; he has a point. They may not be quite so angry if we have a witness. "You'd really do that for me?"

Teddy grins. "Of course. You're the boss! If you're going down in flames, I'll be there right beside you."

Shaking my head, I chortle. "Gee thanks."

"Think nothing of it," he says breezily, opening the refrigerator.

"What are you looking for?"

"Half and half for the coffee."

"We're out, but we can pick some up."

"Okay... how about milk for the corn flakes?" He nods at the cereal box on the counter.

"Um..."

"We're out of that too?" he sighs.

"Yeah... sorry. It's been kind of hectic."

He takes a swallow of his black coffee and then places the mug on a small section of the table that he's managed to clear. "If you make a list of what you want to eat, I can run to the grocery store this afternoon. I'm not much of a cook, but I'm happy to be your errand boy."

"My errand boy?" My mouth tips up at the corners unexpectedly.

Teddy's ears redden. "That does sound a bit... um..."

"About a century out of date. I do hope Auntie Dragonfly never called you her errand boy?"

"Of course not; Miss Dragonfly was always respectful. But we used to watch a lot of old movies together... and some of the terminology just stuck in my head. I'll have to work on updating my vocabulary."

I chuckle. "Probably wise, especially if you want to join the local pack."

Teddy's head snaps up. "Did Jake say anything about me joining his pack?"

"Not exactly. But he did show me the SIU report, which had some history about your last pack."

"I don't want to talk about it," says Teddy; there's a note of warning in his voice I've not heard before. "It has no bearing on my status as your employee."

"I'm sorry about your alpha," I say softly, and I mean it.

Teddy stands abruptly. "I'll meet you at the bakery

shortly; I need to grab something to eat." He walks stiffly to the sink, rinses out his mug for another full thirty seconds, and then leaves without another word.

Wow... I've obviously struck a nerve... but what happened with his old pack in Michigan that makes Teddy so reluctant to discuss it?

CHAPTER 10
SIMPLY DOOMED

TEDDY

Saturday Morning, June 23

I reach into the back seat of my Caddy and grab a handful of granola bars; they'll have to do for breakfast. It's one of those cloudless, perfect, early summer days, the kind that remind me of summer camp and toasted marshmallows and lazy pack meets around the campfire. I can't resist a quick walk down to the harbor; perhaps if I stare long enough at the sparkling waters of Green Bay, I'll be able to settle my edgy nerves.

I plunk down on a park bench and break open my first breakfast bar; a pair of seagulls wander hopefully toward me, but I shake my head. "Sorry fellas, but I don't have anything to spare today."

There are a few old timers out for an early stroll, and some tourists getting ready for a day of fishing or cruising along the coastline. I sigh, wishing I could join them; of course I'm grateful to Miss Dragonfly for this opportunity of a do-over, but my new faerie boss is a complication I hadn't bargained on.

Despite all the ways Sophie and I are incompatible... I'm finding myself increasingly drawn to her... and I know that's a very bad idea. The sight of Sophie in her tiny pajamas this morning lit a flame inside me that I'm still struggling to squelch. And just now, when she expressed remorse over my old alpha, my heart literally flip-flopped in my chest, and I had to get out of that claustrophobic kitchen.

We're about as different as two people can be—we're not even the same supernatural species—which makes it difficult for me to understand why my insides fizzle whenever she draws near, and my head gets wooly like it's stuffed with yarn.

I'd better figure out fast how to manage this unwanted attraction to my new boss; our work arrangement *has* to pan out for me. If I give Sophie a legitimate reason to fire me, then all I'll have left in the world is Miss Dragonfly's old car and the clothes on my back. The Cadillac DTS is certainly large enough to sleep in, but I'd prefer not to be homeless and packless.

I toss the empty wrappers in the trash bin and make my way back to Main Street. Marv the cop is outside the Sit for a Spell Café, issuing a red-faced driver a ticket. Our eyes meet as I pass him, and he gives me a neutral nod. I suppose that bodes well for the pack meet tomorrow night, right?

As I cross the street, my eyes are drawn to the bakery's opaque white windows. What a minute; who installed the white shades? I don't think Sophie would've risked another spell, which means her mom and grandmother have already arrived and magicked some shades for privacy. That's probably not a good sign.

I try the door handle, but it's locked, so I give the door a firm knock. There's no answer, but I detect movement on the other side, so I continue pounding until an elderly faerie with a striking resemblance to Miss Dragonfly pulls open the door. "We're closed, sonny."

When she starts to shut the door, I insert my foot in the opening. Her mouth pulls into a pout, and I have a feeling if I'm not careful, this faerie might decide to teach me a lesson I'll never forget. "Are you Miss Catbeam Spellman? Younger sister of Miss Dragonfly Spellman?"

"Who wants to know?" Her eyes narrow into twin slits.

I extend my hand with a smile, but Catbeam Spellman grunts, so I quickly drop it. "I'm Leslie T. Barker. I was your sister's live-in companion until her untimely death."

"*Untimely?*" The faerie shakes her head. "Dragonfly was so old even she forgot her age most days."

An attractive middle-aged woman stares at me from inside the shop; this must be Phoebe Spellman. I'm a little worried about getting involved in faerie business, but I told Sophie I'd be here for her, and I'm not going to let her down. "Who are you speaking with, Mother?" asks Phoebe.

"A boy named Leslie," quips Catbeam. "Guess he's *that Leslie*, you know, the one Dragonfly employed for the last few years and then left ten percent of the bakery to."

Catbeam hasn't opened the door wider, so I'm perched on the threshold, half in and half out.

"That's correct," I say, drawing myself up to my full height. "And I'd like to be permitted entry to the bakery that I partially own."

"What a hoot!" Catbeam Spellman throws back her head and laughs, reminding me of my late patroness. "I can see why my sister hired you. Come on in, although watch your step; my granddaughter was just explaining to us how that wall disappeared yesterday."

Sophie gives me a barely perceptible head nod, but I sense she's grateful I'm here. She says, "Like I was saying, I tried cleaning the wall... and I guess I tried too hard."

A gargling sound escapes from my throat, which I quickly hide behind a cough. There's no way Sophie was cleaning yesterday; I don't think that girl actually knows the meaning of the word. Sophie shoots daggers at me with her eyes, and I manage to get myself under control.

"What spell did you use, child?" asks Catbeam.

"How do you know I used magic?"

"Because your grandmother and I felt it," snaps Phoebe.

Sophie hangs her head. "It was a combination of a few spells."

"Then which spells did you combine?" asks her grandmother.

Sophie throws her hands in the air. "I don't remember. It all happened so fast, and it felt so right at the time, until Cassia shouted at me to stop and pulled me back."

"I'm glad Cassia had the good sense to stop you." Phoebe folds her arms and addresses Catbeam. "This is a matter for the elder council, Mother. What's your verdict?"

The elderly faerie pins her granddaughter with a hawkish glower, but Sophie doesn't make eye contact; she's staring down at her green sneakers, shuffling them nervously on the dirty flooring. I'm positively itching to start scrubbing the old glue, gobs of wallboard, and general filth off the shop's wooden floorboards. I suspect there's very nice hardwood buried somewhere beneath all that ick.

"Sophie Spellman Brownlee," huffs Catbeam, obviously ready to pronounce her judgment. "You have been found guilty of the misapplication of magic for the third time. The first two times occurred when you were in high school, and I let you off with a warning each time. But you're turning twenty-nine next month; it's time to grow up and face facts. You're a talented kitchen faerie. Period. Save your magic for desserts, not drywall!"

"Does that mean…" Sophie starts to say, as if she's sensed a glimmer of hope that, quite honestly, I'm not detecting. This skinny, silver-haired faerie is all business.

"I'm not finished," Catbeam continues. "Since you have yet to learn your lesson and embrace the wonderful gifts you do have, you leave me with no choice. I'm clipping your wings for six new moons."

I've spent enough time with faeries to know what this archaic expression means; Catbeam is going to bind Sophie's magic, essentially forcing her to live as a nonsuper for half a year. I wince as Sophie shrieks, "Granny, no!" Then she turns to her mother, tears welling in her large, gray eyes. "Mom, please, can't you do something?"

Phoebe Spellman shakes her head, her auburn bob swaying slightly. "I'm sorry, Sophie, but you brought this on yourself."

Catbeam places her hands on Sophie's shoulders and utters an incantation in a low, fast murmur. I sense a vibration in the air, although I don't see anything. When she's finished speaking, Catbeam pats Sophie's back and then leaves the shop with Phoebe.

Sophie just stands there in the middle of her broken bakery with the missing wall and gray dust everywhere, and sobs her heart out.

I don't know what to do, but I'm itching to enfold this woman in my arms and comfort her. The question is... should I? Would that lead to complications neither of us needs?

Then Sophie hiccups and tries wiping her face with the backs of her hands, but it's useless because she's crying even harder, and my resolve crumbles. I pull her into my arms, cradling her soft body against my chest.

To my surprise, Sophie Spellman Brownlee, the slovenly, outspoken faerie with the clipped wings and failing bakery, fits there like the last bars of a melody I've been humming all my life but never got right.

That's when I realize what all the tingly, befuddled feelings have been trying to tell me. They've spelled trouble all along, very big trouble, worse even than winding up living in my old Caddy for a few months or sharing breakfast with a couple of gulls.

My grumpy faerie boss, the woman who's providing me with room, board, and a job, holds one more key to my entire future.

I find it very hard to believe she's going to be happy when I tell her, which won't happen anytime soon, because even though Sophie hasn't moved yet from my arms, as soon as her brain engages, she's going to be pushing me away and pretending this didn't happen. And all the while my heart, which she already possesses without my consent, is going to be mourning even that small separation.

How am I going to survive being in continual proximity to Sophie without being able to touch her, or tell her, or do anything except pine because of this single, irrefutable fact I've just discovered?

Call it love at first sight, call it a soul bond, call it the purest, truest magic; technically it's all the above. What it means is that from this moment forward, I'll have zero control over my emotional response to my boss.

Mongrels and moonbeams... I'm doomed.

Sophie is my fated mate.

CHAPTER 11
CLIPPED WINGS

SOPHIE

SATURDAY MORNING, JUNE 23

Granny's spell to clip my wings struck my magic with the force of a giant sledgehammer hacking out a piece of my soul. It hurt my spirit so much I burst into tears on the spot. But despite my weeping and hiccups, I'm feeling unexpectedly comforted... and warm... and kind of cozy. It slowly dawns on me, I'm leaning against someone's brawny chest.

Wait... is it?

No blasted way!

Teddy Freaking Barker isn't just giving me a little pat on the back; he's wrapped his massive arms around me and pulled me so tight against his body I can feel his heart hammering through his tan safari shirt.

I give him a hard shove in the chest. "What are you doing, Teddy? I'm your boss, remember?"

Teddy drops his arms like I'm radioactive and scurries back a few steps. Although I miss the warmth of his arms around me, it's inappropriate, even if he was trying to be nice. "I'm sorry, Sophie." Teddy glances down at the toes of his giant combat boots. "You were so sad, and I wanted to help."

"Well don't! We have to maintain professional decorum."

He mumbles. "Of course."

"Make sure it doesn't happen again."

"I'll try."

"What do you mean you'll try?" I snap at him.

"I... I mean yes, of course, it won't happen again."

Then he reaches into his breast pocket, pulls out a neatly pressed, white handkerchief, and hands it to me. Since my nose is dripping like a leaky faucet, and I don't have a tissue handy, I accept it and start mopping my face. By the time I'm done, black mascara streaks Teddy's formerly pristine hanky, which is now damp with my tears and snot. Even a normal guy wouldn't want this thing back; Mr. Clean would probably gag if I tried.

I stuff the balled-up hanky down my front pocket and survey the interior of my shop, which looks even worse in the morning light, probably because Granny magically cleaned the plate glass windows when she installed the shades. She wanted to protect our privacy, and I think also give me a little parting gift before she stripped away my magic; new window shades are one less thing I'll have to invest in later.

"I don't even know where to start," I say lamely, feeling sorry for myself while also trying to process the fact that being held by Teddy wasn't really all that bad. In fact… it was pretty nice.

But I remind myself it's a bad idea. Besides, there's another werewolf who promises to be more edgy and less uptight than Teddy, and who comes without any of the employer-employee complications to worry about. My phone pings, and I pull it out of my back pocket.

Speak of the devil—it's Rafe!

I grin at his message. "Vreeland is taking Pru out on his boat tomorrow afternoon. He invited me and said I could bring a plus one. You're the only plus one I want to bring. Can you make it?"

"What time are they leaving?" I text back.

"Five-thirty. They want to do a sunset cruise, and Pru's packing a picnic dinner."

I know where Vreeland docks his boat; it's about a half-hour drive for me. "I can make it work. I'll meet you at the dock at five-thirty."

Rafe sends me a thumbs up. "Cool. See you then."

I'm still smiling as I tuck my phone back into my shorts. When I glance up, I notice Teddy's brow is puckered. "What was that about?" he asks. "You went from tears to grins in a matter of seconds."

I fold my arms. "Not that it's any of your business, but that was my prospective boyfriend."

"*Your what?*" Teddy screeches.

I jump back, startled. "What's wrong with you? You just scared me half to death."

"Sorry," Teddy mumbles and then walks stiffly toward the storage area in the back of the shop. He returns with the broom and dustpan and starts sweeping in large, methodical strokes.

My phone buzzes again, and this time it's a message from Cassia, who wants to know what happened with Mom and Granny. I fill her in about my clipped wings—which I'm super upset about, but the date with Rafe has momentarily overshadowed my despair—and I tell her about seeing Rafe, Vreeland, and Pru tomorrow.

Cassia doesn't respond right away, which happens a lot because she's working in my parents' restaurant. Then she texts, "I'm glad it's a double date."

I blow out a puff of air. Cassia means well, but she's such a fuddy-duddy; I know she's worried about Rafe's lone wolf status. She's probably heard all sorts of negative stories from Jake about the problems caused by loners. "He's Vreeland's friend. What can go wrong?"

"He gives off bad-boy vibes."

"Exactly!" I text her. "I'm bored."

Cassia sends me an eye roll. "Just be safe."

When I slip my phone into my back pocket for the second time, I sense Teddy's eyes on me, but he quickly glances away. He's acting weird today, which is exactly why employees should never embrace their bosses; it messes up everyone's pheromones.

When Teddy finishes sweeping the floor, he bags up all the dirt, dust, and broken bits of wallboard and then carts it outside to the trash bin. He's gone maybe ten minutes, which gives me time to make a hair appointment tomorrow with Spectra, who squeezes me into her schedule. I know I'm going on a boat, and my hair will be wild in a matter of minutes, but I want to start my date with Rafe looking my best.

Teddy returns carrying a lined pad of paper, a pencil, and a tape measure. "What's all that for?" I ask.

"To take measurements so I know how much wallboard we need."

"Why?"

Teddy waves a hand at the gaping hole I made in the shop. "So I can put up a new wall. How else were you planning on repairing it?"

I shrug. "I thought I'd have to hire a contractor."

"You should save what you have left of your inheritance for buying supplies later."

"Do you know how to install dry wall?" The skepticism is evident in my voice. Perhaps I'm being unfair, but Teddy's singular skill seems to be cleaning.

"I wouldn't offer if I didn't know how," Teddy chides me gently. "My next-door neighbor owned a construction company; I worked for him every summer until I graduated from college. I can do the repairs, put in new light fixtures, put up new trim, and paint the shop. But if we're going to get this place ready for its grand opening in time, you're going to need to do your part."

I sputter. "What's that supposed to mean?"

"It means it's time for you to put your phone away and do some manual labor. You can begin by stripping the wallpaper from the rest of the walls using glue remover, a scraper, and some elbow grease. Getting this bakeshop ready is a two-person job. You need to pull your weight every single day until we open."

"How dare you speak to me like... like..."

"Like you've been addressing me since I arrived yesterday? Like I'm little more than a nuisance, someone you're stuck with because of Miss Dragonfly's will?" Teddy heaves a sigh. "Look... we both want this bakery to succeed, which won't happen if we spend our time arguing. Here—" he hands me one end of the tape measure "—let's just get to work."

I stare down at the tape measure, then up at Teddy. It's true I've been treating him like a nuisance, because he is. And like someone I'm stuck with, because I am. But if he really can help me get this bakery ready for the grand opening, Teddy deserves a little respect, even if I'm still resentful about his ten percent ownership stake. "I agree we need to work together, and of course I'll pitch in and do my part. But just to be clear, I already have plans for tomorrow." Then I add, because I feel like I need to say it aloud. "I have a date."

"With your 'prospective boyfriend'?" Teddy says it with annoying little air quotes.

"Yes."

Did Teddy just wince? It was so fleeting I can't be certain. He doesn't say anything else, and we get to work taking the measurements. Then he shows me how to strip the wallpaper, which I hadn't been doing correctly. It goes much faster once I score the paper first, then soak it with the glue remover, and then scrape it off. It's still tedious, but it's no longer impossible.

Around noon, Teddy straightens from hand-scrubbing the floor. I have to admit, the portion he's cleaned does look remarkably better. "I'm going to run out and pick up some lunch. What would you like?"

"You don't need to get me anything," I say with a sniff, even though I'm half starved.

"Actually, I do. Your stomach's been growling for the past thirty minutes." When Teddy smiles, the corners of his eyes crinkle ever so slightly.

"Well, I certainly wouldn't want my growly stomach to interfere with your concentration, so I suppose a turkey sandwich wouldn't go amiss. And some iced tea. And maybe some apple chips." I pause and retrieve my purse. "Here, I can contribute."

"I've got this."

A short while later I hear the purr of his car engine as he returns, pulling into the driveway. I open the rear door, surprised to see Teddy lugging a blanket along with a bag of food and a cardboard tray with two iced teas.

"What's all this?" I ask, helping him spread out the blanket.

"Indoor picnic." He waits until we're both seated on the blanket and then hands over my drink, sandwich, and apple chips.

"Ooh, you went to Vlad's Victuals."

"It seemed safer than going to your parents' café. I don't think your mom likes me very much," says Teddy. "She scowled at me the whole time she was here."

"She probably can't figure out why Auntie Dragonfly left you ten percent of this bakeshop." I unwrap my turkey and Havarti on rye. "And frankly neither can I."

"I didn't twist Miss Dragonfly's arm or anything, if that's what you're wondering." Teddy takes a bite of his roast beef sandwich, chews carefully, and swallows. "She told me her plans after her attorney visited for the last time, which was about three months ago."

"Were you surprised?"

"Shocked... and incredibly grateful. But I refused at first, explaining to Miss Dragonfly that you and your family would resent me. But she said her mind was made up, and what was done was done."

"Did she tell you why she made you partial owner of my bakery?"

"Our bakery," replies Teddy with a twinkle in his eye.

"As ninety-percent owner, I think I can safely call it mine," I huff.

"Fair enough. You're the baker, after all." Teddy glances down at the blanket for so long that I'm not sure he's going to answer my question. When he looks at me, his blue eyes have a sheen that makes them even bluer, if that's possible.

"Miss Dragonfly wanted to give me a fresh start in a new supernatural village, a place where she knew the local pack was well run, and where I'd have a fighting chance at making friends... or at least, not making enemies." He gives me a sheepish grin. "She also felt you needed someone with a good head on their shoulders to help you with the business; your auntie said you were an 'impetuous faerie'—her words, not mine."

Shaking my head, I snort. "She knew me better than I realized." Then I think about what else Teddy said, about the need to start over, find a pack, and make friends. He shared a lot in very few words. "Why do you need to start over in Riddle Hill? Don't you have any family?"

Teddy's shoulders slump. "My parents split up

recently; my dad took a new job on the west coast, my mom is sweet but unreliable, and my sister is busy with her own family." Teddy shrugs. "My dad was an only child, and my mom's extended family lives in Scotland. So... I do kind of need to figure things out for myself."

I think about my mom and dad, Cassia, Jake, Granny Catbeam, and all my unalive ancestors hanging on the walls of my parents' café. "My cup is overflowing with relatives; too bad we can't trade."

"You don't really mean that."

"My grandmother clipped my wings today, and my mother did nothing to stop her. What do you think?"

"I think you know, deep down, they love you."

I shrug. "I'd still trade places with you."

"Actually Sophie, I don't think you would," says Teddy so softly I have to lean closer to hear him.

CHAPTER 12
ASSERTIVENESS TRAINING

TEDDY

Afternoon, June 23

Sophie is making excellent progress stripping the wallpaper, while I've been scrubbing a decade of grime and gook off the hardwood floors. It's a little after three, and we both pause when we hear the shop's back door opening. "It's me! I've come bearing gifts," calls a female voice.

"Cassia! Thank the stars! Teddy has been an absolute taskmaster all day," shouts Sophie, who promptly drops her scraper on the floor. She's obviously done for the day, which is just as well. I need a long run to decompress and figure out how I'm going to win Sophie's heart. I don't know how, and I don't know when, but I *will* make it happen; the idea of finding my fated mate but losing her to someone else hollows out my chest.

I wipe my hands on a rag and rise from the floor, curious to meet Cassia, a petite blonde faerie with a friendly smile. She's holding a carryout tray with three coffees and a bag of pastries. Sophie makes the introductions, waving her hand between us. "Cassia, this is Leslie T. Barker, also known as Teddy. Teddy, this is my cousin, Cassia Spellman."

"It's nice to meet you." I take the tray from Cassia. "Thanks for the coffee."

"I've been dying to meet you," says Cassia, her smile widening. "Granny Catbeam likes you, which is no small feat. Aunt Phoebe is cautiously optimistic, and Uncle Nash said Sophie's place is already showing signs of improvement." She turns to Sophie to explain. "Your dad just picked up the eel."

Sophie rolls her eyes. "Am I the only person around here who doesn't mind a little mess?"

"Yes!" Cassia and I reply with a chuckle, and even Sophie laughs.

I let Cassia and Sophie sit on the blanket, while I perch on a step stool with the coffee. Cassia holds up the bag. "Want a croissant? I've got chocolate and almond in here."

I shake my head. "No thanks. I'm not hungry." Which is true; my stomach clenched into knots as soon Sophie told me why she couldn't work tomorrow. My mate is going on a date with someone she deems boyfriend material, and I can't shake off this desperate sort of dread whenever my head reminds my heart of that fact.

But I do enjoy watching Sophie take her first bite of the pastry; she closes her eyes and makes a little *hmm* sound as she savors the flavors. She must sense my eyes on her, because she glances up with a little scowl, so I quickly look away.

Cassia squeezes Sophie's arm. "So how are you doing, really? I can't imagine how horrible it is… to have magic… and then have it taken away." She bites her lower lip, and I sense there's some history with her own magic.

"It's absolutely awful." Sophie sniffles. "And it hurt—not physically, but on the inside, like something was being ripped out of me—I wanted to die on the spot. The only thing that made me feel any better—" Sophie hesitates; is she going to mention that I took her in my arms to comfort her? "—was that text message from Rafe. At least I have something to look forward to tomorrow."

Suddenly I'm choking, the coffee going down the wrong way. Cassia gives me a worried glance. "You okay?"

I wave my hand. "I'm fine."

Sophie arches her eyebrow; I think she thinks I did that on purpose. Perhaps on a subconscious level I did. "I'm thinking of wearing my new red bathing suit. But should I wear it under my clothes or change on Vreeland's boat later? What do you think?"

Stars above! She's going to wear a bathing suit tomorrow? This is worse than I thought! Her prospective boyfriend is going to take one look at her curvaceous loveliness, and the man won't be able to keep his hands to himself.

I clear my throat a few times, and Sophie narrows her eyes at me. Cassia ignores us both and shrugs. "I think it's easier to wear your bathing suit and bring a dry change of underclothes for later."

They're talking about female lingerie! Bras and panties! A small gargling sound escapes from my throat. This is too much for a guy who's been living with an ancient faerie for the past three years and hasn't dated since college.

I leap up from the stool, knocking it over. I take my time righting it and then say, "Ah… I think I'll leave the discussion of proper boating attire to the two of you. Thanks again for the coffee, Cassia; it was nice to meet you. See you later, Sophie."

Dashing out the back door, I inhale several large gulps of fresh air and then jog toward the cottage. As I step inside, I hear a "*Meep!*" from Zosia, who raises her head from one of the chairs lining the wall. The kit has been alone all day and probably wants some attention, but I'm desperate for exercise; Zosia's needs will have to wait a bit longer.

"Sophie will be back soon… and er, I need to go for a run before my head explodes."

Zosia yawns, hops down from the chair, and arches her back in a long stretch. As I head toward my bedroom to change into my running gear, I notice Zosia prancing behind me, all nine tails streaming behind her. I pause at the threshold, my hand on the doorknob, and stare down at the white puff of fur by my feet.

"What do you think you're doing?" My voice rumbles low, just like Jarrod used to do when he was asserting himself.

"*Wump.*" Zosia gazes back at me through her silver eyes, clearly not intimidated by my attempt at dominance. My shoulders droop; while I have no desire to ever be an alpha or even a beta, I would like to project enough self-confidence to earn the respect of my future pack-mates... and of this baby fox.

"You're not allowed in my bedroom; I believe I've made that quite clear." I had to shut the door in Zosia's face twice last night; once when I went to bed, and a second time when I returned from the bathroom and she was prowling by my door.

As Zosia starts to groom one of her tails, I inch the door open, intending to slip inside without her. Fat chance; I'm a big, bulky shifter, and she streaks past me like a lightning bolt.

"No, Zosia!" I grumble. "This is my space, and you're not invited."

Zosia trots over to the ugly chair in need of reuphol-stering and hops up, kneading the lumpy cushion with her front paws. "Down, Zosia! Right now."

The fox tilts her head to the side, jumps down from the chair, and trots past me. Good; perhaps I'm making progress. But instead of leaving my room, the little stinker leaps onto my bed—my clean sheets are going to be smothered with white fox fur!

I wave my hands to shoo her off my bed. "No, no, no!"

"*Pah.*" Zosia stalks toward the head of my bed, but before she can put any of her nine tails and fuzzy derriere on my pillow, I snatch it up. Undeterred, Zosia curls up where my pillow would have been and gives a contented sigh.

I drop onto the bed, hug my pillow to my chest, and groan. "Why won't you listen to me?" Somehow this feels like one more test I'm failing; I never completed the assertiveness training course that Miss Dragonfly paid for because I couldn't pass the midterm exam.

I feel a warm lump against my thigh and glance down; Zosia has nestled in next to me and is licking her front paw.

Sighing, I reach down and scratch behind her ears. She purrs and rubs her face against my leg. As we sit there in contented silence for several minutes, a strange sense of being wanted—even if it's just by Zosia—settles over me. Maybe having a pet isn't so awful after all.

I leave her lying on my bed as I change into my gym shorts, tee, and running shoes. When I turn to go, I call out, "See you later, Zosia."

Zosia opens one silver eye and says, "*Pah.*"

As I pull closed the door to the cottage, it occurs to me that sounds an awful lot like *Pa*.

Great stars... I hope the little fluffball doesn't think I'm her father!

CHAPTER 13
GIRL TALK

SOPHIE

Afternoon, June 23

Cassia and I are sitting cross-legged on the blanket inside the bakery, sipping our coffee. After I hear the back door clack shut behind Teddy, I heave a sigh. "Finally; a little peace! Teddy is such a workaholic... and he's so persnickety. How am I going to survive a year without killing him?"

Cassia tents her blonde eyebrows. "Are you kidding me? Teddy is hot! And he seems genuinely nice. On first impressions alone, I like him a thousand times better than Rafe. Why bother dating Rafe when you could get to know Teddy better?"

"You can't be serious! For one thing, Teddy has a cleanliness disorder." Cassia chortles, but I hold up my hand. "I'm serious! I think he cleans to unwind or something. Plus he's my employee, and I refuse to date anyone on my staff."

"Teddy is the only person on your staff," points out Cassia. "Who cares?"

I shake my head. "I'm determined to keep Teddy at arm's length. It's not a good idea for us to get involved... not with Auntie's will and all. Besides, I'm really excited to see Rafe tomorrow."

Cassia huffs out a breath. "It's so unfair."

"What's so unfair?"

"You get to work with a gorgeous werewolf, and I'm stuck working with five nasty gargoyles who make rude gestures all day. Well, if Teddy needs an extra job, please send him to the café. The customers would adore him."

"I don't think he has any restaurant experience."

"So what? His looks alone would bring in more business."

"Wait a minute, are you interested in dating Teddy?" I recall the feeling of Teddy's arms around me and frown slightly. I might not want to become romantically involved with Teddy, but I'm not sure I want my cousin getting any ideas about him either. He's still my house-mate and business partner.

"Nope, he's cute, but I'm not into werewolves. I grew up with one, remember?" Cassia waves her go-cup around. "I'm merely suggesting you might want to reconsider your stance on not dating Teddy. See where things go. You never know; he could be *the one*."

"The odds of Teddy being *the one* are zilch." I sniff. "He actually called me a frumpy, grumpy faerie last night, after I went to the trouble of picking him up from jail." I don't bother giving Cassia the full context or telling her that Teddy also called me beautiful.

"Oh, well that doesn't sound very nice. But he'd just been arrested, so maybe he was venting."

"Maybe." I shrug and change the subject. "So how's Olivia enjoying day camp?"

Cassia's face brightens as she talks about her daughter, who's the sweetest kid around; that's all Cassia's doing, since her immature ex-husband lacks basic parenting skills. Cassia helps me clean up before she heads home, and I walk back to the cottage.

I desperately want to shower after stripping wallpaper all day, but then I recall the eel and realize I need to clean out the tub first. Ugh! Where's that fastidious werewolf when I need him? Teddy would probably douse it with bleach and then scour it three times.

Grumbling under my breath, I grab my cleaning supplies, pull aside the white plastic shower liner, and kneel down on the tiled floor. "Gross!" I mutter; the eel left a sandy bath ring around the tub and a disgusting fishy smell. I scrub and rinse, but I can still feel a gritty residue in places, so I repeat the process.

I'm listening to music through my earbuds while rinsing out the tub for the second time when I detect movement at my back. "Zosia?" I call out. The little kit didn't greet me when I came in, probably because she was fast asleep somewhere she shouldn't be, like Teddy's room.

"It's me," murmurs Teddy from behind me. "I could use... um... do you have, er..."

Of course it's Teddy, and of course he needs something, but his voice trails off before he tells me what he needs. I remove my earbuds, stuff them in my pocket, and pivot around on my knees, which are starting to ache from kneeling for so long. I'm scowling at the interruption, but all my grumpiness flees when I see blood running down both of Teddy's legs.

"What happened to you?" I cry, leaping up from the floor. I grab Teddy's arm, drag him to the kitchen, and push him down into one of the chairs over his objections.

"I took a tumble while I was running and skinned my knees." Teddy lifts his massive shoulders. "But if you just get me your first aid kit, I can bandage myself up."

"Really? How are you going to bandage yourself with these?" I grab his large hands and turn over his palms, both of which are scraped raw and bleeding.

"I... I can manage," he mumbles, his eyes downcast.

I squint at him and grumble, "*Humph.*"

Then it dawns on me, I'm standing over a huge, ridiculously handsome werewolf with bulging, sweaty muscles, and I'm holding both his hands in mine. I'm so close I notice the blond hairs on his strong forearms, and the rise and fall of his broad chest beneath the fabric of his performance tee.

My face heats up; clearing my throat, I place Teddy's hands back in his lap. "Just sit there while I get a clean washcloth and some bandages."

Teddy nods but doesn't reply; maybe he feels as self-conscious right now as I do.

Grateful for the distraction, I gather what I need from the hall closet. Then I take a few stabilizing breaths before re-entering the kitchen, reminding myself this is Leslie T. Barker, my annoying employee. I blame Cassia and her chatter about Teddy's hotness for this awkward-ness I'm feeling.

I fill a pot with warm, soapy water and carry it over to the table, which is piled high with cookbooks, pads of paper filled with my ideas for the bakery, pens, high-lighters, and sticky notes; this kitchen functions as my office, at least for now.

Teddy clears a space so I can set down the water, and then I start by cleaning his hands. After I've washed and dried them, I apply antibiotic ointment and stick a large bandage on each palm. Then I change out the water and return to work on his knees, which look even worse than his hands. Stooping over, I wash the scrapes, which have a lot of sand and grime ground into them. Teddy tenses, probably because it stings, but I continue cleaning his wounds and neither of us speaks. Once I'm satisfied, I apply ointment and bandages to each leg.

As I straighten, I glance at Teddy and our eyes lock. The flecks of gold around his irises darken, and he gives me a look so tender it takes my breath away and makes my knees go wobbly.

This is *not* good... not at all! Teddy is affecting me in ways he shouldn't.

I carry the pot over to the sink, dump out the dirty water, and start scrubbing like my life depends on it; my sanity certainly does. Despite the heat swirling around inside me, I have absolutely no intention of encouraging Teddy.

I hear the chair scrape the floor behind me and sense him approaching. "Sophie."

His voice rumbles low and soft, and my stomach

drops to my knees. I know it would be a mistake to turn around and look him in the face, so I don't. But then Teddy leans past me, his arm brushing mine, and turns off the water. "The pot's clean, Sophie." His breath is warm on my neck.

Then I hear his footsteps retreating; when he reaches the kitchen doorway, he says to my back, "Thank you." I hear the front door open and close, and then the soft purr of his car's engine as he backs down the driveway.

I can only hope when Teddy returns I can look him in the face without melting into a puddle.

My date with Rafe can't come soon enough, but now I'm worried whether even Rafe is a strong enough distraction from Teddy Freaking Barker.

CHAPTER 14

JUST DRIVE

TEDDY

LATER, JUNE 23

I start driving, so distracted I'm not even sure where I'm going. I pass through a crowded village with families out for a stroll, couples headed to dinner, a group of teens tossing a football on the beach, and huff out a ragged breath. Everyone is with someone else, so I drive on, seeking a quieter spot for reflection.

Eventually I find a widening of the road on the Lake Michigan side of the peninsula that forms Door County; here the surf is rougher, the water chillier, and the towns less congested. I pull off, parking at an overlook with a twisty path down to the beach. I take my time climbing down; after falling once already today, I don't want to stumble on the tree roots and loose rocks. I finally reach a quiet stretch of shoreline and wander over to a boulder; perching on top of it, I stare out at the curling waves, too deep in thought to really see them.

When Sophie was cleaning and bandaging my cuts in the kitchen, something happened that made her feel really uncomfortable; she was so unsettled she continued scrubbing that pot until I shut off the water. I think Sophie must have sensed my inner wolf, yearning for my fated mate; it took all my self-control not to reach out, cup her face in my hands, and claim her full, pillowy lips.

Of course she'd probably evict me if I even tried, and I wouldn't blame her. A werewolf needs to restrain his impulses at all times, even more so around his mate.

Growling, I drop my head in my hands. What am I going to do?

The last thing I want is for Sophie to tense up around me, but I can't possibly avoid her either. Other than when we're sleeping in our separate bedrooms, we're going to be together nearly non-stop, agonizingly close and yet so far apart.

Maybe it's just as well she's taking tomorrow off; it'll give us both some time to cool off. But Sophie is going on a date with her prospective boyfriend... even worse, she'll be wearing a bathing suit.

Aargh! I'll be worrying about her the entire time we're apart. I growl aloud again.

I need some counseling from a werewolf with more experience, ideally an alpha. But I'm not in a pack, and the last person I should discuss this with is Jake Spellman.

On the other hand, if Jake's as smart as I think he is... I'm not going to be able to hide my feelings for his tantalizing faerie cousin.

Not for the first time I find myself asking: *Miss Drag-onfly, what were you thinking?*

Eventually my stomach tells me I need to eat, and I head south toward Sturgeon Bay, the largest town in the county and the only place to find fast food restaurants.

It's almost eight p.m.; I have just enough time to grab some to-go burgers and then watch the sunset over the bay. I'm in the drive-through line, waiting to place my order, when I see a bulked-up, dark-haired werewolf stride past, hop on his motorcycle, and zoom out of the lot.

Despite the warmth of the summer evening, an icy chill courses through me; that wolf looks vaguely famil-iar, but it can't be *him*. Last I saw of him, he was loping away from the fight that claimed Jarrod's life and nearly took mine. I never did learn his name; he appeared in the woods that day and disappeared just as quickly.

Shrugging, I head over to the harbor; I doubt it's the same guy, and I have more pressing concerns than reliving painful history. Munching on a cheeseburger, I watch as the sun dips down below the horizon, the sky darkening from golds and peaches to reds and violets.

By the time the sky is a deep indigo, my mind's made up.

I need to find the man I hope will be my next alpha: Jake Spellman.

I TAKE my time driving back to Riddle Hill; I'm not ready

to return to the cottage I share with Sophie, not until I can get some advice.

As I plunk down on the only available barstool inside Howling Shores Pub, Wes quirks his dark eyebrows at me. "What can I get you?"

I glance around the nautical-themed werewolf hangout. "I need to find Jake Spellman."

The black-bearded pub owner grunts, "You sure about that?"

"Positive."

"He's in a mood; don't say I didn't warn you. But if you're sure..." Wes nods at a booth in the corner, where Jake Spellman is sipping a beer with another fellow, a werewolf with dark blond hair and beard.

I order a root beer from Wes and carry my mug over to the corner. Jake Spellman glances up and gives me a hard nod. Not unfriendly, but not welcoming either, exactly as an alpha should respond to an outsider intruding on his privacy.

The other werewolf looks over and cocks his head. "Let me guess. Are you Leslie 'T is for Teddy' Barker?"

"That's right."

The man introduces himself. "I'm Rob Wolferman, Jake's beta. I thought you were stopping by our pack meet *tomorrow* night. You're early."

"I need to speak with Jake tonight," I reply stiffly.

"What gives you the right—"

"It's alright, Rob," Jake interrupts. "I'll catch up with you later."

Rob takes his mug and leaves, but not before giving me a sidelong glance.

Jake waves his hand at Rob's vacated bench. "Have a seat."

"Thanks." I slide into the booth and place my drink on the table. "Um... I have a problem that requires an alpha's guidance."

Jake squints at me. "I'm not your alpha."

"I hope to remedy that."

"Is that so?" Jake takes a long swallow from his glass, sets it aside, and leans forward. "You have a lot of nerve, Barker."

Maybe Wes was right, and I should have waited until Jake was in a better mood, but it's too late now. "I have no one else I can discuss this with."

Jake's scowl softens somewhat. "Alright. I'm listening, but before you ask for any guidance, I'd like to hear about your last pack; what went down, why you're a loner, and how you wound up working for Dragonfly Spellman."

I've been preparing to have this conversation with Jake, the one man who deserves to know the details. I stare down at the caramel-colored liquid in my mug, gathering my nerve.

"Let me start by answering the last part of your question. Two of Miss Dragonfly's garden gnomes found me lying unconscious near the edge of her estate. I was bloody and bruised, but still breathing; unfortunately, the same couldn't be said for my alpha, Jarrod Huntley, who was discovered in the woods half a mile away. I'd crawled on my hands and knees, seeking help from the nearest home, when I'd collapsed on her property.

"Miss Dragonfly ordered the gnomes to carry me into

her mansion, where she and her healer nursed me back to health. Once I was well, Miss Dragonfly offered me a position as her companion. She was a very kind and astute faerie; she must have realized I needed a break from the pressures of pack life so I could heal from the trauma."

"Pressures? What sort of pressures?" asks Jake.

"The need to be looking over my shoulder, to be prepared to defend myself from bullying."

Jake shakes his head. "That doesn't sound like a healthy pack at all."

When I put up my hand, Jake arches an eyebrow at my bandaged palm but nods at me to continue. "Jarrod was a good, decent man, but he wasn't ready for the alpha role. He inherited it from his brother, who'd passed away unexpectedly six months earlier. I think Jarrod was still grieving, so he didn't see the warning signs I did."

"Such as?" prompts Jake.

"Such as the charming loner named Drew who turned up out of the blue, seeking entry into our pack. Jarrod was eager for new members, so he promptly accepted him, but the guy never fit in. Just the opposite in fact; he was a disrupter."

"Is that when the bullying started?"

"Yeah. I wound up tussling with him at least once a week." I lock eyes with Jake. "I'm no coward, but I prefer to settle things without my fists, if possible."

"That's not cowardice, but common sense," grunts Jake. "Tell me, what was Jarrod's beta doing during all this pack upheaval?"

"That's the worst part. Jarrod had been our beta

when his brother died, and he'd left that spot vacant until the loner showed up."

"Don't tell me he promoted the loner into the beta role."

Nodding, I continue. "I suppose in some ways it was a logical move, since Drew was the best fighter in our pack, next to Jarrod, but he was also a prime bully. Drew eventually challenged Jarrod to a fight, but not at a pack meet with witnesses. No... he had other plans.

"Drew told Jarrod he wanted to show him some property the pack could acquire for a new hangout. I followed behind them, remaining downwind so they couldn't pick up my scent. When Jarrod's back was turned, Drew and another werewolf, a complete stranger, attacked. I joined the fight, desperate to defend Jarrod, but it was too late. Jarrod went down, and I took a lot of blows, unable to fend off two aggressive were-wolves. I don't think they wanted to kill Jarrod, just scare him enough so he'd step aside and let Drew take over, but Jarrod hit his head when he fell... and he was gone."

"Did you ever find out why Drew attacked in such an underhanded fashion? What was his ultimate goal?"

"Miss Dragonfly later learned that my old pack—the few werewolves who stuck with Drew after Jarrod's death—had been arrested for some phony security scam. I guess they hired out as security guards and proceeded to steal from their customers." Shrugging, I add, "You know the trouble werewolves can get into with the wrong sort of alpha. I can only assume Drew had broached the topic with Jarrod, who would have shut him down cold."

"I'm surprised Jarrod didn't kick him out on the spot."

I shake my head. "Old Jarrod would have, but grieving Jarrod wasn't fully engaged."

"Sounds like a recipe for a full pack meltdown." Jake grimaces, sighs, and then says, "I appreciate you telling me how it went down... and now maybe you can explain what sort of guidance you're needing from me. I'm not making any promises, mind you, but I'm willing to hear you out."

"Thanks." I glance away from Jake's piercing gaze; discussing that last fight still roils me up inside. "I didn't think I'd make it that night." My voice cracks just a little, and I take a fortifying breath. "As I lay there on the ground, I was consumed with regret for many things, but mostly for my fated mate."

"Your fated mate? Who's your mate?" Jake's brow wrinkles in confusion.

"That's the point; I hadn't met her back then, and I was regretting that fact." I gulp down some of my root beer before continuing. "And believe me, if you knew my parents—who married out of convenience and were never happy together—you'd wait for your true love too."

"Fated mate? True love?" says Jake, who has a dreamy look in his eyes but then shakes himself. "Yeah, well, not everyone's so lucky."

"Perhaps not... but some of us are." I pause and add, "However, even when we find them, things can get mighty complicated, mighty fast."

Jake is back to scowling again and folds his arms

across his chest. "I think you better tell me what this is really about."

"I swear, Jake, I never expected to find my fated mate in Riddle Hill... and in your family."

The gold around his irises darkens, and he barks, "Don't tell me... just no. I can't see you and my sister together."

"Your *sister*? My mate isn't Cassia—it's Sophie!"

Jake's mouth gapes open. "Sophie? Are you sure? The two of you are about as different as sunshine and shadow."

"Oh, I'm sure." My mouth turns up at the corners as I think about my Sophie. "She smells like springtime, and she has the most lustrous chestnut waves and perfect curves and makes me feel tingly all over. And then there's my heart, which nearly exploded in my chest the first time I held her."

A vein pops out on Jake's forehead. "You *held* Sophie?" He leans across the table and grips my sweaty performance tee with two beefy hands. "How dare you!"

"It's not what you think! Sophie was sobbing after your grandmother clipped her wings this morning... and I gave her a hug to comfort her... and that's when I *knew* she was my mate."

Jake purses his lips, lets go of my shirt, and sits back down with a growl. "Granny Catbeam actually clipped Sophie's wings?"

When I nod, he says, "Poor Sophie." Then he sharpens his gaze at me. "But that doesn't give you the right—"

"I realize that!" I huff. "You don't have to worry

about Sophie; she's got plenty of spunk. She gave me a hard shove and told me to never, ever do it again. And I never will, without her consent. But it's going to be really, really hard... knowing she's my fated mate and not being able to tell her or hold her... or, er... well, you get the picture."

"Confound it all—you've just lobbed a huge problem in my lap! I'd look out for any woman in this town, but Sophie is family; she's like a sister to me." Jake rubs the back of his neck, obviously thinking about what to do. I cling to the hope he's a decent man and won't run me out of town, which is his prerogative as the alpha and mayor of a supernatural village.

"If Sophie is truly your fated mate—"

"She is," I reply with full conviction.

"Then it's going to be really hard working with her if she doesn't feel the same way—and since Sophie's not a werewolf, she may never feel what you do. At the same time, you're part owner of the bakery and have every right to work there. But that's not what worries me."

I'm pretty sure I know what Jake's going to say next, so I remain silent. But he surprises me with a question. "Do you have any idea what happens on the first full moon after a werewolf meets his fated mate, but she's either unaware of their connection—which can happen for a variety of reasons—or even worse, she soundly rejects him?"

"N-no," I stammer, realizing how little I really know about this whole fated mate thing.

"It's called mate blight. Basically, the werewolf becomes a howling, snarling, whimpering mess and needs to be locked up for everyone's safety, including his own."

An icy chill settles around my heart; what Jake is really saying is that I could lose my self-control during the next full moon, and possibly say things… or do things… I'd regret later. I run both my hands through my hair. "In that case I definitely can't stay with Sophie. I've been avoiding going back to the cottage tonight… but other than living in my car… I'm kind of out of options."

Jake rolls his eyes. "Honestly, if it weren't for the fact Auntie Dragonfly trusted you enough to hire you and then bequeath part of the bakeshop to you, I'd send you packing right now. You're the most troublesome were-wolf I've had to deal with in… in forever. You get yourself arrested your first day here; you discover my cousin is your fated mate your second day here… and you're all banged up."

I guess Jake must have noticed my bandaged knees when I approached him earlier. He waves a hand. "Let me guess. You went for a run to clear your head and took a tumble. Am I right?"

"You're right… and then I went back to the cottage to ask Sophie for bandages… but rather than pointing me to the supplies, she washed my cuts and bandaged them up for me. And I could tell she was suddenly uncomfortable around me afterward. That's when I left."

"You're telling me Sophie actually patched you up?"

"Yes." I nod. "And her touch was soft and gentle and—"

"You can stop right there; I get the picture." Jake stares up at the ceiling for a moment and then heaves out a long, growly breath. "I'm probably going to regret this, but under the circumstances, it's the only thing I can think of on such short notice."

"What're you thinking?"

"I'm going to let you stay in one of the dorm rooms at the fire station. But it's temporary, only until you can find an apartment."

I straighten. "The fire station? That's... that's great!"

"It's just a dorm room."

"But in a fire station... it's better than I could've hoped for."

"Why's that?" asks Jake, furrowing his brow.

"I guess I never mentioned I have a fire science degree, and I've always wanted to be a firefighter."

"Is that so? You're full of surprises, Barker." Jake snorts and shakes his head. "It just so happens I'm Riddle Hill's fire chief."

Jake must see the eager gleam in my eye, because he puts up a hand. "Maybe... just maybe... we can discuss you joining the volunteer roster. But first, you need to be a pack member. Second, you need to pass all your training."

A little burble of hope blooms in my chest. Perhaps I can make a go of things in Riddle Hill after all.

But then my world caves in again when Jake adds, "And third, you need to survive the next full moon alone."

CHAPTER 15
TEDDY FREAKING BARKER

SOPHIE

VERY LATE, JUNE 23

I'm pacing around the neat rows of boxes that Teddy stacked in my living room, not sure what to do. Teddy's not back yet, and it's almost eleven. I don't know whether to be grateful he's not underfoot or aggravated he's gotten inside my head despite my best efforts to shove him away. I remind myself for at least the tenth time that I'm not responsible for Teddy Freaking Barker; his whereabouts don't warrant a second thought.

But what if Teddy is lying in a ditch somewhere? His car is ancient, he's not familiar with the roads, and he's clearly accident prone.

I give myself a good mental shake; this is ridiculous! Teddy can take care of himself. He's a big, strong werewolf and very muscular. In fact, Teddy has lots of rippling muscles... and strong thighs and forearms... and it's impossible *not* to notice how his biceps bunch beneath his tee.

Gah! What am I doing?

I don't even like Teddy, well, not much anyway. And I'm still miffed he owns ten percent of my bakery. That man can't even boil water without a microwave, for star's sake!

I stomp off toward my bedroom, ready to call it a night, when my phone pings with a text from Teddy. "Hey, Sophie. Just wanted to let you know I'm bunking at the fire station tonight."

I stare down at the message, completely flummoxed. Why is Teddy staying at the fire station? And who's letting him inside?

I have to satisfy my curiosity. "Only firefighters can stay at the station. You're not doing anything illegal... again... are you?"

Teddy responds with a smiley face. "Nothing illegal, I assure you. This is Jake's idea."

My overprotective cousin is allowing Teddy to stay at the fire station? This makes no sense, but I'm too tired to try and reason it out tonight; I'll have to pump Jake for information later. "Okay. Thanks for letting me know."

"Please give Zosia a head scratch for me."

Give Zosia a head scratch? Teddy wanted nothing to do with my baby fox yesterday. Come to think of it, I haven't seen Zosia for a few hours; she disappeared after dinner. I glance up, notice Teddy's bedroom door is slightly ajar, and take a peek inside. Zosia, who's curled up in the middle of Teddy's mattress, opens one silver eye, yawns, and goes back to sleep.

Huh. Looks like Teddy and Zosia have reached détente... or have they?

I snap a photo of the little white furball on Teddy's bed and send it to him. "Looks like Zosia has made herself at home."

Smirking, I wait for Teddy's reply, expecting outrage or at least disgust. Instead, Teddy *hearts the picture*.

I bite my lower lip, more confused than ever. Then Teddy texts, "Sweet dreams, Sophie."

Trying hard to ignore the flutter those words create inside my chest, my fingers hover over the screen. What should I say? Should I wish him goodnight? Tell him I'll see him in the shop on Monday? Tell him good luck at the pack meet tomorrow night?

I finally give up and send Teddy a nice, noncommittal thumbs up.

Under the circumstances, it's the best I can do.

CHAPTER 16
HAND OF FATE

SOPHIE

SUNDAY, JUNE 24

I'm having my third cup of coffee... or maybe it's my fourth... at my kitchen table, surrounded by cookbooks and notes and a half-eaten bowl of oatmeal. I should be eager for my hair appointment in an hour and thrilled about my date later with Rafe, but I have this unsettled feeling in the pit of my stomach I can't shake.

I knew this morning would be rough, and that I'd probably be a little weepy. After all, it's not every day a faerie has her wings clipped; it's not even every decade. I decided to scan Riddle Hill's online archives this morning, and I nearly fell off my chair when I discovered the last time a faerie's wings had been clipped was 1932.

But the best part was finding out the name of that infamous faerie—Auntie Dragonfly!

Apparently my great aunt had used magic to disintegrate her ex-boyfriend's boat... when he was sailing on the lake! He wasn't hurt; he was a merman, so really, it was more of a prank, a pretty spectacular one if you ask me. I've always known Auntie Dragonfly was feisty, but this little fact gives me renewed respect for my deceased faerie auntie.

All of which is making me wonder whether I should trust her judgement a bit more when it comes to Teddy. I haven't exactly welcomed him with open arms... not that I intend to hug him or anything... but maybe I could be more understanding of his situation.

The doorbell rings, and Zosia dashes out of the kitchen with a loud, *"Pah!"* I guess Zosia is expanding her vocabulary from *wumps* and *meeps*. Shrugging, I pull open the door, surprised to find Jake and Teddy on my doorstep. "Hey guys... come on in. Can I get you some coffee?"

Jake shakes his head. "No thanks. We're here to pick up Teddy's things."

"Oh, I see." I glance over at Teddy, not sure what's going on. Yes, we had an awkward moment in the kitchen yesterday when I was patching him up... and also in the bakery when he held me in his arms... but that doesn't explain why he's moving out.

I clear my throat, hoping Teddy will look at me, but he's bending down to pet Zosia. My baby fox has wrapped all nine of her tails around Teddy's ankles, and rather than trying to escape, he's smiling down at her. "Has something happened that I should know about?" I ask.

Without glancing up, Teddy murmurs, "Nothing's happened."

Jake claps a hand on his shoulder. "Why don't you go pack? I'll wait here." Teddy nods and heads into his room, Zosia hot on his heels.

Once the bedroom door closes, I turn to Jake and hiss, "What's going on? A few days ago I needed to rearrange my home to accommodate a werewolf named Leslie, who had nowhere else to live, and now you're helping him move out. This makes no sense; you're not even Teddy's alpha."

Jake rubs the back of his neck. "Teddy and I had a long chat about a lot of things, and under the circumstances, it's prudent for him to relocate."

"What circumstances?"

"This is werewolf business, Sophie; I can't disclose it."

Stars above! I hate it when werewolves get all mysterious. Sometimes I wish I could be a werewolf for a day, just so I could know what happens at a pack meet. I'll bet it's actually pretty boring; the werewolves probably do a lot of chest bumping, howling, and chomping on beef jerky. Besides, I love being a faerie... well, I did before my grandmother stripped away my magic.

I'm feeling guilty about Teddy's sudden departure, like maybe I'm to blame. "Did I do something wrong?"

"Of course not," says Teddy quietly, coming up behind me. When I spin around he finally meets my gaze, and I take a step back. The gold flecks in Teddy's irises flare and then wink out, and now I'm staring at the saddest puppy-dog eyes imaginable. My insides twist; if I saw those eyes on a dog in the street I'd have to take him home with me.

Jake goes into the bedroom and returns with an armful of boxes that Teddy hasn't gotten around to unpacking. Nodding at the suitcase and backpack he's holding, Teddy gives me a tentative smile. "I think that's everything... Oh, I almost forgot." He puts down his stuff, withdraws his key ring, and hands me the house key. When his fingers brush mine, he pulls his hand back so quickly you'd think I just burned him.

I narrow my eyes at Teddy, but he grabs his belongings and hurries out the door. "See you tomorrow, Sophie—" he calls over his shoulder "—and... um... I hope you have a nice day off."

"Geesh," I mutter when he's out of earshot. "I don't get him at all."

Jake pauses at the door with the boxes. "I like him; if things go well at our meeting tonight, I suspect he'll be joining my pack."

"That's... surprising. I thought you didn't trust lone wolves who eschew pack life."

"As a rule, I don't. But sometimes we all need a second chance."

After I close the door, Zosia whimpers and flails all nine tails in the air. Then she trots into the spare room that's no longer Teddy's and starts whining, *"Pah! Pah! Pah!"*

She can't possibly be missing Teddy already... Can she?

It's time to shake off my melancholy mood, which has nothing to do with Teddy's departure and everything to do with my clipped wings. I need to get in the proper frame of mind for my date with Rafe, and I know just the gal to help me: Spectra Twinkler, a middle-aged, platinum-blonde faerie who can turn even my wild waves into something stylish. She's also one of the best sources of gossip in our town.

"Sophie!" calls out Spectra in her sing-song voice. "I've been so worried about you!" Spectra is high strung and speaks with a lot of verbal exclamation points.

"You've been worried?"

She hugs me and then guides me over to the sink for a shampoo. "Of course! We all heard about your clipped wings; you must be positively devastated!"

"It's been a rough twenty-four hours."

"You poor thing! Let's get you all fixed up for your date with that gorgeous werewolf." Spectra drapes a cape over my t-shirt and cutoffs; I'll change later into my cute boating attire.

"How do you know my date is with a werewolf?" When I made the appointment yesterday and begged Spectra to fit me in, I told her I had a date... but I didn't mention with whom.

Spectra massages my scalp as she lathers my hair, and for the first time since Teddy showed up on my doorstep two days ago, I feel myself start to relax... until she says, "Who else could it be? We've all seen that strapping Norse god wandering around town, and we know he's part owner of your bakeshop. Lucky you; I hear he's as sweet as he is good looking! I'd love to inherit a man like that!"

My eyes are closed to prevent soap from getting in, so I can't give Spectra an eye roll. "Why does everyone assume I should be delighted to have a big, clumsy, finnicky werewolf as my business partner? Teddy can't cook or bake; the only thing he seems to excel at is cleaning."

Spectra says something I can't hear over the running water, so she stops rinsing my hair and repeats herself. "Please send him over here; I'd hire him on the spot!"

"Whatever for? He's obviously not a hair stylist."

"That handsome young man could sweep floors for me all day; he'd be good for business. My customers would go gaga for him!"

This is getting ridiculous; first Cassia suggests I send Teddy to my parents' café for a job, and now Spectra wants to hire him. "Well," I reply stiffly, "Teddy's not available. We have a lot of work to do to get the bakery ready for its grand opening."

Done shampooing, I sit in one of the cushioned salon chairs and watch Spectra's mirror image as she sprays my wet hair with her patented conditioner, which has been liberally infused with her magic. Spectra is an aura faerie and a master at enhancing hair, makeup, and overall appearance. Her clients are both supers and non-supers (who don't have a clue why they look so amazing after a few hours in her chair).

As she tackles my tangled locks, she says, "Okay, spill the jumping beans. Who *are* you going out with today?"

I tell her about the sunset cruise with Vreeland, Pru, and Rafe. "So you were right that I'll be on a date with a werewolf, just not the one you assumed."

Spectra shakes her head. "You've met another werewolf? Do you think the universe is trying to tell you something?"

I quirk my eyebrow. "Like what?"

"Like maybe you need to pay careful attention to all the cues. This seems like more than coincidence, Sophie."

"If it's not a coincidence, then what could it be?" I start to shrug but stop because Spectra is snipping off my split ends.

"The hand of fate!" says Spectra with a completely straight face.

I snort. "You've got to be kidding me. Do you really believe in that nonsense?"

Spectra stops scissoring my hair long enough to murmur, "Of course I do!" Then she gets a dreamy look on her face and proceeds to tell me how she met her husband. It's a sweet and romantic story I've heard before, but I smile as she recounts it again.

When Spectra's finally finished, she spins me around so I can see my image in the mirror, and I clap my hands. "You're a regular miracle worker." My hair falls in long, shiny, chestnut waves around my shoulders; she's done my makeup too, keeping it minimal and natural looking, perfect for sailing around the bay.

Spectra grins. "I appreciate the compliment, but it's easy to make a pretty girl like you look spectacular."

"You must be mistaking me for Cassia; she got all the looks in our family."

"I hope you're joking!" exclaims Spectra, placing a hand on my shoulder. "You're two of the prettiest girls in this town; Cassia's beauty is ethereal and delicate, while yours is earthy and natural. In fact, I wouldn't be surprised if that's one of the reasons why you're attracting werewolves; they adore sassy, curvy girls like you."

I burst out laughing. "I'm not sure how I feel about that last remark, but thanks anyway."

As I'm leaving the shop, Spectra calls out, "Remember to be on the lookout for any signs from the hand of fate!"

Rolling my eyes, I wave goodbye.

CHAPTER 17
SNIFF AND TUSSLE

TEDDY

Sunday, June 24

After I neatly stack my boxes in one corner of the minimally furnished dorm room, I sort through the suitcase for some clean clothes and head to the men's locker room, desperate for a shower. As the water streams down my head and back, I recall Sophie's glower as I was leaving the cottage and heave sigh. She's obviously confused by my sudden departure, especially after I insisted on adhering to all the requirements of Miss Dragonfly's will—including the need for Sophie to provide me with room and board.

Sophie probably thinks I'm too dimwitted to date, let alone become a proper boyfriend. Then I remember she'll be seeing her prospective boyfriend later today, and I smack the damp tiles with the palm of my hand.

"Ouch!" I howl, forgetting about my cuts.

"You alright over there?" asks a man in the next

shower stall. It takes me a few beats to place the voice; he's Jake's beta.

"Um... yeah... just having a moment," I mumble.

"You up for a run? If you don't mind talking while you jog, I don't mind listening."

I wonder what's gotten into Jake's beta, Rob Somebody; the guy was downright snippy last night. Then it dawns on me Jake probably filled him in; as the pack's number two, Rob has as much of a right as Jake to know what happened with my last pack, and why I need to put some distance between Sophie and me during non-work hours. He's probably the guy who'll monitor me when the full moon comes around, which isn't for another few weeks.

"That sounds good. I'll be ready in ten minutes."

"Meet you out front," says Rob, turning off the water; his feet make squishy sounds on the floor as he pads away.

I stand under the shower spray for a couple more minutes, wondering if Sophie is thinking about me at all.

Nah... She's not giving me a second thought.

On the other hand, I can't get that feisty faerie out of my head. It's almost like Sophie has taken up residence inside my heart, filling up all the vacant places with her sass and beauty and kindness, which she carefully hides beneath a layer of grump.

The fire station is quiet as I head toward the lobby, which is painted a soothing blue. Pausing by the front door, I scan the assorted posters tacked onto the walls: fire safety tips, an estate sale, the dates of the various summer festivals, and a recruitment poster for volunteer firefighters, which I tap with my forefinger. Evening training classes start this week.

"Sign me up," I whisper, pulling open the door.

Rob is doing stretches on the sidewalk and straightens as I approach. His hair and beard look a bit paler in the sunshine, more of a sandy blond; he's as tall as me and a bit stockier. "You up for five miles?"

"At least," I reply. "Yesterday's run was interrupted when I took a tumble, and the day before I drove for eight hours. I'm desperate for a good head-clearing."

"Gotcha." Rob nods. "The beach is too crowded at this time of day; let's head inland."

After I do some leg stretches, Rob leads me down a picturesque side street, past small cottages and larger homes, up a rather steep hill, and then onto a two-lane county road. We jog in companionable silence, passing farmhouses, orchards, barking dogs, grazing cows, and even a llama farm. I realize he's waiting for me to say something, so I clear my throat and ask, "How much has Jake shared with you?"

Rob glances over. "Pretty much everything. I heard about your last pack, which sounds like a sorry mess; my condolences on your alpha. And Jake told me about Sophie. I didn't see that coming... and to be honest, I find it hard to picture the two of you together... not that I'm doubting your feelings. Werewolves know when they've met their mate. I'm just saying I've known Sophie all my life, and she's a force all her own. It's going to take a strong, assertive man to win her heart. And... er..." Rob hesitates.

"Just say what's on your mind. It's not anything I haven't heard before."

"Fine." Rob quirks an eyebrow in my direction. "You appear to be a pleasant, well-organized, rule-following werewolf—and not at all Sophie's type."

"But she's my mate," I huff out a breath. "So I'm going to have to find a way to win her heart."

We run in silence for a spell, and then I ask, "What's her type?"

"Tall, dark, and dreary," quips Rob.

"Huh?"

Rob snorts. "Sophie appears attracted to troubled, broody guys; I'm not sure if she thinks she can 'fix' them, or she merely likes their edgy personalities. She's not into squeaky-clean guys like you... or me."

"Did you ask her out?" I snap, my pulse rising along with my temper, which is unexpected. I'm generally even-tempered and rarely roused to anything remotely approaching the hot anger suddenly coursing through me.

Holy conflagration! How much worse will my reactions become when the full moon comes around, and I'll be without Sophie?

"Chill out, wolf," growls Rob in a commanding voice, and I'm grateful. I take some deep breaths and get my overactive imagination and racing heart back under control.

"Yeah, I asked her out a few times," he continues. "Sophie turned me down flat each time... in the nicest possible way, of course, since I'm Jake's beta and best friend."

"Good." My spike of unreasonable jealousy subsides, and we both laugh. After a quarter mile or so, I say, "You said Sophie likes tall men; I'm tall."

Rob chuckles. "Okay, you've got that going for you... and she does seem to like werewolves. So perhaps you have a chance, a slim one, of convincing Sophie to date you. But you and I share those attributes, and they didn't work for me."

I shake my head. "I don't understand how I can yearn for a woman who won't even give me a second glance. It makes no sense."

Rob sighs. "Who ever said love makes sense?"

I'm jittery as I climb the stairs inside Howling Shores Pub that lead to the second story, a large, open space with fitness equipment at one end and locker rooms at the other.

If I can't join Jake's pack, then I don't stand a chance of being able to remain in Riddle Hill. Where would I go? And how could I woo Sophie if I'm packless and homeless? I glance down at my white, Oxford-cloth shirt and neatly pressed khaki slacks; maybe I should have worn something looser since I'll need to shift, but how could I make a good impression in baggy sweats?

Pausing at the top step, I grit my teeth, determined not to allow self-doubt to gain the upper hand. I try recalling something useful from my assertiveness train-ing, but my mind's a blank. Then Jarrod's grinning face pops into my head, and I can almost hear him say, *"Hey, wolf cub. Lighten up and have some fun!"*

I smile at the memory. *You're on, Jarrod.*

"Hey, Teddy." Rob must have been waiting for me by the stairs. "Let me introduce you around."

We head toward Marv, who grins. "Teddy and I are well acquainted."

"Oh yeah, that's right." Rob chuckles and then takes me over to Wes and his mate, a pretty werewolf named Maisie. By the time we've made the rounds, I've met nineteen adult pack members; I'm good with names, but even I'm having a difficult time remembering all of them. Most of the adults are married; their children are home with sitters this evening, but Rob told me when they have family events, their full pack numbers forty-nine.

Jake calls the meeting to order, and we sit on the workout mats scattered around the center of the wooden floor. He runs through a pretty typical pack agenda: several complaints that Jake delegates to Rob and Marv to investigate, an update on the Riddle Hill Summer Fest in a few weeks, and a report on lone wolves in the area. Apparently there's a werewolf in Sturgeon Bay who's not checked in with the pack, and then there's me.

Everyone swivels their heads toward me, and I look at Jake, who gives me a nod. "Teddy Barker worked for my step-dad's aunt, Dragonfly Spellman, for three years. During that time he was not a member of any pack." There are a few murmurs, but Jake raises his hand, and the room grows silent. "Teddy has explained to me the circumstances in detail, which align with what I know about his last pack. Teddy has indicated his desire to join our pack, but as you know, I don't make unilateral decisions when it comes to new members. This is something for the pack to decide."

Jake waves his hand, and I stand up. "Teddy, it's time for us to meet your wolf."

The ladies head toward their locker room to change, giving us all some privacy as we strip down to gym shorts or loose sweatpants before transforming. In an actual fight, everyone would shift on the spot, shredding a lot of garments in the process. Werewolf families probably spend more on attire than any other species, given the number of times young cubs lose control and shift before peeling off their layers.

While I'm folding my clothes in a neat stack next to the wall, most of the guys are tossing their stuff onto the floor. Arching my eyebrow at the messy piles, I transform slowly and methodically, retaining full control throughout the process. I hear more than a few whines and even some whimpers escaping from some of the other guys, and I'm glad I've managed to remain quiet despite the discomfort.

I turn toward Jake and wait, not sure how he wants to run this part of the meeting. The women re-enter from their locker room and gather in a loose knot in the center of the room.

"Line up-p," barks Jake through his muzzle. "R-reverss or-rderr!" Nineteen werewolves jostle into position; clearly they've done this before and know what their alpha expects. I notice Rob is at the end of the line, standing behind Marv, and I figure reverse order means weakest to strongest.

Looks like I'll be challenging each adult wolf in the pack; it's certainly the best way to assess my stamina and skills, but I've never fought nineteen adults in a row before.

"Ted-dy." Jake waits until I join him before providing instructions in wolf-speak. "Walk-k dow-n-n the line, look-k each wolf-f in the eye... an' you kno-ow the dril-l-l. Chal-l-lenge me last-t."

I nod and take several deep breaths, hoping to quell my nerves enough to not lose my supper. My stomach is nothing but a fistful of knots as I head over to the first werewolf, Maisie. When we lock eyes, she lowers her gaze. I tap her shoulder with my right paw to indicate dominance, and she steps out of line, heading over to the opposite wall.

Well, that was easy... perhaps I'll only need to fight half a dozen or so tonight.

Hah! Wishful thinking on my part; when I reach the fourteenth werewolf in line, a sturdy female, she locks eyes and then charges, knocking me to the floor. I'm temporarily winded, but I'm larger and stronger. We wrestle for a few moments before I manage to flip her onto her back, pinning her shoulders. She looks away, breaking eye contact, which is the signal I'm looking for; she accepts my dominance, and the fight's over. As I give her a hand up, she smiles.

I'm panting heavily by the time I reach Marv, who gives me a cheeky grin; I get the sense this big guy can't wait to repay me for getting arrested. I've managed to best every werewolf up until this point, but my cuts have re-opened on my hands and knees, and the last werewolf landed a punch to my gut that's left me nauseous.

Our eyes lock, and Marv starts to look away, but it's a feint; he charges sideways, slamming into me and sending me skidding across the polished wooden boards.

"Oof!" I mutter, scrambling to my feet. We lock arms in a semi-crouch and spin ourselves around, each of us trying to hook a foot around the other guy's leg to trip him.

Marv taunts me through his snout, "Wittle Wolf-fy, what'z wro-ng-g?" Then he breaks free, jams his head into my stomach, and sends me reeling backward onto the floor. He pins me down, and I glance away to indicate he's won.

We slowly rise from the floor, and he nods at me before accepting a towel from one of the women... but I'm not done yet. I still have to face the pack beta and alpha.

When I look into Rob's eyes, he wrinkles his nose and folds his arms across his chest, never breaking eye contact. Confused, I cock my head to the side. Wrong move; Rob spins around, landing a flying kick to my stomach, and I drop like a stone. When he kneels over me, I avert my gaze, and he gives me a hand up.

I turn toward Jake and stare into the golden flecks in his irises; by now I'm bruised, bloody, and wheezing. Jake takes two steps, throws a right hook that catches me in the jaw, and I crumple to my knees. Jake flips me onto the floor, pins my shoulders, and I close my eyes; it's finally over.

All that remains is for the Bay Howlers to decide if

they'll accept me into their pack. Rob helps me up and guides me into the locker room. Dropping my clothes onto one of the benches, he barks at me in wolf-speak, "Fir-rst aid-d kit... Bath-R-room. Shift-t. Wash-sh. Dr-r-ress. Wait-t."

After he leaves, I lean one hand wearily against a locker, grimace at the bloody pawprint I've left on it, and head into the shower.

Thirty minutes later I'm bandaged, dressed, and standing in front of Jake, who's flanked by his pack on either side of him; they form a semicircle around me. Someone's cleaned up the blood stains on the floor, which smells of fresh lemon oil.

Everyone has shifted back into their human forms and clothes, but they look so solemn and serious that I can't read the room. I swallow nervously, figuring I must have failed to win their approval. Then Jake grins and shouts, "Let's welcome our newest pack member, Teddy Barker!"

After nearly dying in a fight with my last pack beta three years ago and wondering whether I'd ever fit in elsewhere, it's finally happened—I belong to a pack again!

The room erupts in cheers and applause, and suddenly men and women are pumping my hand and clapping me on the back. I feel my eyes growing moist with gratitude, but I inhale a shaky breath, stuffing down my emotions.

There's only one thing that would make this night perfect, and that's having Sophie by my side.

Unfortunately, she has other plans for this evening.

I choose to ignore the pang in my chest when I think of Sophie out with someone else tonight. Instead, I follow Jake, Rob, and the rest of the pack downstairs for a celebratory brew, or in my case, root beer.

Tomorrow is soon enough for me to begin planning my campaign to win over Sophie Spellman Brownlee, my somewhat disheveled but undeniably delectable faerie boss.

CHAPTER 18
SUNSET CRUISE

Later, June 24

It's nearly three; I'm staring out the kitchen window, thinking about clipped wings and pack meetings, when my smoke detector starts blaring. Zosia shrieks, "*Pah!*" and tears out of the kitchen as I dash over to the oven and pull open the door. Dang! I just burned the batch of almond-crunch cookies I was planning on bringing tonight.

I grab a pair of oven mitts, pull out the offending tray of singed cookies, and put them on the stove to cool before dumping them. Then I climb up on one of my kitchen chairs, twist off the smoke detector's cover, pull out the battery, and pitch in in the trash.

I'm sure Teddy would lecture me about fire safety if he saw me, but I'm so frustrated with him and Jake for their mysterious "werewolf business" that I feel like stomping right over to the fire station and demanding an explanation. And then there's Granny Catbeam, who utterly humiliated me by binding my magic *for half a year!* That's practically barbaric! Auntie Dragonfly's magic was only bound for one lunar cycle, according to the archives.

Frowning, I'm surprised to discover I'm just as upset about Teddy's weird departure as I am about my missing magic... which is a revelation I'll need to ponder when I have more time.

Staring at my pan of ruined cookies, I realize it's time for me to choke down my pride and beg my mom for a tray of her caramel-fudge brownies; I can't turn up empty-handed at the boat, and I don't know anyone who can resist Phoebe Spellman's brownies.

The last of the café's customers have just left when I slip through the back entrance. I poke my head inside my dad's shiny, stainless steel kitchen; he's whistling as he wipes down the counters, but he glances up when he hears me enter. Then he opens his arms and wraps me in a bear hug that makes my eyes water.

"How are you holding up, honey?" My dad's a huge, baldheaded, bearded Irish kitchen faerie, commonly referred to as a brownie; he's also a big softy, and I absolutely adore him. Since it's after hours, he's dropped his glamour. Dad's wings are tightly furled against his back to prevent any feathers from catching fire; his dark eyebrows slant upward, and his faerie ears rise into points.

"I'm alright," I sniffle. "I don't have any choice but to carry on."

"If you need any... er..." Dad lowers his voice. "Help of a magical nature, let me know. Just between us."

"Thanks, Dad."

"Are you talking to yourself again, Nash?" asks my mother from the passthrough; she's heard whispering but hasn't spotted me yet.

"No, Mom. I'm here too," I step around my dad, go through the swinging doors, and enter the restaurant's sunshine-yellow dining room. Our faerie ancestors, dressed in Renaissance-style garb or old-fashioned military uniforms, are in various states of repose on the walls, dozing inside their picture frames. Antique oak booths line three walls, and a large counter runs along the back wall. Five gargoyles, one per carved corbel, stand beneath the counter. They're behaving for now, but they're cheeky little monsters.

A pretty, middle-aged woman, my mom is still glamoured; not a single hair is out of place in her auburn bob. We're complete opposites; Mom can work a fourteen-hour day and still look fresh as a newborn unicorn (I suspect her faerie magic is involved), while I'm barely functional after eight hours, with wild hair, streaky mascara, and droopy wings.

I wait for Mom to say something, anything, but she purses her lips and gazes steadily at me; looks like it's up to me to break the silence. My lower lip wobbles slightly as I say, "I thought you would've defended me yesterday with Granny. It really hurts to know your own mother won't stick up for you with the elder council."

Mom blinks rapidly, like I've wounded her somehow, and now I feel both sad *and* guilty. "It tore me up inside to watch my mother strip away your magic; I cried myself to sleep last night."

"You did?"

She nods. "Yes, but that doesn't mean I disagreed with the punishment. Your grandmother has to follow the ordinances established centuries ago to protect supernaturals everywhere… and the misapplication of magic is a serious violation."

I heave a sigh. "All I've ever wanted was to be like you and Granny… a powerful gatekeeping faerie… and not just an ordinary kitchen faerie."

Since Mom is still in her human form, it's a lot less dramatic when she quirks one auburn eyebrow. "I love kitchen faeries; they have amazing magic! It was your father's incredible cooking that first attracted me… and then when I got to know him… well, I was lost." Her face softens as she gazes at me. "You have no idea how relieved I was when I realized you'd inherited your father's magic—and not mine."

My forehead puckers in surprise; my mom has never told me this before. "You were *relieved*? But why? I'd think you would have wanted your daughter to inherit your magic."

"Quite the opposite; I never wanted you to be encumbered with the weight of my magic."

"But you can do practically anything! You instinctively know what our customers need to eat as soon as they enter the restaurant; you make incredible desserts. You pinch-hit for Granny when she can't attend the elder council meetings, and you keep those little stone fiends in line." I point at the five gargoyles beneath the counter, who are fake-crying and patting each other's wings.

Stars above! Those stinkers are making fun of my clipped wings!

Mom turns around, glares at the horrid creatures, and murmurs an incantation. I hear five loud *thwacks*; each nasty gargoyle hops to attention and stares straight ahead. "Did you just—"

"I just spanked their bottoms."

"See... that's what I mean!" I exclaim. "You have wonderful magic."

"No, sweetheart, I have burdensome magic. Sure, I enjoy helping my customers, and I love baking treats with a little extra faerie dust inside... but not the rest of it... and especially not looking after those gargoyles. Ugh! I wish I'd never crossed their mother."

I pause, not sure I heard her correctly; Mom has *never* disclosed how she wound up with those five obnoxious gargoyles. "What are you talking about?"

"Do you think you're the only impetuous faerie in the family?" My mom shakes her head. "I challenged Matron Verda, one of the gargoyle elders, to a 'friendly' magical competition many years ago... and I lost. Now I'm stuck babysitting her five sons for a hundred years!"

My mouth gapes open. "So *that's* what really happened? There are all sorts of stories floating around town about how you bravely battled five horrid gargoyles and eventually won, forcing them into a hundred years of servitude for their wicked behavior."

"Hmm..." says Mom. "I wonder who could have spread such falsehoods?"

"*You* started those rumors?" I'm shocked that my Goody Two-Wings mother was ever such a baddie.

My mother winks. "Some secrets are best kept within the family." Then she drapes an arm around my shoulders. "I think you need some of my caramel-fudge brownies to go... don't you?"

"How did you... oh never mind," I chuckle, realizing Mom's magic is giving her insight into what food would make me feel better. "Actually, I could use a dozen."

We both laugh, and some of the tightness in my chest loosens. Mom sends me away with brownies, a fresh batch of sugar cookies, and another hug.

AFTER MUCH INTERNAL DEBATE, I decide to wear my red, two-piece swimsuit under a long, red-and-gold sarong and a golden linen top that floats just above my waistline. I have strappy, flat sandals on my feet, the kind with rubber soles so I don't slip if the deck gets wet.

I arrive early at the dock to help Pru carry the food and beverages onto Vreeland's sleek new yacht. At five-thirty we're ready to depart, but there's no sign of Rafe. Vreeland and I both check our phones; there's no message from him either, but we're in an area with poor reception. Vreeland glances over at me. "I'll wait fifteen minutes, but then we should head out."

"Fair enough." I know how antsy sailors get when they're ready to depart and something or someone holds them up.

"I'm sorry everyone," says Rafe sheepishly, turning

up at five-thirty-eight. "I wound up at the wrong marina and had to backtrack." In black jeans and a long-sleeved gray tee, Rafe is just as muscular and good-looking as I recall, and he's giving off the same tough-guy vibes as the first time we met.

But all the talk about stranger-danger, lone wolves, and the hand of fate must have shaken something loose inside my head, because suddenly I'm a lot less attracted to him. In fact, I really don't like how his eyes are raking over my figure. A little male appreciation is one thing... but there's a possessive quality in the way Rafe's irises darken that makes me extremely uncomfortable.

Why, oh why, does Cassia always have to be right? Probably because she wound up falling for the wrong guy and then having her heart smashed to bits.

I resign myself to making the best of the situation. I adore Pru and Vreeland, it's a perfect night for a cruise, and I'm on a low-risk double date. What could possibly go wrong?

Vreeland points his boat toward one of the small, heavily wooded, private islands in the bay, which happens to be owned by his uncle. He drops anchor near the sandy shoreline, and we all decide to take a dip before dinner.

I'm rethinking the whole idea and wish I'd left my bathing suit at home; then I'd have a ready excuse not to get in the water with Rafe, who's been invading my personal space since we set sail. Pru, Vreeland, and Rafe have already shed their outer layers, ready to take the plunge, and they're all waiting for me. Pru knows me well enough to sense I'm uneasy and turns to her fiancé and Rafe. "Why don't you two dive in first. We'll be along in a minute."

"What's the matter?" she hisses as soon as we hear two splashes off the port side.

"Rafe's paying way too much attention to me. Gives me the heebie-jeebies."

"But I thought he was your type!"

"So did I... until tonight," I whisper. "Don't worry... it's just for one evening."

"Oh no!" Pru's fangs catch on her bottom lip.

I arch an eyebrow. "What's that supposed to mean?"

"One of Vreeland's cousins is having surgery next month and can't be a groomsman, so I encouraged Vreeland to ask Rafe because I thought you liked him. Rafe immediately accepted when he found out you were my maid of honor, and Vreeland sort of promised you'd be paired up together."

Why do these things always happen to me? Seriously, can't the hand of fate pick on some other magicless faerie?

I huff out a breath. "It's... it's alright—how could you know? Besides, it's only the rehearsal and the wedding. No problem!"

"And the joint bridal shower too."

"Okay, so I just need to remind Rafe to keep his hands to himself for three more nights... got it!" I say with more cheer than I'm feeling.

"Sorry," says Pru, who looks so remorseful I punch her lightly in the arm.

"Lighten up!" I peel off my sarong and top and follow Pru to the railing. "Just don't leave me in the water alone with him."

Which is exactly what Pru does ten minutes later, but it's not her fault. Vreeland and Rafe were horsing around with an inflatable frisbee, and Rafe's elbow accidentally poked Vreeland in the mouth. Vreeland's lip started bleeding heavily, so Pru followed her fiancé into the boat to get him an icepack.

"Sorry, man!" Rafe calls after them.

Vreeland waves off his apology. "It's all good, since I won."

Rafe chortles as he treads water. "I demand a rematch."

"It'll have to wait until after the wedding!" says Pru. "I don't want my groom showing up with a fat lip!"

I start paddling toward the yacht, intent on following Pru and Vreeland, but Rafe intercepts me, his broad, muscular chest bobbing in the water in front of me. "What's your hurry?"

"Um... I just wanted to check on Vreeland." I try swimming past Rafe, but he starts circling around me in the water; with every one of my attempts to paddle past him, he shortens the distance between us.

"But the water's mighty fine this evening," he murmurs, closing in on me. "And so are you."

Argh! I grit my teeth at the lame pick-up line; why did I think this guy was attractive for even five seconds?

Rafe's hands encircle my waist, drawing me toward him, but I smack his shoulder, shoving him away. "Keep your hands to yourself!" I growl low in my throat.

Any super from Riddle Hill would immediately back off, but this lone wolf isn't taking the hint. He's tightened his grip, and I'm piping mad. I raise my arm, ready to slap him in the face, but Rafe is lightning fast. He catches my wrist, gives me a sly grin, and chuckles softly. "I enjoy a woman who plays hard to get... After all, I'm a wolf."

"I'm not playing anything," I hiss. "Let me go, or I'll scream."

Rafe winks. "Anything you say, darlin'." He releases me slowly, trailing his fingers down my back.

I *hate* this guy! And there's no way I'm going to be able to stomach him for Pru's wedding. I need to come up with an alternate plan that won't ruin my friend's special day... and will ensure Rafe keeps his distance.

I scramble into the boat, grab my bag, and head into the cabin reserved for guests, where I change into light-colored jeans and a lightweight, white hoodie; the air temperature is already dropping as the sun slowly sinks to the horizon.

As I'm wrestling with how to put Rafe in his place, it dawns on me I know a lot more than the average faerie about werewolves. Knowledge is power; let's see if I can make Rafe as acutely uncomfortable as he's making me. I rub my hands together as I ascend the steps, ready for a little payback.

We're sitting at the table mounted to the deck, enjoying the cold chicken dinner Pru packed. I'm sipping lemonade; Rafe is having a beer, and my vampire friends are drinking tart cherry juice to help manage their cravings for that other red liquid. Unfortunately, the juice also stains their lips bright red, which is off-putting if you're not used to it. I notice Rafe keeps glancing up at them and then quickly looking away. He also keeps bumping into me, despite the number of times I've shifted away from him on the bench seat.

Biding my time, I wait until there's a lull in the conversation, and then I turn to him. "Remind me again... how long ago did you move to Sturgeon Bay?"

Rafe takes a long swallow before placing his beer can on the table. "It's been seven weeks."

"O-oh." I draw out the syllable. "What do you think of the local pack? Do you like them?"

I can feel Rafe stiffen slightly next to me, but his voice is cool as ever. "How should I know?"

"But aren't werewolves supposed to check in with the pack alpha soon after they relocate?"

A muscle in Rafe's jaw tightens. "Some do and some don't."

"You mean you don't have to check in at all?" I bat my eyelashes innocently.

"Only if I feel like it." Rafe places his hand over mine and squeezes. "I appreciate the concern, but I think I know a bit more about werewolf culture than you do."

Gah! This guy is so arrogant. Smiling sweetly, I withdraw my hand and reply, "Of course."

Pru and Vreeland have been watching our exchange with interest, and Vreeland starts to say, "Oh, but Sophie's—"

Pru knocks into her glass of cherry juice, spilling some on Vreeland's shirt. "Oh no! I'm so sorry, Vee! Why don't you go change your shirt, and I'll soak this one right away so the juice doesn't leave a stain."

I arch an eyebrow at Pru to let her know I know what she just did, and I definitely owe her. She's savvy enough to realize I was probing Rafe for information about his werewolf status, and she figured I wouldn't want Vreeland mentioning my close ties to the local pack.

"Okay." Vreeland shrugs, oblivious to his fiancée's shenanigans, and retreats to his cabin below deck to change.

"Poor guy." Rafe shakes his head. "He seems kind of accident prone tonight."

As soon as the boat docks, I thank Vreeland and Pru for a lovely evening, say goodbye to Rafe, and walk briskly toward my car, anxious to get home.

Rafe falls into step beside me, and I smother a sigh. "When can I see you again?"

"I guess the next time will be at Pru and Vreeland's joint wedding shower."

Rafe flashes his most charming smile, which might make some women swoon, but it's not working on me. "You can't fit me in any sooner?"

"Afraid not," I reply, trying to sound sincere. "I'm on a really tight deadline to get the bakery ready for its grand opening."

"Well, if you could use some help..."

"Thanks, but I'm fine. My new employee has turned out to be very helpful."

"Oh really?" he sounds surprised. "I thought your new employee was giving you trouble."

Now I could kick myself for oversharing about my personal life when we first met. When will I learn to keep my big mouth shut? "Not at all... it was just a misunderstanding."

"I'm glad to hear it, but if anything changes, my offer still stands."

We've reached my car, and I want him to leave; I'm dying to be alone. "Your offer?"

"To take care of your employee so thoroughly he won't bother you ever again."

A chill ripples down my spine that has nothing to do with the gust of wind tousling my hair. "That won't be necessary, Rafe." I open my car door. "Goodnight."

"Thank you for a provocative evening," says Rafe as he saunters away.

A provocative evening? I clench my jaw, start my car, and pull away, relief washing over me when I see his retreating form in my rearview mirror.

I check the time; it's nine-thirty, which means the pack meeting is long since over. I wonder how Teddy made out? I want to call him to ask but decide against it; Teddy moved out for some reason he can't or won't discuss with me... which is a clear signal about setting boundaries, something I've lectured him about a few times.

I'm tempted to call Jake and ask him, but he's as tight-lipped as a vacuum-sealed Mason jar when it comes to werewolf business.

I cover a yawn with one hand and sigh.

Guess I'll just have to wait until tomorrow to find out.

CHAPTER 19
A VISIT TO THE VET

TEDDY

Monday, June 25

When I enter the bakery promptly at seven, I'm surprised to see Sophie is already stripping wallpaper. I move stiffly; every muscle aches, I'm covered with cuts and scrapes, and the side of my jaw where Jake punched me is swollen and discolored. But I feel like a million bucks—I'm a member of the Bay Howlers pack!

Sophie turns toward me, drops her sponge, and shrieks. "Oh, great stars above—what happened to your face! And... and the rest of you! Did the whole pack beat on you last night?"

"Pretty much." I try to smile but it ends in a grimace.

"That looks so painful." Sophie tips her head at my jaw. Concern clouds her large, solemn eyes, the color of molten pewter; I could happily drown myself in those depths.

"I'm fine, really," I mumble through the swelling; it's

149

impossible for me to speak clearly. "And, er… you're looking at the newest member of Jake's pack."

"Really?" asks Sophie, and when I nod, she beams up at me. "I'm happy for you, Teddy, truly happy."

My mouth starts to curve up at the corners again, but I wince at the spike of pain. I murmur through clenched teeth, "Thanks. I'm happy too."

Sophie steps closer and tenderly probes my face. Her fingers feel cool on my flushed skin; she smells like a spring rainstorm, and little flecks of wallpaper dot her glossy chestnut hair. I briefly consider pulling her into my arms and declaring my intentions to woo her until she falls for me the way I've fallen for her, but I close my eyes, managing to tamp down the urge to make an utter fool of myself.

"Have you seen the doctor yet?" she asks.

"Not yet."

Sophie draws her brows together. "I'll bet you all went down to the pub for a drink after the pack meeting, didn't you?"

She pauses long enough for me to nod and then sputters, "Did anyone bother to ask the pack's doctor to examine you?"

When I shake my head, she throws her hands in the air. "Werewolves! Honestly, I don't understand how your species has survived this long!"

Sophie pulls her phone out of her pocket and places a call. "Elvira? Hey, it's Sophie Spellman Brownlee." She nods, a fleeting sadness dimming her features. "I was pretty upset, but I'm doing okay; thanks for asking. Actually, I'm calling for my business partner, Teddy Barker.

He's the newest member of Jake's pack; they met last night and—" she nods her head and chuckles "—You guessed it; he's a *mess*. And I don't like the swelling on his face. Can you fit him into Doc's schedule?" There's a slight pause, and then Sophie gives me a thumbs up. "Perfect; see you in twenty minutes."

Sophie grabs her purse. "Come on, wolf-boy. It's time for you to meet Doc Demetrius."

"Wolf-boy?" I grumble as I slide into the passenger seat of her ancient Subaru.

Sophie grins. "I think it suits you."

"*Humph*," I mutter, pretending to be offended, but secretly I'm pleased Sophie has given me a nickname, however ridiculous.

She heads south on Highway 42, passing stone cottages with kids playing out front, thick stands of evergreen trees, and occasional glimpses of the teal waters of Green Bay visible through the trees.

"How was your evening?" I ask, hoping she didn't enjoy herself, which makes me feel like an ungrateful heel.

"It was fine. But I actually think you had more fun." We both chuckle, and my heart lightens in my chest.

At the risk of annoying her, I push Sophie for more details because I have to know. "And your prospective boyfriend?"

Sophie snorts. "A real turkey."

"I see," I say casually, but enough fireworks to light up all of Door County are going off inside my head. "Are you... um, disappointed?"

Sophie shakes her head but keeps her focus on the

two-lane highway as we round a couple of twisty curves. "Nope; just annoyed that I have to spend three more evenings with him."

I know I took a few blows to the head last night, but this doesn't make any sense. "Why do you have to see him again?"

Sighing, Sophie explains about her friend Pru's upcoming wedding, and the fact she's a bridesmaid and the non-boyfriend is a groomsman. I get the sense she's not disclosing everything, which makes me uneasy, but she's obviously done talking about him. "Tell me about last night," she says, changing the subject.

I'm careful to avoid anything Jake would consider sensitive pack information as we chat. When she asks me how many werewolves I wound up besting, I shrug. "Enough."

Sophie chortles and turns into the driveway of a rustic log cabin. A hand-painted sign in the yard says, "Doc Demetrius, Serving Your Pets Since 1898."

"You're taking me to see a veterinarian?" I stammer, feeling indignant on behalf of my species. "I'm entirely human at the moment; there's not a snout or tail in sight."

"Very funny," says Sophie. "Doc serves as the staff doctor for Jake's pack and for the Riddle Hill Fire Department, which consists of mostly werewolves. He's board certified in both veterinary medicine and internal medicine, which makes sense since many of his patients are shifters."

I pull open the door to the clinic and usher Sophie in ahead of me. Stepping into the gloomy interior, she waves at a vampire with a Bride of Frankenstein beehive; the woman must have a pound of white-and-black hair piled on top of her head. Sophie introduces me to Elvira, who collects some basic information from me and asks us to wait until the doctor is ready.

"The doctor's a vampire?" I hiss, noting the dim lighting, the dark burgundy drapes and wallpaper, and the odd assortment of photos on the walls. Apparently Doc Demetrius treats everything from griffins to dragons.

"What were you expecting? The Faerie Queen herself?" Sophie shakes her head at me, but her eyes are sparkling with good humor at the unhappy expression on my battered face.

"I've never been examined by a vampire before," I whisper. "Our two species were not quite so cozy back in Michigan."

"Ooh. I'd love to hear all the details sometime," Sophie teases; I roll my eyes, which appears to be the only part of my face I'm able to move without flinching.

"Just… never mind," I stammer helplessly, unable to resist smiling at Sophie.

A deep voice booms, "Mr. Leslie Theodore Barker, I presume?"

We both rise, and a tall, slender, silver-haired man with spectacles offers me his hand. "Doc Demetrius." After we shake, he adds, "Congratulations on joining the Bay Howlers; it's a fine pack."

"Thank you."

He gives Sophie a sympathetic smile. "You know I never interfere in faerie matters, and I trust Catbeam's judgement. Nonetheless, I was sorry to hear about the wing-clipping."

Sophie sniffs. "I guess it was bound to happen sooner or later; I haven't exactly been a model faerie—" she waves her hand at me "—but we're here for Teddy; just look at him!"

I stare adoringly at Sophie, my heart thrumming in my chest. I think she's actually concerned about me—at least a little—until she adds, "I'll never get the bakery opened in time without Teddy's help."

My mouth twists, but I don't want Sophie to see how much her words sting, so I glance away. What did I expect? Just because her date last night was disappointing, it doesn't mean Sophie is suddenly going to see me as anything other than her business associate.

"Help yourself to some coffee," says Doc kindly to her. "Teddy and I won't be too long."

The vampire doctor impresses me with his professionalism and quiet efficiency. He checks me over, cleans and re-bandages the deeper cuts, and prescribes an anti-inflammatory to help reduce the swelling in my jaw and hands, which are bloodied and bruised. "I recommend you avoid any more 'sniff and tussles' for the time being; your body needs time to heal."

"Since I prefer conversation over fisticuffs, that won't be an issue."

"Good; that solves at least one of your problems." Doc Demetrius claps a hand gently on my shoulder. "Does she know?"

I frown at the doctor. "Does she know what?"

"Come now, son. It doesn't take a hundred-and-fifty-year-old vampire to recognize the signs. That spunky faerie sitting in the waiting room is your mate, isn't she?"

My head drops to my chest. "Is it that obvious?

"To a physician accustomed to working with shifters, it is." Doc removes his wire-rimmed spectacles. "Sophie deserves to know the truth."

I shake my head. "It's too early… and besides, she thinks of me as her employee, not as boyfriend material."

"She's going to be mighty suspicious when you vanish for thirty-six hours during the next full moon."

"Thirty-six hours? I thought I needed to disappear for ten hours, tops."

"Not a chance." Doc sucks in a breath, his upper fangs glinting. "I'm going to recommend thirty-six hours at a minimum, and you must begin your confinement at least twenty-four hours before the moon waxes full."

"But why do I need to be confined for that long?"

"A young werewolf spending his first full moon alone after meeting his mate needs time to master his powerful emotions," says Doc. "Unless you and Sophie establish a firm mate bond before the next full moon, your mate blight will set in—and trust me on this—it won't be pretty."

"But you heard Sophie," I remind him, "she needs my help getting her bakery sorted out!"

"You'll be in no condition to sort out anything during the full moon. In fact, you could do more harm than good if you're not careful."

"Fine," I mumble. "Message delivered."

"Good." The vampire hesitates. "And… er… may I offer a word of advice?"

"Of course."

"Sophie wouldn't have insisted on scheduling the appointment and driving you to the clinic if she didn't have some feelings for you. I believe you can trust her with the truth."

"With all due respect, I believe you're very much mistaken." I shake my head firmly. "We argue almost constantly—about everything—and Sophie shoved me away when I tried to comfort her after Catbeam Spellman clipped her wings. Sometimes I think Sophie barely tolerates my presence."

Doc chuckles. "My wife and I have been married for a long time." He adds with a wink, "Oh, how I miss those heady days of falling in love. So much misunderstanding and drama."

"I don't understand."

"Sophie may be resisting your considerable charms for now, but with a little persistence on your part, I believe she will realize she likes you—quite a lot. Don't be discouraged, Teddy... and don't wait too long to reveal what's truly in your heart."

CHAPTER 20
GREENEST GREEN

SOPHIE

MONDAY, JULY 2

"No, no, no. I don't like any of them. Why is this so hard?" I shake my head at the six samples of green paint Teddy has dabbed on the bakery's wall. It's been a week since I drove him to Doc's, and thankfully his cuts and bruises are mostly healed. Not that his injuries have slowed him down; far from it. If anything, Teddy has been pushing himself hard, almost too hard, like he has an internal deadline that's driving him to finish the bakery's repairs in record time.

Consequently, I've felt obligated to pitch in and work just as hard, which has made me grumpier than usual. I've broken every single fingernail, gotten glue and primer stuck in my hair more than once, and banged up both knees scrubbing the floor, which I took over so Teddy could finish the walls. I'm so tired I could sleep for a month, except there's no time; the bakery's grand opening is less than two weeks away.

Teddy taps one of the samples on the wall. "What about this one? You said you wanted emerald green, and that's what this is called."

I wrinkle my nose. "That looks nothing like emeralds. Besides, I've changed my mind."

"O-okay." The corners of Teddy's mouth twitch.

I glower at him. "What's so amusing?"

"Nothing," he says, but now he's smiling at me, his sea-blue eyes sparkling with humor. Teddy looks so endearing...er, I mean efficient... in his white painter's overalls, and his grin is so infectious that I feel my lips curving upward of their own accord.

"Stop it!" I cross my arms. "This isn't funny." But then Teddy starts to chuckle... and I wind up laughing, both of us practically slap-happy with fatigue.

When we get our giggles back under control, Teddy looks at the swaths of green paint and tilts his head to the side. "Actually, I think they're all too dark; you might want to consider a lighter green altogether."

I tap my chin with one finger, thinking about all the shades of green I've ever seen. Then it comes to me, and I dash over to the back door. "I know the perfect color! Come on."

"Hang on," calls Teddy, who puts the paint brush in water and closes the lids on the various samples before following me out the door. "Where are we going?"

"The beach."

"Sophie, I don't think we have time to—"

"I know just the color for the bakery—" I break into a

jog, and Teddy easily keeps up "—but I've only ever seen it by the shore."

We jog the four blocks down to the water's edge, and then I lead him up a hill toward the dune grasses clinging to the rocky incline. I bend down, break off a clump, and turn around, holding up the tall grass in my hands. Grinning, I say, "See? It's perfect!"

"It certainly is," murmurs Teddy softly. He pulls out his phone and snaps a few photos of me holding the cluster of grass against my chest like a bouquet.

"What's that for?"

"It's for the *Before and After* scrapbook," he explains.

Teddy has been taking photos of the bakery in each stage of repair for his scrapbook, but he's also taken a lot of photos of me—with paint on my nose, or a glob of glue on my cheek, or a smudge of dirt on my forehead. Once, when I was in a particularly foul mood, I accused him of taking photos that could be used to blackmail me later, but at the hurt look in Teddy's eyes, I told him I'd only been joking.

"But I don't have paint, or glue, or dirt on my face... do I?" I ask, suddenly suspicious.

"Nope. I merely wanted to capture the moment when you found the right shade of green." He holds up his phone. "Do you mind if I take a few closeups?"

I arch an eyebrow but shrug. "Suit yourself."

Teddy steps closer, so close he looms above me, the sunlight making his shoulder-length, blond hair look like spun gold. He tenderly pushes a lock of my plain, brown hair off my cheek, and I inhale sharply as my face tingles at his touch.

When did my skin become so sensitive that even a simple brush of Teddy's fingers causes a reaction?

He steps back, snaps a few more pictures, and reaches out to take my hand. A pleasant warmth that has nothing to do with the summer weather spreads up my arm and into my chest, and my pulse accelerates like the lead car at the Indy 500. Despite my resolve to keep Teddy at arm's length, I don't pull back when his fingers wrap firmly around mine.

"Let's get to the paint store before that grass dries out," he says. "They'll be able to produce a custom paint color for us; I think we should call it 'Sophie's Greenest Green.' What do you think?"

A burble of laughter escapes from me as Teddy helps me climb down the rocky hillside. As we head toward the road, my eyes glimpse a movement between two cottages. I spot a tall, dark-haired, muscular man in jeans and a black tee; when he gazes at me, my joyful mood crashes, and I stumble.

Teddy catches me; when he notices I've gone still, he frowns and then starts turning toward Rafe, but I squeeze his hand. "It's alright; I thought I saw someone I knew, but I'm mistaken."

Teddy nods, and we jog back to the bakery. I think he senses I'm not being truthful, but the last thing I want is for Teddy to confront Rafe on my behalf; I can take care of myself. Besides, I don't think it would end well for Teddy, who doesn't need a bully like Rafe on his case.

I'm preoccupied as Teddy drives us to the paint store, debating whether to talk to Jake. I decide to wait and see;

if Rafe makes another appearance in Riddle Hill, then I'll tell Jake everything I know.

"Are you okay?" asks Teddy.

"I'm fine," I reply curtly, and he doesn't press me for details I'm obviously not willing to share. I blow out a puff of air. "Sorry; I don't mean to be cranky, it's just... " My voice trails off.

"I get it; you have a lot on your mind right now. Just remember I'm here to help. Don't feel like you need to shoulder all the responsibility by yourself."

"Thanks... I appreciate it." And I really do; I'd never have been able to get the bakery refurbished this quickly without Teddy's tireless dedication.

But he's not being entirely frank with me either. Teddy never speaks about his last pack; I've tried probing a few times, but he instantly shuts down, his face turning into an impassive mask. He's seen me at my worst, when my wings were clipped, and it hurts he doesn't trust me enough to be vulnerable about his past. Even worse, Teddy has never explained why he suddenly moved out of the cottage; he's now living in a studio apartment above Rob Wolferman's garage, paying rent he obviously can't afford.

Teddy's behavior doesn't add up... and until he explains himself, I won't be opening up to him either.

"WELL, WHAT DO YOU THINK?" It's after five, and Teddy has been painting since we returned from the store. Sophie's

Greenest Green now covers one entire wall, and it looks amazing, exactly what I've been envisioning all along.

"I *love* it!"

"Good; that's what I want to hear." Teddy gives me a smile so tender it takes my breath away, and we lock eyes for a heartbeat. Then my phone rings in my pocket; thankful for the intrusion, I hastily withdraw it.

"My father is calling." Somewhat confused, I swipe to answer. Dad rarely calls me, preferring to text or merely show up on my doorstep.

"Honey… it's your mom," Dad's voice sounds strained. "We're at the hospital; the doctors think she's had a heart attack."

"What?" I gasp. "How is she? Will she be alright?" This can't be happening; my mother is a strong, healthy faerie who hardly ever gets sick. Quite the opposite— she's the one who takes care of the rest of us.

"Phoebe's still being evaluated… I don't know." My dad huffs out a long, shaky breath. "I've called your grandmother, who's on her way. Can you tell Jake and Cassia for me?"

"Of course, and then I'll be right over too." After I tell Dad I love him and hang up, I promptly burst into tears. I sense Teddy hovering, but given how I pushed him away with a stern lecture the last time he tried comforting me, he's giving me some space.

"What is it? What's wrong?"

"It's my mom." Sobbing, I struggle to say, "She's had a heart attack." The last words end on a wail as I fling myself into Teddy's chest.

Without hesitation, he wraps his powerful arms

around me and draws me close. "I'm so sorry, Sophie." He holds me as I weep all over his white overalls. "Tell me what I can do to help."

Nestled against Teddy's broad chest, I feel so safe and protected that I don't want to leave his embrace. Odd. These feelings aren't something I normally crave, especially not from a man as persnickety and perfect as Teddy, who can paint an entire wall without getting himself covered in spatter. We're as different as any two people I've ever known, and yet there's something about his sweetness and solidness that draws me to him... until he lectures me about fire safety, or the proper way to dispose of old paint cans, or the nutritional balance of Zosia's diet.

I had to chuckle when Teddy, the werewolf who claims he doesn't like pets, purchased a vitamin supplement for Zosia's fur. He insists I add it to her food every day; even when he's aggravating, he's adorably well-meaning.

With a small sigh, I step out of Teddy's arms, already missing their warmth. "I... I need to tell Jake and Cassia... and then meet my dad at the hospital."

"Let's make those calls right now, and then we'll go to the hospital together. Where's your phone?"

"Here..." I unlock my phone, go to my favorites tab, and hand it to him. "Cassia first, and then Jake."

Teddy puts the phone on speaker and places an arm around my shoulders as I tell Cassia, who begins to cry, which reopens my floodgates. "I'll meet you at the hospital," she chokes out between sobs.

Jake is more stoic; no tears for him, but his voice

drops so low I barely hear him rasp, "She'll be fine, Sophie. She *has* to be." Then he coughs and grumbles, "I'll be there as soon as I can find someone to cover my shift."

I've been wiping my eyes with the backs of my hands, but now Teddy produces another of his clean, white hankies, which I gratefully accept. I mop myself up as best I can in the bathroom.

When I emerge, Teddy holds out my phone, which I drop into my purse. He casts me an anxious look, his brow deeply furrowed. "I'll drive."

"Thanks," I whisper, grateful for his strong, calming presence.

Teddy drops me off before searching for a parking spot in the hospital's crowded lot. I race through the special entrance reserved for supernatural visitors, which is tucked in the back of the hospital, hidden by a wooden fence and climbing ivy to prevent unsuspecting humans from wandering inside. This waiting room is one of the few places in Riddle Hill where supers don't have to hide our wings, fangs, fins, and fur from the public; given the amount of stress involved in waiting for news of a loved one's condition, it makes sense we can be ourselves here.

As soon as I enter, I release my wings, which I've been keeping tightly closed on the drive over here. As they unfurl through the slits in the back of my pink tee, I spot my dad and race over to him.

Dad grips my shoulders as my wing feathers brush against him. "It turns out the doctor's initial assessment was wrong." When he sees my lower lip begin to wobble, he hastily adds, "It's good news! Phoebe didn't have a heart attack after all—she has a severe case of faerie flu!"

"Faerie flu? But I thought Mom couldn't catch it!" I'm simultaneously confused and relieved; faerie flu is a nasty illness and highly contagious if you've never been exposed to it before, but it's not fatal. When I was fourteen our entire family came down with it—except for my mother. Even Dad and Jake were bedridden. (Werewolves can catch it too.) Mom had to close the Sit for a Spell Café for a week so she could nurse us back to health. After that incident, we all assumed she'd developed immunity.

"Apparently not," says my grandmother. "Poor Phoebe; they're putting her in isolation right now. The doctor says she needs to stay here for five days, and then she'll need to rest at home for another week." Granny Catbeam pats my wing feathers, like she's trying to apologize for binding my magic, but I'm not ready to forgive her yet.

Teddy arrives in the waiting room at the same time as Cassia, who sheds happy tears when Dad shares the news. Before any of us have time to inform Jake, he arrives, his face pale and drawn. Poor Jake; everyone sees him as the big, strong alpha, but I remember the frightened, grieving, twelve-year-old boy who'd just lost his mother and stepdad in a car accident. While Cassia sobbed at their funeral and teared up often at school afterward, Jake remained stolid and stone-faced, but at night I'd hear him crying quietly in his bedroom across the hall.

When Dad tells Jake, he shudders and throws his

arms around my father, who immediately wraps his huge, coppery wings around him, giving them both some privacy. The two men finally separate, both of them swiping away the moisture from their eyes.

"Are we closing the café, Uncle Nash?" asks Cassia.

My dad's wings droop. "I don't know what to do. It's the busiest time of the year, so I hate to close even for a few days, but without Phoebe, I don't have much of a choice."

"I can help," I offer. "I don't have Mom's gift of discernment, but I can take orders and help Cassia with the customers."

My dad looks at me and shakes his head. "But you have the bakery's grand opening to prepare for. I can't ask you to sacrifice that."

"I think we can manage both." Teddy has been standing off to the side, obviously not wanting to intrude, but now he steps forward. "I can help Sophie and Cassia during the morning rush, and the rest of the time I'll focus on the bakery."

"And I can give Teddy a hand at the bakery when I'm off work; the remodeling will go more quickly with the two of us," says Jake.

Dad sniffs a few times before giving us a grateful nod, and then his thick, brown beard cracks into a wide grin. "Thank you... all of you." Then he reaches his hand toward Teddy, and I realize I've not introduced them. "Dad, this is Teddy Barker; Teddy, this is Nash Brownlee."

They shake hands, and Dad gives Teddy one of his,

"I'm her father, and I'm watching you" looks. I stifle a sigh; why are the men in my family so ridiculously overprotective?

"Phoebe will be happy to know the Sit for a Spell Café is staying open," says Granny. "And it's a good thing too; someone has to keep an eye on those gargoyles." Everyone groans except for Teddy, who quirks a brow.

"Just you wait," chortles Jake, who claps Teddy on the shoulder. "They're nasty little terrors."

We all chuckle, even Teddy, but I get the sense something is bothering him that has nothing to do with my mom, the bakery, or the gargoyles. After I'm allowed to peek through the two-way glass inside the isolation unit and blow my mom a kiss, Teddy drives me home.

As I'm about to exit the car, he clears his throat; I know this means he has something to say. I wait, my hand resting on the car door. "What is it, Teddy?"

He hesitates and then says in a rush, "If you need help... of a more personal nature... you know I'm here for you, anytime. Just ask." Teddy doesn't look at me but continues staring out the windshield.

I'm not sure what he's talking about or why he's suddenly avoiding eye contact. "Um... thanks?"

After Teddy drives away, I open my front door and scoop up Zosia, who gives me a lot of *meeps* and *wumps*. I settle into the green chair, Zosia in my lap, and drop my handbag on the floor by my feet. My phone tumbles out, and despite my weariness, I decide to thumb through my text messages; I haven't checked them since this morning.

My posture goes rigid, and Zosia whines, sensing my distress.

Now I know why Teddy's brow was so furrowed earlier when he handed me my phone, and why he offered his help just now; he must have seen these messages.

Rafe's first text arrived earlier today, around the time he spotted me and Teddy leaving the beach. "I stopped by to say hi, but then I saw you with another werewolf. Who is he?"

How did Rafe know I'd be on the beach, unless he'd been watching the bakery and followed me when I left with Teddy? Goosebumps prickle my flesh, and I shiver at the thought.

His second text arrived an hour later. "If he's your new employee, I'll gladly teach him a lesson he'll never forget." Sweet moonglow... now he's threatening Teddy? The memory of Teddy holding me sours, and I clutch the phone more tightly; would Rafe really go so far as to hurt him?

Rafe's final text arrived shortly before Dad called to tell me about my mom. "You shouldn't be holding his hand, Sophie. That's not right."

I sit there for a long time, running my hands through Zosia's warm fur, trying to convince myself not to freak out.

It's not working; eventually I stumble into bed and fall asleep, only to dream of Rafe smirking cruelly as he beats up Teddy.

As I wake up feeling more exhausted than when I

turned in, I decide that I need to push Teddy away in order to keep him safe from Rafe's fists. It's time to reassert our employer-employee relationship.

No more hugs or handholding or anything else until I'm sure the obsessive werewolf has moved on.

CHAPTER 21
GARGOYLE ENCOUNTER

TEDDY

Monday to Tuesday, July 2-3

Cruising slowly with my windows rolled down, I circle twice around the block, sniffing the air for any scent of strange werewolf. Satisfied whoever sent Sophie those text messages isn't hanging around at this late hour, I head to my one-room flat above Rob Wolferman's garage, wishing I'd never moved out of Sophie's cottage; if I'd stayed, I could keep her safe at night.

Well... at least until the full moon, when Jake and Rob think I'll turn into some raving mad werewolf. That idea fills me with such dread I shudder as I park the Caddy and trudge wearily up the steps.

My apartment suits my needs for now; I have a kitchenette on one wall, a table with two chairs under the window, and a sofa, couple of lamps, and flat panel TV on the opposite side of the cozy space. Best of all, Rob is charging me half the going rate, in exchange for mowing his lawn and clipping his hedges.

I don't bother turning on the lights; I can see just fine with my night vision, and there's no clutter to trip over anyway, unlike at Sophie's place. I sure miss Zosia though, whom I visit a couple times a day when I need a short break from the remodeling; Sophie has even returned her cottage key to me, just so I can spend some quality time with the little white fluffball.

But I miss Sophie even more, despite the fact we're together all day long. We had a breakthrough on the beach today when she took my hand, and later in the bakery when she threw herself into my arms, although that probably doesn't count. I was the only available source of comfort when she learned her mother was in the hospital; Sophie probably would've been satisfied with any pair of arms in that moment.

Even so, my heart leapt as I held her against my chest, and I planted a tiny kiss on top of her lustrous brown curls; I was so gentle she didn't even notice. I adore that gorgeous, impetuous faerie, and each day it becomes more of a struggle not to tell Sophie about the mate bond, but it's obviously so one-sided that some-times I find myself rubbing the spot over my chest where my heart aches with yearning.

Unfortunately Sophie's not very discerning about other people, especially other men, and she doesn't like asking for advice or help, trusting in her own judgment more than she ought. I'm pretty sure the werewolf who sent those texts is the same guy she called her "prospec-tive boyfriend" not that long ago. At least she realizes he's bad news, but that knowledge alone isn't enough to keep her safe.

I wish I could tell Jake, but that would mean admitting I was snooping through Sophie's phone, which makes me sound almost as creepy as the other guy. I didn't intend to invade her privacy, but I couldn't stop myself from scrolling when I saw that unsettling message on her screen, *You shouldn't be holding his hand, Sophie. That's not right.*

Turns out he's the same guy she went on that sunset cruise with, the one she'd called a turkey. He must have some connection to the vampire couple getting married later this summer, but what was he doing in Riddle Hill today? The werewolf obviously isn't local. Where's his pack located?

I peel off my clothes, slip on my sleeping pants and a clean tee, and tumble onto the sofa; it has a pull-out bed, but I'm too exhausted and upset to bother with it tonight.

On top of trying to get Sophie's bakery ready in time for her grand opening—which I'm going to miss entirely because it coincides with the full moon—now I'll be helping her at the restaurant and keeping an eye out for this lowlife, who's bound to turn up again.

Yawning, I close my eyes, and despite all the worries swirling around inside my head, I fall instantly asleep.

I KNOCK on the café's back door early the next morning, and Sophie pulls it open. Her glorious waves are pulled into a bouncy ponytail, and she's wearing a black apron over a lavender tee and blue jeans. She ducks her head, probably so I don't notice the dark circles beneath her eyes. I need to confess now, before I lose my nerve... and because she can't just ignore this problem named Rafe.

"Let me show you around," she says, turning away, but I tap her on the shoulder. Sophie pauses but doesn't glance back at me.

"I'm sorry, but I read those messages—all of them—from a creep named Rafe," I whisper quickly. "Jake should know there's a strange werewolf hanging around you."

Sophie spins around, pinning me with a hard glare. "You had no right to scroll through my personal texts, even if I handed you my phone; it was wrong and you know it. This situation with Rafe is my business, and... and besides, I've already handled it."

My stomach churns, because I have a sneaking suspicion Sophie probably sent him a message that will only provoke him further. "How did you handle it?"

Sophie hesitates and then pulls out her phone, holding it up so I can see the text she sent Rafe a short while ago. "We went on one date, Rafe, and I can assure you, there won't be any more. You have no right to spy on me, threaten my employee, or lecture me about whose hand I can hold. If I see you in Riddle Hill again, I'll report you to the local pack alpha, who happens to be my cousin. Don't bother replying to this message."

My gut twists when I read it, because Sophie just blasted an unstable werewolf with the cold, hard truth. It's like poking a grizzly with a hairpin. And yet I have to admire this gutsy spitfire of a faerie; Sophie Spellman Brownlee takes no prisoners.

I reach for her hand, but she snatches it back. "I'm still mad at you," she hisses.

Of course she's mad at me; what else is new?

"Fine, you're mad. I get it," I say softly so her father, who's clanging pans in the kitchen, doesn't overhear us. "But I think you just made matters worse."

Sophie's eyes cloud over with fresh worry, but then she shakes her head, her pretty, chestnut-colored ponytail swishing behind her. "I think you're wrong, but we don't have time for second-guessing now. We've got to get ready to open the café. Come on."

Sophie hands me a black apron like hers, with Sit for a Spell embroidered in golden thread across the top. After I pull it over my head and tie the strings in back, she hands me a scrunchie. I hold it up, wrinkling my nose. "What's this for?"

She rolls her eyes and points at my hair. "You need to pull it back into a ponytail like mine."

I scowl at the scrunchie. I've never tied my hair back before; I prefer to leave it loose.

"It's the law," she adds firmly, waiting for me to comply.

"Fine," I grumble. "Is there a mirror somewhere?"

"Oh, just turn around; I'll do it for you," grumps Sophie.

She snatches the scrunchie from me and then runs her fingers through my hair several times to smooth back all the strands; each time I nearly moan in pleasure at the glorious sensation. It seems to be taking Sophie longer than necessary to finish the task, and now I'm gritting my teeth so I don't make any awkward noises.

Finally she's done, and I wipe my brow, which is moist with perspiration. Nash sticks his head out of the kitchen long enough to give me a friendly nod as we pass, and then he disappears to continue his meal prep.

We enter the dining area, and I'm immediately drawn to the portraits on the walls, which must be Sophie's ancestors. A lady in a purple gauzy gown smiles down at me, flaps her wings, and plays a chord on her harp, while an admiral with a hook for a hand glowers at me; nearly everyone else waves and nods, although a few remain sleeping.

I'm anxiously awaiting the arrival of Miss Dragonfly's portrait, which the faerie undertaker will ship as soon as he confirms her ghost has taken up residence. Although unalive supernatural ancestors sleep most of the time, I'll be able to converse with Miss Dragonfly when she's awake; I can't wait to tell her I've joined a pack again... and that Sophie is my fated mate.

"Are you Aunt Sophie's boyfriend?"

"What?" Both Sophie and I turn toward an adorable faerie child with delicate tipped-up eyebrows, teardrop-shaped ears, and small purple-and-silver wings. I'm assuming she'll glamour her features once the doors open.

Cassia rushes over. "Olivia, that's not a polite question. Mr. Barker is part owner of the Rhyme 'N Riddle bakery."

"But Aunt Sophie was touching his hair... a lot."

Cassia quirks her brow at Sophie, who blushes.

Maybe Sophie liked the feel of my hair in her fingers as much as I did. "I was helping Mr. Barker tie back his hair," she explains.

"Oh," says Olivia, who promptly dissolves into giggles. She points at the long counter that runs along the café's back wall, which is supported by five stone gargoyles mounted on corbels.

The gargoyles are smoothing down the tops of their heads with their three-fingered hands, slowly blinking their stony eyes as if in ecstasy, and grinning wickedly. Even though they're making fun of me, I can't help myself; I burst out laughing.

"Oh, please don't laugh; they crave attention. It's best to ignore them completely," says Cassia under her breath.

But Sophie has other ideas; she stomps over to them, crosses her arms, and growls, "I'm keeping a record of your misdeeds for my mother. Every time you act up, I'm writing it down; so far you've earned one good spanking from her. Want to make it two?"

The gargoyles immediately drop their act, shuffle their feet, and shake their heads. "That's more like it. Now stand up straight and stop goofing around. We have work to do."

The stone creatures listen to her! My chest swells in pride at Sophie, who can command a troop of gargoyles without using magic.

I feel a tug on my apron and glance down to find a pair of bright green eyes staring up at me. "Yes, Olivia?"

"I'm hungry."

Cassia, who's reviewing the daily specials with

Sophie, looks up. "Uncle Nash is making you breakfast. I'll go check—"

"I'll make sure Olivia has her breakfast," I tell her. "Finish what you're doing."

Cassia nods her thanks, and Olivia takes my hand, leading me over to the counter. "This way, Mr. Barker."

"You can call me Teddy."

Olivia giggles at me.

"What's so funny?" I lift Olivia onto one of the counter stools just as Nash delivers her a short stack of strawberry pancakes, two slices of bacon, and a glass of orange-mango juice.

"I'll call you Teddy Bear!"

"No, Olivia, you may not call him that," scolds Cassia. "Please address him as Mr. Teddy or Mr. Barker."

"Okay." The little girl sighs. "But he reminds me of a great, big teddy bear."

Sophie snorts and then turns away, while Cassia compresses her lips to keep from laughing out loud. I suppose I ought to be offended, but I think it's kind of cute, even if it hits a bit too close to the mark. Even this little faerie realizes I'm as harmless as a stuffed animal.

Sophie decides the best way for me to learn my way around the café is to shadow Cassia, who knows all the regulars by name and recites the menu from memory. I'm surprised at the number of non-supers who stop in for a meal, but Cassia explains that a lot of human tourists vacation in Door County during the summer season.

My original plan was to head over to the bakery after the breakfast rush, but the café is still full as noon approaches, so I stay on to bus tables and refill beverages. A platinum-blonde faerie named Spectra picks up a chicken-veggie wrap to go and tells me to stop into her salon anytime; the first trim will be on the house. The takeout line is long and comprised mostly of women, who introduce themselves to me and want to chat. Nash is struggling to keep up with all the orders, but when I offer to give him a hand in the kitchen, Sophie glares at me and stomps off to help her dad.

I stare after her, unsure why she's mad at me again. Cassia must notice my confusion because she whispers, "Sophie's just mad because I was right, and she was wrong."

My brow furrows. "What were you right about?"

Cassia chuckles softly. "I told Sophie you'd be good for business—and clearly that's true. Besides, I don't think she likes all those women fawning over you."

"Are you sure about that?" I cock my head to the side. "Because Sophie is constantly pushing me away."

"Well, that's between the two of you," says Cassia. "But if you like Sophie, then you need to make sure she knows. Sophie isn't very good at reading signals."

"Don't I know it," I mumble, embarrassed by the extra attention I seem to be attracting from the other women. They're all customers of the café who deserve prompt service and a friendly smile. How else should I behave?

Sophie continues to shoot me salty glowers for the remainder of the morning, which I'm not sure how to interpret. Does that mean she might like me, just a little, as Cassia seems to be implying? Cassia is her best friend and knows her better than anyone else, so perhaps I should take comfort in her advice, but I can't.

By one-thirty the café is beginning to thin out, and I hang up my apron. "I'm heading over to the bakery now."

"Thanks for all the help today," says Cassia. Nash steps out of the kitchen long enough to say thanks, but Sophie doesn't reemerge.

I pull open the back door, my shoulders slumped with dejection; even the warm sunshine doesn't cheer me up. I recall Doc Demetrius's advice to tell Sophie she's my fated mate, but given how often I annoy her, I don't think that's wise.

The truth is I want Sophie to fall for me; *I want her to choose me.* Until that happens—if it happens—I won't burden her with my needs and the depth of my feelings.

I never want Sophie to feel guilty because she doesn't love me back.

CHAPTER 22

LIKE BEES TO NECTAR

SOPHIE

Thursday, July 12

"This is ridiculous!" I hiss into Cassia's ear, who nods in agreement as we stare at the long line of customers, mostly women, waiting for a table at the café.

"I know," she whispers. "Teddy draws the ladies like bees to nectar." We've been run ragged for the past week as word has spread about the handsome werewolf bussing tables at my parents' restaurant. With so many women batting their eyelashes at Teddy or giggling at everything he says, you'd think his head would puff up as much as his biceps. But not Teddy; he's as humble as ever... and he doesn't flirt back.

I can confirm this because I watch many of those interactions closely; a few times he's caught me in the act of scowling at a particularly aggressive flirt, and he gives me a gentle smile that heats up my insides like the flames of a Wisconsin bonfire. But I just nod curtly and try not to notice the fleeting sadness in his sea-blue eyes at my coldness.

I have no choice; I need to maintain our arm's-length relationship for the time being. Rafe sent me one more text this week, and my stomach twists every time I read it.

"Hey, that's a great suggestion. Even a loner like me enjoys an occasional sniff and tussle. I look forward to meeting up with your employee and your cousin sometime. See you at Pru and Vreeland's shower." Rafe added a couple of kissy face emoticons that made me gag.

Given Rafe's subtle threat toward Jake, I can't confide in him either. Jake would probably track down Rafe and have it out with him. While I'm certain my cousin would prevail, a defeated Rafe would have even more reason to pound on Teddy for revenge.

All I can do is continue to tell Rafe I'm not interested, and hope he finds some other girl to obsess over soon.

Great stars above! At least Rafe has cured me of bad boys for good.

I just hope by the time Rafe moves on, Teddy can forgive me for being so cool and aloof, especially given the long hours he's putting in to finish the bakery.

Teddy lightly taps my shoulder after the lunch rush; when I spin around, our eyes lock, and the golden flecks around his blue irises darken. He gives me a tentative smile, like he's afraid I might bite his head off for touching me, and I feel lower than an eel's belly. I wish I could tell Teddy why I've been especially prickly lately, but until I speak with Rafe at the shower tomorrow night, I don't want to take any chances. I'm hoping Rafe will move on after I reiterate, once again, that we won't be dating.

"I'm heading to the bakery now. Come as soon as you can—I have a surprise, well actually, two surprises!" says Teddy.

I can't help myself; I break into a grin at his boyish enthusiasm.

"I'll see you as soon as I check on my mother," I tell him. Mom came home from the hospital a few days ago, and Granny's been looking after her while Dad's at work. My mom will gradually resume her duties at the café; her doctors expect a full recovery within the next month.

Teddy nods. "Of course. I'll be there until six."

I cock an eyebrow. "What happens at six?"

"I have my first exam tonight at the fire station. And I spoke with Jake about my schedule; he says the only time my volunteer duties would interfere with bakery hours is if there's an active fire and all hands are needed." Teddy's eyes sparkle with excitement. What is it with guys and bright, red, fire engines? "Er... I hope that's okay?"

"Of course it's okay. Riddle Hill needs dedicated fire-fighters."

Teddy nods. "Exactly. I knew you'd say that, but Rob didn't think you'd be so... um... accommodating."

"Oh really?" I snort. "Tell Rob he doesn't know me as well as he thinks he does."

I park in front of the two-story stone cottage with cobalt-blue shutters, tucked down a small lane near the town's harbor. I adore my childhood home, with its scraped wood floors and shabby-chic décor; this is where I learned to love, and laugh, and cook.

Grabbing a tray of freshly baked caramel-fudge brownies from the car seat, I head toward the front door. When we ran out of my mother's brownies at the café and our customers kept asking for them, I figured I'd give them a try. I can't magically enhance the flavor or sprinkle a bit of faerie dust for good measure like Mom does, so they can't really compare, but the customers don't seem to notice or care.

My mother is sitting on one of the large, yellow sofas in the front room, and as I sit next to her, two nine-tailed foxes charge into the room and hop in my lap; they're mates and Zosia's mama and papa. After I pet and coo over them for a few minutes, Granny shoos them away.

Mom picks up a brownie from the tray and takes a bite, her auburn eyebrows arching in appreciation. "Sophie, these are so good! I can't believe you made them without any kitchen magic—and is that a hint of cinnamon I'm tasting?"

When I nod, she smiles. "You are such a natural. Your bakery is going to be the talk of the town."

Granny helps herself to a brownie, slowly munching and puckering her lips between each bite. When she's finished, she slaps her knee. "As good as Dragonfly's caramel-fudge brownies."

"Auntie Dragonfly made caramel-fudge brownies?" Mom and I ask in the same breath.

"Darn tootin'. Where do you think I got that recipe in the first place? Dragonfly won nearly every baking contest in Western Michigan for two decades. Every time she broke up with a boyfriend and wanted to meet someone new, she entered another competition."

Mom and I look at each other; Mom grins, but I howl with laughter. "I had no idea Auntie Dragonfly liked the boys quite so much."

Granny chuckles. "Dragonfly was a hoot... She was also my big sister and a mighty pain in my butt."

I'm still laughing as I rise from the couch. "Thanks for the taste test; I better get going."

When I bend down to kiss my mom, she squeezes my hand. "You look tired, honey. I'm so sorry I got the flu during the busiest time of the year—and with everything else you need to get done at the bakery too."

"I'm fine, Mom. Besides, Teddy has done the lion's share of the remodeling at the shop."

"That boy's a real keeper," pipes up Granny, who's chomping down her second brownie. "I hope you're being nice to him."

"Of course I'm being nice." I scowl at my impossible grandmother.

"That's funny; all the gals down at Spectra's Salon claim you're downright snippy with the lad. They're taking bets on how long he'll stick around."

"That's ridiculous!" I stomp toward the door, spinning back to add, "Besides, if Teddy skips out, he'll lose his portion of the inheritance. Trust me, he's not going anywhere."

"Whatever you say, dearie." Granny gives me a shrewd look. "Just the same, I'd advise you not to take that nice, young werewolf for granted. Some other pretty faerie or werewolf with a sweeter personality than yours will snap up Teddy Barker in a heartbeat."

I yank open the front door and march outside without another word.

TEDDY AND JAKE finished painting the shop's walls in Sophie's Greenest Green, added crown molding around the ceiling, and painted the windows, trim, and adjoining kitchen a warm white. They also installed my stainless steel coolers and new convection oven (a gift from my parents), and Jake scheduled my first inspection with the city engineer; I have my provisional permit to open!

While there are still some finishing touches needed for my little bakery, we're mostly ready for the grand opening during the Riddle Hill Summer Fest this weekend. So what's Teddy been up to?

As I pull open the bakery's back door, Teddy calls out, "Wait! You need to close your eyes first."

"Why?" I huff, still fuming over my interfering, brownie-consuming, wing-clipping grandmother. But then Teddy's warm hand engulfs mine, and the tension in my shoulders starts to release. Somehow, in the span of a few weeks, a simple touch from Teddy has become a balm to my jangly nerves.

Teddy guides me from the kitchen to the front of the bakery before releasing my hand. "Okay. You can look now."

I blink open my eyes and squeal as I spin around.

Teddy has dug up old travel posters, which he's framed in black and hung on the walls; they lend the shop a kitschy, bistro vibe that I love. I dash over to three small, wrought-iron tables with various mismatched chairs, all painted white, which Teddy has positioned near the plate glass windows. Running my hand over one of the tables, I'm awestruck by how well he's brought my vision for the bakery to life.

"Oh Teddy... this is..." As I struggle to find the words, Teddy's brow crinkles.

"Don't you like it?"

"Are you kidding? I *love* it! This is amazing... it's like you've been inside my head and knew exactly what I wanted to achieve. How did you do it?"

Teddy's handsome face lights up as he chuckles. "I listened to you; every time you told me about your vision for the bakery, I made a mental note. I want you to be happy, Sophie."

Teddy's eyes lock onto mine with a gaze so sweet and inviting that I begin moving toward him, a moth fluttering helplessly toward the flame. I can only pray that Rafe's threats are idle ramblings, because I'm falling for Teddy despite my best efforts to push him away.

Teddy's lips part, his chiseled features softening as I approach him.

I'm moving closer and closer... we're only three feet apart... then two... then one.

This is it; I'm going to throw my arms around Teddy and kiss this gentle giant, this gorgeous, kindhearted werewolf who's taken all my gruffness in stride and worked tirelessly to turn my dreams into reality.

But then Teddy inhales sharply and steps away; I pause, confused by his mixed signals.

"I'm glad you're happy," he murmurs softly, "and that... um... you'll be ready for your grand opening."

"Don't you mean *our* grand opening?" I smile up at him.

Teddy swallows and shakes his head. "Since the grand opening coincides with the full moon, I won't be here; that's why I wanted everything to be ready ahead of time."

"But the full moon's on Saturday *night*, when the bakery is closed, so I don't see what the big deal is." I shrug and start moving toward Teddy again, but he skirts behind a table to avoid me.

Geesh. What's gotten into him?

"The thing is... I need to leave for the entire weekend. It's... um... a werewolf thing," says Teddy.

"A werewolf thing?" I stop moving and cross my arms with a frown; something doesn't add up. Is this another of Teddy's secrets? "I grew up with Jake and his pals. I know all about the pull of the moon. A young wolf cub may need to be isolated while he learns to adjust to the waxing moon, but you're a grown man."

As Teddy runs both hands through his long, blond locks, I recall the silky feel of those strands between my fingers. Little Olivia was right; I took my time pulling Teddy's hair into a scrunchie. I've wanted to run my fingers through his hair since that first day he walked into my wrecked bakery, lecturing me about Auntie Dragonfly's will and the forfeiture clause in Appendix C.

"Adult werewolves sometimes have... um... a certain condition that requires more time away."

I narrow my eyes. "What sort of a condition? Are you

sick?" My voice drops low; should I be worried about him?

"In a manner of speaking." Teddy puts up a hand. "But it's not contagious or anything. Like I said, it's a werewolf thing."

"And that's all you're willing to share with me?" My voice rises in frustration. "Can't you trust me with the truth for once?"

"What's that supposed to mean?" Teddy's forehead creases.

"You never told me what happened with your last pack, even though you obviously told Auntie Dragonfly and Jake. You never told me why you suddenly moved out like I had the plague or something. And now you refuse to tell me the real reason you can't be here for the bakery's grand opening. You're keeping an awful lot of secrets."

"*I'm* keeping secrets? What about you? I find it impossible to believe that creep hasn't tried contacting you again, but every time I bring it up, you steer me away. If you don't want to discuss it with me, fine. But at least tell Jake there's a strange werewolf harassing you."

"Don't try changing the subject," I fume. "This isn't about me—it's about how you're hiding behind your werewolf nature to avoid the truth!"

Teddy reaches one hand toward me, and then lets it drop down to his side. "I don't want to hide anything from you."

"Is that so? Then tell me the real reason you can't be here for the grand opening."

He doesn't reply; instead, he glances away from me

and takes a couple of deep breaths, like he's getting ready to sprint out the door any second.

I'm so frustrated with Teddy that my filter is gone, not that I have much of a filter to begin with. "What are you hiding from me? What's so important you're willing to risk everything you've worked so hard for?"

Teddy's gaze snaps back to me, and his mouth gapes open. "What are you trying to say, Sophie? Are you considering *firing me*?"

I feel a twinge of remorse, given everything he's done to get the Rhyme 'N Riddle Bakeshop ready, but this is the most important weekend of the season, and Teddy is my only employee. I'm going to really struggle to run this bakery by myself. "I don't want to take such drastic measures, but you're refusing to work during our grand opening without giving me a valid excuse."

Teddy's chest heaves a few times, like he's having trouble getting enough air in his lungs. "I already told you—I have a werewolf condition."

"And you're sticking with that story?" My face flushes, hot anger coursing through my veins.

"It's the truth." Teddy is obviously lying through his dazzlingly white teeth.

"Then you leave me with no choice," I say firmly, despite the churn in my stomach and lump in my throat. "Since you refuse to show up for work on a critically important weekend, and you refuse to give me a reasonable explanation, I'm exercising Appendix C."

Teddy's eyes grow misty, like I've wounded him deeply. "Wow. You're firing me *and* you're asking me to forfeit my ownership interest in the bakery?"

"Yes." I bite my lower lip to keep it from wobbling. "I'll purchase your shares at the end of the twelve-month period, and... um... I'll reimburse you for any out-of-pocket expenses. I want to be fair."

"You want to be fair?" says Teddy through his clenched jaw.

I raise my chin. "Yes, of course."

Teddy stalks around the little tables and exits through the back door; I hear him open and close his car door. When he returns, he's holding a legal document, which he slaps on top of the bakery case. "Here you go! Signed, sealed, and delivered."

I pick up the document in trembling fingers and scan it quickly; Teddy is *giving me* his ten percent ownership in the bakery, and he's asking for nothing in return. He signed it in front of two witnesses, Jake and Rob, a week ago. "I... I don't understand."

"I wanted to take you to dinner after the grand opening to celebrate... and, er... to give you my share of the bakery, no strings attached." Teddy's breath hitches. "But there's no point now; it's all yours."

"I...I don't know what to say."

"You've said quite enough already." The door slams shut, followed by the purr of Teddy's old Caddy as he drives away.

Tears spring to my eyes that I quickly swipe away. What's wrong with me? I should be celebrating, not crying.

I've gotten everything I ever wanted—I'm the proud owner of a chic new bakery on Main Street. This is something I've dreamed about since high school.

But I'm having trouble ignoring the ache lodged in the center of my chest and the fistful of knots twisting in my stomach. I'm feeling bluer than Granny Catbeam's hair after she visits Spectra's Salon.

Why am I so weepy over Teddy Freaking Barker?

He's the one who walked out on me.

CHAPTER 23
FOOLHARDY FAERIE

TEDDY

Thursday, July 12

I accelerate down Main Street in a foul mood, deeply hurt by Sophie's lack of trust in me and shocked she exercised Appendix C. I'm also piping mad—but more with myself than Sophie. How did I manage to wreck such a beautiful moment? Sophie was so close, and I could see in her eyes she was ready to take the next step in our relationship, but then I blasted it all to moondust.

I should've told Sophie sooner that I'd have to miss the bakery's grand opening, especially since she was counting on my help. But I kept chickening out, not wanting to disappoint her. So instead of kissing those lush lips of hers, I backed away and finally fessed up.

Then I compounded my error with the lame "werewolf condition" excuse, which Sophie didn't buy for a minute. I bang my hand on the steering wheel. Confound it all!

Who scheduled the Riddle Hill Summer Fest for this weekend anyway? What a ridiculous lack of planning for a supernatural village to be hosting the event during a full moon!

On the other hand, as Sophie rightly pointed out, it's really only an issue for very young wolf cubs... and for lovelorn werewolves like me.

Still muttering to myself, I park by the harbor, grab the brown bag dinner Nash packed for me before I left the café, and find a secluded bench where I can stare at the water. I need to get my roiling emotions under control before I show up at the fire station and take my first written exam.

But I can't focus; I'm too worried about Sophie. She may not want me around anymore, but she's still my fated mate—and that fact will never change. Perhaps, if I'm persistent and really, really lucky, she may change her mind about me someday. I guess I'm in for a really rough full moon this weekend, given everything Doc's told me about mate blight, and the number of times Rob and Jake remind me about my upcoming confinement.

But in the meantime, I'm concerned about here and now.

How can I ensure Sophie's safety when I'll be locked up for most of the weekend? Shaking my head, I realize there's only one right answer; I need to tell Jake about this Rafe character. Sophie will be mad at me all over again, but that's a small price to pay.

Besides, I don't mind Sophie's grumpy side; if anything, it makes me want to kiss away her frowny face all the more. As I think about nuzzling that foolhardy spitfire of a faerie, my mouth twitches into a smile, and a small sigh escapes from my lips. But then I recall she's just fired me, which means I'll have no reason to hang around her all day in the bakery, secretly pining. At least I'll see her tomorrow at the café for one final shift before the weekend; maybe she won't be as angry with me in the morning.

I finish my cheddar cheese and roast beef on rye, feeling better now that I've decided to speak with Jake. I'm gathering up my sandwich wrapper when the hair on the back of my neck stands up, and my muscles tense. I leap to my feet, scanning my surroundings for whoever or whatever triggered my fight response.

It's a lovely, warm evening by the bay; families and couples are picnicking or swimming, and a group of teens is playing volleyball on the beach. I don't detect the scent of a strange werewolf or any other potential danger as I sniff the air; on the other hand, a smart predator would ensure he's downwind.

I chalk it up to a case of nerves as I head to my car. I'm definitely more jittery than usual, anxious about doing well in my firefighter training, upset about my argument with Sophie, and worried about this weekend.

But I can't shake loose the feeling in my gut that someone is watching me.

~

"HOLY CONFLAGRATION!" hollers Jake.

We're standing in the now-empty training room at the fire station; the rest of the class has already departed.

I'm learning how to read my alpha's mood. When Jake is in a really foul temper, a vein pops out on his forehead.

Yep… there it is.

Jake is probably madder at me for not telling him sooner than Sophie will be when she finds out I snitched. This is a classic example of a no-win scenario; either way, I'm in the dog house.

"Why didn't you tell me about this creep right away? Now I have to worry about him stalking Sophie—on top of the Riddle Hill Summer Fest, Sophie's grand opening, my aunt's health, the full moon, and your mate blight. Is there anything else you want to pile on? Hmm? I'm all ears."

"No, sir." I shuffle my feet nervously and gaze at the floor.

Jake rubs the back of his neck wearily and grunts. "I don't mean to be taking this out on you. Sophie should have confided in me immediately; she's just so stubborn." He heaves a sigh. "I'll tell Rob and Marv; they can keep an eye out too."

"Thanks, Jake." I turn to leave, my shoulders hunched forward, but he calls me back.

"What's wrong with you? You look like you lost your best friend."

"Sophie and I… argued today." I shake my head. "She doesn't understand why I can't help her this weekend, and I won't tell her the real reason. I don't want Sophie to feel forced into a relationship; I want *her* to choose *me*."

"I'm sorry… that's got to hurt," says Jake quietly. "It's all the more reason why you need to be back here tomorrow night by eleven. Doc Demetrius wants you in lockdown before midnight."

"Yes, sir." I head for the door.

"If you're going out to your car, I'll walk out with you."

"You go on without me. I still have something I need to do here," I say, hoping he won't ask any questions.

But Jake cocks his head to the side. "What are you up to?"

Everyone in the pack already knows I'm fastidious, and I brace myself for some more good-natured teasing. "If you really want to know... "

"Yes, Barker, I really want to know." Jake quirks an eyebrow at me, waiting.

"Fine," I huff. "I'm going downstairs to clean out the disgusting padded cell where I'll be living for thirty-six hours. When was the last time that room was fumigated?"

To his credit, Jake rolls his lips together to keep from laughing in my face. Once he gets himself under control, he claps a hand on my shoulder and says, "That's a very good idea, Barker. Thanks for handling it." But as he heads outside, I hear him chuckling under his breath.

What I'm not telling Jake or anyone else is that I have a plan of my own for tomorrow night. Sophie and Cassia were chatting about the wedding shower this morning, and I just might have overheard when and where the vampire couple will be having their party.

Alright, I'm not proud of myself; I intentionally snooped while I was cleaning the café's countertop, which took me way longer than usual. The wedding shower is being held tomorrow evening at the Sage Mage Supper Club, which I gather is quite posh in an Old World, Transylvanian sort of a way.

While Sophie is inside the supper club attending the party, I'll be waiting outside in the parking lot, in case there's any trouble from a werewolf named Rafe.

It's time he and I had a little chat about my mate... who hates my guts and broke my heart... but that's beside the point.

CHAPTER 24
ALWAYS THE BRIDESMAID

SOPHIE

FRIDAY, JULY 13

I've been avoiding Teddy all morning at the café, which isn't as hard as you might think. Whenever he casts me a wounded look, my heart constricts a little tighter in my chest, my breathing turns a little raspier in my throat, and I quickly find something for him to do.

So far he's cleaned the bathrooms, dusted all the ancestors' gold-leaf picture frames, and polished each gargoyle, which turned out to be the worst chore of all. Each little fiend made gagging noises in Teddy's ears; by the time he finished, he looked pale, sweaty, and nauseous.

I didn't realize Teddy had such a sensitive stomach, or I wouldn't have put him through that experience. But at least he's stopped all attempts at eye contact; he must realize his flimsy excuse about having a "werewolf condition" won't fly with me. I probably know as much about werewolves as any faerie in Riddle Hill, and there's no such thing as a condition that forces adult werewolves to disappear for a few days at a time.

Even so, I feel really bad about our fight yesterday, and I definitely regret firing him. I think if I hadn't been ready to kiss him, I might not have reacted so strongly when he told me he couldn't work this weekend. I'm also shocked Teddy handed over his ownership interest in the bakery without asking for anything in return. I don't feel right keeping it, and I'm too mad at him to return it, which goes to show how muddled I've become over the whole thing.

At one o'clock I hang up my Sit for a Spell apron and cross the street to the Rhyme 'N Riddle Bakeshop. It's time for me to start baking for tomorrow's grand opening!

I just wish I didn't have this heaviness deep down in the pit of my stomach over the whole Teddy debacle; I feel like I swallowed a bucket of sand, and it's weighing me down. I also wish I didn't have to stop, get cleaned up, and go to Pru and Vreeland's shower tonight. Not only would I prefer to continue baking, but I'm nervous about seeing Rafe. I finally told Cassia she'd been right about him all along, but I didn't tell her about the text messages because I didn't want to alarm her; she has enough anxiety issues without dealing with mine.

After donning my apron and headwrap, I let my faerie form emerge; I may not have any magic, but at least I can be myself in my own kitchen. My ears slope into points, my eyebrows tip upward, and I partially extend my wings; if I let them unfurl completely, I'll be knocking over all my pans.

Since the summer fest is the busiest weekend of the year, and I have no employees to help me, I'm going to keep things simple. I'll bake two desserts, caramel-fudge brownies and chocolate chip cookie bars; I've come up with catchy titles for them, Spelled for You Brownies and Riddler's Magic Bars. I plan to cut them into sample sizes and serve them for free, along with a cute card displaying my hours of operation. The business card was Teddy's idea; I'll admit he's whip smart. He's also a whiz at remodeling, and if cleaning were an Olympic sport, he'd take the gold medal.

But Teddy skipped out just when I needed him most, which makes him pretty unreliable in my book. I'm stirring up another batch of dough, but I flip off the mixer, upset with him all over again.

I wander out of the kitchen, hoping for some fresh inspiration to tamp down my sadness. I smile at the lovely shade of dune-grass green on the walls, the cheery travel posters in their black frames, the cute tables and chairs perched by the window, and the neatly painted white trim.

It's perfect—and ninety percent of it is Teddy's doing.

My wings droop; he's holding back something very important from me, something related to his phony werewolf condition. When this weekend is over, I'm going to get to the bottom of Teddy's secrets—every single one of them.

I'M STANDING in the lobby of the castle-like supper club, where a larger-than-life statue of a knight in shining armor perches on his silvery steed; he's holding a staff in his right hand and looks ready to charge down Highway 42. Sir Reginald is one of Jake's werewolf ancestors, so I feel like he's a member of my quirky, extended family.

"Hey, Sir Reginald," I nod, since his ghost still inhabits the armor.

His helmeted head creaks slightly in greeting.

"I might need some help tonight," I whisper.

There's a clang, and then Sir Reginald goes quiet. Well, it was worth a try.

I smooth down my short, violet cocktail dress and blow out a puff of air. It's showtime; one of my closest friends is getting married, and she deserves my happy face.

But it's kind of hard always being the bridesmaid… you know? I was Cassia's maid of honor, of course, and I've been a regular bridesmaid four other times. Everyone looks so happy on their wedding day, so in love, that my heart twists up inside my chest each time. Honestly, I think the real reason most women cry at weddings is because they're lonely and want a man to look at them the way the groom gazes lovingly at his bride.

Take me, for example; the one man I want to kiss has vanished, and the one man I never want to see again is walking into the lobby now.

I swallow nervously and take a step back, resting my

hand on Sir Reginald's horse. "That's the guy," I mumble, but the ghostly old knight is probably sleeping, because he doesn't stir.

Rafe is dressed in a black, unstructured jacket, navy V-neck tee, and black jeans. "Hey, darling, you look stunning," he drawls in a low voice that he might think is sexy but makes me want to stomp all over his highly polished cowboy boots.

"I'm not your darling." I glare at him, but he merely smirks as if this is a game we're playing. Then he invades my personal space and reaches an arm around my waist like we're dating, which I've made abundantly clear we're not.

Thunk!

Sir Reginald's long staff drops down on Rafe's shoulder, and he yips in surprise. I quickly extract myself from his grasp and clack down the hall in my spiky heels, anxious to join the party and escape from Rafe.

"Hey, Sophie... um... I could use a little help here!"

I glance over my shoulder and compress my lips to keep from laughing. Sir Reginald's staff is now pressed in front of Rafe's chest, pinning him against the large mare. "If you promise to keep your hands to yourself and stop bothering me, he might let you go."

"Huh?" Rafe is such a clueless oaf.

"You're a big, bad wolf; figure it out yourself," I tell him and push open the door to the private party room.

For the first twenty minutes I actually have some fun, and then Rafe turns up. But he's looking pretty disheveled; his jacket is gone, he's limping slightly, and the V-neck of his tee is all stretched out.

Score one for the ghost of Sir Reginald!

Cassia has rearranged the seating, placing Rafe as far away from me as possible. I should be able to enjoy myself, but I feel Rafe's eyes boring into me from the other side of the room. I wait until one of Pru's other friends gets up to leave, and I stand up too; I need to get away from Rafe's glower, and I need some sleep before I have to be up at three to finish my baking.

"Not so fast, Sophie," growls Rafe behind me.

I turn around to face him, my pulse skittering nervously. "What's the problem?"

"I thought we were friends."

"Friends don't send threatening messages and place their hands where they're not wanted."

"I haven't threatened anyone," he protests, adding, "I thought you were a fun girl, but you're just a dud."

"Well, this is one dud who wants to be left alone," I hiss. "Got it?"

He squints at me through hooded eyes and snarls, "Yeah, I got it."

Julien, the wedding photographer, wanders into the hall with Cassia; he has a camera slung over one shoulder and a tripod under his arm. He glances from me to Rafe and says, "Hey, Sophie, I was just heading out to my truck; why don't I escort you."

Cassia obviously put him up to it, and I'm grateful to them both. "Sounds good, Julien. Thanks."

Julien waits until I've started my car before walking to his truck. As I drive away, I notice Rafe standing in the parking lot. But he's no longer tracking my departure;

instead he's sniffing the air, like he's caught the scent of something he doesn't like.

So long as he stays away from me and my loved ones, I don't care who he's chasing next.

CHAPTER 25

A WHIFF OF TROUBLE

TEDDY

Friday, July 13

I left my car in an inconspicuous spot at the edge of the parking lot, where the asphalt ends and the woods begin. I'm leaning against a sturdy tree trunk, my arms folded across my chest, on the lookout for whoever is hassling Sophie.

My breath hitches as she emerges from the restaurant wearing a shimmery purple dress and high heels, her long hair falling in soft, silky waves around her shoulders. My heart cracks a bit more at the realization we won't be working together any longer; not only did Sophie fire me from my job at the bakery, but Phoebe Spellman will be back at work next week, which means the café will be fully staffed. I rub the ache in the center of my chest, which feels hollowed out as I gaze at my mate.

As Sophie strides into the parking lot I creep closer,

using the thick bushes at the edge of the woods to remain hidden. Tracking a strange werewolf would be a lot easier if I could shift, but there are too many non-supers inside the supper club, and I don't want to scare anyone with my fuzzy muzzle and tail.

Hang on! Who's the guy walking Sophie out to her dented silver Forester? I raise my nose and sniff; he's a vampire! Growling low, my hands curl into fists at my sides. Sophie and Jake may have vampire friends here in Riddle Hill, but the vamps back home were smug, superior, and never helped anyone outside their own clan.

"Thanks, Julien," whispers Sophie.

"No problem," replies the vampire. "Do you need me to follow you home?"

Sophie shakes her head. "I'll be fine."

The vampire waits until Sophie starts her car before he moves away; that's when I notice he's lugging camera equipment, and I realize this is the wedding photographer. I suppose if Cassia trusts this vampire, he must be alright.

That's when I smell *him*.

My heart seizes in my chest, my body goes rigid with fear and fury, and then the flashback hits, sending me reeling backward. Beads of perspiration form on my brow as I break into a clammy sweat. Shuddering, I grip the nearest tree branch for support as memories of that night descend on me with the strength of a gale-force wind.

Jarrod is lying on the ground, surrounded by two were-wolves: Drew, our disloyal beta, and his dark-furred, anony-mous companion with the pungent, ashy scent. Both wolves turn toward me, their lips curling to reveal razor-sharp fangs. When they attack, I flail my limbs and howl, completely outmatched. I cringe even now as I recall that horrific beating and my accompanying shame; not only was my alpha dying, but I could do nothing to help him or defend myself.

Drew had called me a useless werewolf more than once, and he wasn't wrong. But that other werewolf, the one I now realize is Rafe, was even crueler. As I lay curled up in a ball on the grass, Drew barked, turned, and loped away. But Rafe pulled back his leg and gave me one more swift, hard kick before leaving.

And now that same werewolf is swiveling his head in my direction—Rafe's caught my scent!

He bares his teeth and barrels toward me in his human form. I'm immobile, still stuck in the past, still smelling the coppery tang of Jarrod's blood and hearing my own cries for help, when Rafe pounces on me, shifting in mid-air as he knocks me down.

Stunned out of my stupor, I transform from man to beast in mere seconds. The change happens so quickly I'm only dimly aware of my surroundings; I hear my clothes shredding and my anguished yelp as Rafe sinks his fangs into my left shoulder. Snarling, I rake my sharp claws down his flank, and he rears back in surprise.

I'm no longer the same young, useless werewolf without any survival skills; Miss Dragonfly made sure of that. She hired a half-gnome, half-werewolf to tutor me, and I spent the last three years learning how to fight. I still prefer negotiating to fighting, but some thugs need to be taught a lesson.

Roaring, I flip Rafe over, and we wrestle, rolling

around on the hard ground as leaves and twigs stab into our hides. One instant he's on his back, the next it's me, looking up at the dark outlines of the trees, and the nearly full moon overhead. We struggle and tussle, punching, slashing, biting, and grunting.

I finally manage to break free from Rafe's grasp and stand, blood dripping from a gash on my brow, the bite on my shoulder, and numerous cuts and slashes on my arms and legs. Panting to catch my breath, I give Rafe a chance to climb to his feet, even though I know full well he'd never extend the same courtesy to me. This time when he charges I'm ready; pulling back my fist, I ram it into his muzzle.

"Oof!" he yelps, backing away.

Rafe raises one shaky paw to his snout and yips in wolf-speak, "Big-g MISS-take." Then he turns and lopes away with a howl.

I brace myself against a tree and wait for my legs to stop shaking and my breathing to return to normal. There isn't a single part of my body that isn't bruised or bloodied or aching. Once I'm sure Rafe isn't returning for another bout, I slowly, painfully shift back into my man form.

Gazing down at my ripped-up khaki shorts, shredded tee, and battered limbs, I realize I can't return to my car until the parking lot empties out. It looks like I'll be late for my lockdown, and my beta is going to be furious. Since I locked my phone and wallet in my glove compartment earlier, I can't call or text Rob either.

It's well after midnight when I finally climb into my car; there's only one vehicle left in the lot, a motorcycle that I suspect belongs to Rafe. As I pull away, I notice some movement in the trees on the other side of the lot; it's probably Rafe, but I'm not concerned. He isn't going to be bothering Sophie or anyone else for a while, at least until his broken nose is healed.

"Barker!" hollers Rob. "Is that your sorry butt you're dragging down here?" He obviously hears my footsteps as I slowly, painfully descend the steps to the fire station's basement.

"Yup," I mumble through my split lip.

"You're late!" he snaps, "You better have a really good excuse, because—" Rob races over to me as I stumble on the last step. "Where did this happen? And who did you fight?"

"Supper club," I rasp, "Wolf named Rafe." Then I crumple onto the floor.

When I wake up, I'm lying on a table someone's hauled into the basement, Doc Demetrius is bending over me, and Rob and Jake are hovering nearby. A nurse with a massive hair-do—Elvira?—hands Doc a syringe. He's preparing to put me under so he can stitch me up, but I raise my palm. "Wait a sec," I whisper.

Groaning, I turn my head so I'm facing Rob and Jake; my alpha peers into my eyes, and his breath quickens. "Was it him? The werewolf who's been harassing Sophie?"

I nod. "But that's not all. He... he was there that night in Michigan."

Jake and Rob glance at each other and then down at me, clearly not tracking. As I cough and then wince at the pain, Doc says, "He needs medical attention *now*."

"Rafe..." I mutter through gritted teeth. "He was one of the wolves who attacked Jarrod."

"Alright, that's enough talking," says Doc, who jabs my arm with a needle.

As the anesthesia trickles into my veins, I hear Jake whisper. "I'll take it from here, Barker. I'll make sure he doesn't hurt anyone else."

I try to mumble a warning about Rafe's tricky ways, but my words are nothing but garbled noise. My last thought is of Sophie, beautiful as always in her purple dress, and a tear dribbles onto my cheek.

CHAPTER 26
A NOT-SO-GRAND OPENING

SOPHIE

Saturday, July 14

The chorus of compliments is nonstop—"Congratulations!" "Your bakery is adorable!" "This is SO delicious!"—as I stand behind my bakery display case, handing out samples to a steady stream of friends, neighbors, and out-of-towners.

"Where's that scrumptious werewolf you've been hiding?" asks a pert little faerie who's a few years younger than me; come to think of it, she's probably Teddy's age.

"He's busy," I tell her with a mighty scowl.

"Oh!" she says, her squeaky voice pitched even higher. I think I might've scared her off. Good; Teddy doesn't need bimbos like that flirty faerie hanging around him.

It's almost three in the afternoon, and I've been on my feet for twelve hours straight. Cassia dashed over with some lunch for me and then scurried right back to the café, which is just as busy as every other shop on Main Street. Our festival has been blessed with ideal weather—mid-seventies, low humidity, and blue skies— and the folks keep on coming.

Taking advantage of a lull in the foot traffic, I dash into the kitchen to grab another tray of bars just as the bell above the shop door tinkles. Stifling a yawn, I return to the front, a welcoming smile plastered on my face... only to find the one woman I don't want to see standing inside my shop, humming off-key.

She's wearing a pink flannel shirt over a gray tee that reads "Manga Mama," red Converses, and baggy, yellow hiking shorts; sticking out of her shorts are a pair of skinny legs that a razor hasn't touched in fifty years.

"Hi, Granny." I place the tray of samples inside my display case and straighten. "Can I get you something?"

"So it's true," says my cryptic grandmother.

As usual, I have no idea what she's talking about. "What's true?"

"Your werewolf is off somewhere, waiting out the full moon."

"He's not *my* werewolf," I snort. "And while he's getting ready to commune with moonbeams, I'm here working off my wing feathers."

My grandmother purses her lips. "So you really don't know, do you?"

It takes every ounce of self-control not to roll my eyes. "I guess not... Can you please enlighten me? What am I missing?"

Granny's wrinkly face transforms; her frown lines

are smoother, her complexion more radiant, and her white hair takes on a faint silvery glow. When she smiles at me, I smile back, suddenly remembering all the fun we used to have before I became a sulky, rebellious teen. I guess I'd forgotten that I actually love this growly old faerie.

"I'm afraid I can't say, dearie; it's against the rules for elders to get involved. I can only tell you this—your young werewolf deserves another chance, and another after that—and he needs *you* to provide them."

Then Granny swipes three of my samples and shuffles out of the shop. But instead of scowling at her departing back, I stare after her in wonder. She's trying to help me... not that I have a clue what she's talking about.

I don't have another free moment until after five, when it's finally time to close up. I see Marv walking past in his black police uniform, grab my last two brownies, and poke my head out the door. "Hey, Marv, take some samples. I'm heading home shortly."

Marv pauses, breaking into a grin. "Thanks, Sophie. How'd it go today?"

"Really well, except I sort of lost my employee at the last minute." Hmm... maybe Marv knows something about Teddy's mysterious werewolf condition. "You wouldn't happen to know anything about Teddy's... er... condition, would you?"

Marv's eyes widen, and he nods to indicate we should step into the shop. "How did you hear about the fight?" he whispers urgently, closing the door behind us.

"Fight? What fight?"

"Oh... um... so you haven't heard?" says Marv, backing away, like he's going to sprint back outside.

"Oh no you don't, Marvin Maxwell Maywood, Junior." I plant myself firmly in front of the door. "What's this about a fight? Is Teddy hurt?"

Marv puts up his hands, palms facing outward like he's trying to ward off an invasive species, but I've known him all my life. Next to Rob Wolferman, Marv is Jake's closest buddy and his second beta. "There's an ongoing police investigation; I'm not supposed to say a word."

I grab the front of Marv's uniform; he's at least six inches taller than me and weighs twice as much, but he lets me anyway. "Tell me what happened to Teddy, or I'll tell Jake you're the one who ruined his science project in eighth grade."

"That was an accident... and... you promised not to tattle!" Marv glares at me.

Shrugging, I pat his shoulder. "I only promised not to tell Jake that you accidentally *sat on* his science project. I never said I wouldn't tell him you're the one who broke it... Now, what's this about Teddy and a fight?"

"Never trust a faerie," grumbles Marv. "Fine. But you better not tell Jake I'm the one you heard it from."

When I fold my arms and arch my eyebrows, Marv caves in. "Teddy and another werewolf got in a fight last night in the woods near the Sage Mage Supper Club. Teddy was pretty beat up—"

I gasp, "How badly is he hurt?" I remember how awful Teddy looked after his first pack meeting, and that was a "friendly" fight.

"Cuts, bruises, bites; the usual. He'll be fine... he's, er... resting now."

I'm pretty sure I know the answer, but I ask anyway. "You said the supper club. Who did Teddy fight?"

"We think he's a loner, the same wolf who's been hanging around Sturgeon Bay lately."

"O-oh... this is all my fault." I bring my hands up to my mouth, horrified that Teddy was injured in a fight with stupid, smirking Rafe.

"How can a fight between two werewolves possibly be your fault?"

"I've known about that loner for a while; I dated him once... and... and—" I'm having trouble catching my breath all of a sudden.

"It's okay, Sophie," says Marv gently. "We know Rafaellus MacTire has been harassing you."

"How do you know that?" I sniffle.

"Teddy was worried and told Jake, who asked Rob and me to keep an eye out."

Of course Teddy blabbed, but that doesn't matter now. "Where's Teddy? I want to see him."

Marv crosses his beefy arms and shakes his head. "That's out of the question. The full moon is hours away; no one outside the pack gets in."

"But... but... "

"No buts about it; you know the rules. You're going to have to wait until the full moon wanes, and Doc Demetrius says it's alright for you to see Teddy."

"If someone called Doc, then Teddy must be pretty badly hurt." An image of Teddy's chiseled, gorgeous face flits across my weary brain. I blink rapidly, trying to shake off the same picture of Teddy's face, now battered and bruised.

"Yeah." Then Marv adds softly, "But not all his injuries are physical."

"That's my fault too," I whisper, swiping my leaky eyes. "I said some things I shouldn't have."

Marv goes to the door. "When Teddy wakes up, I'll let him know you were asking after him."

I lock up and lean against the door, my head in the crook of my arm. This time, when the tears start flowing, I don't bother wiping them away.

CHAPTER 27

MEDS, MOONS, AND MATES

TEDDY

Saturday to Sunday, July 14-15

"Soo-phie! Soo-phie!" I howl through my muzzle, knowing she can't hear me, knowing she doesn't love me, knowing she won't come. I'm thrashing around on a thin mattress inside a dim, windowless room. I'm in agony; every part of my body aches, but my greatest torment comes from the chasm inside my chest, where my heart's been cleaved in two.

"Soo-phie!" I moan, my long snout muffling my words. "Pain... o-oh... such pain!" I begin tearing at my chest and limbs, seeking relief from the relentless anguish; I'm cracking, my soul is splintering.

"Doc!" A woman shouts on the other side of the door, probably the vampire nurse. "He's reopened several wounds—he needs more sedation!"

Paws pound and footsteps scramble on concrete flooring; harsh light spills in from the open doorway.

"Soo-phie?" I whimper. "Where she?" I push against the furry hands holding me down, arching my back in frustration.

"No-o... meds!" I screech as the vampire doctor with wire-rimmed spectacles sticks me with a needle. "Need. Her-r-r. But... she... no-o... need... me-e." Slurring my words, I begin to drift off.

"How. He. Doing?" demands my alpha in wolf-speak.

"Physically, he'll heal," murmurs the vampire. "But his mate blight..."

The room darkens, the door swings shut, and I fall into a fitful slumber. I'm pursued relentlessly by a massive werewolf with fur as black as midnight; he's constantly nipping at my heels, despite how hard I'm running. When he finally catches me, something glints wickedly in his paw: a dagger, which he thrusts into my heart. As I tumble backward with a loud cry, the face of my assailant peers down at me... but it's no longer the werewolf who's holding the blade... it's *her*.

"Teddy!" shouts Rob through a small opening in the padded door. "Doc says you can come out now."

"Go. 'Way!" I growl. "Not-t. R-ready." The inexorable pull of the full moon receded hours ago, but I have no desire to shift out of my wolf form and emerge from my cell. I'm bruised, battered, and most of all, bereft; I want to be left alone to lick my wounds in private.

There's a low hum of voices—my pack has obviously returned to their human forms—and Doc Demetrius calls out, "I need to examine your injuries, Teddy."

"No-o!" I grumble.

I hear shuffling around the door and then my alpha's

dominant voice. "Barker, you need to shift back *now*, so Doc can see to your injuries. That's an order."

I hesitate before whining through my canine lips, "Fi-ine." I reach for the blanket, which the nice vampire nurse left for me, and drape it across my lower extremities before transforming.

"I… hur-rt!" I yelp as the full weight of my pain—both physical and emotional—crashes over me with the force of a maelstrom. Like others of my species, I have far better pain tolerance in my werewolf shape.

The door opens, and Doc and Jake enter; Rob hangs back, blocking the doorway, probably so he can prevent anyone else from witnessing my humiliation.

Doc gives me an assessing gaze and kneels beside me with his black bag, but Jake grimaces, bringing a hand to his nose and gagging slightly.

I take a whiff and wrinkle my nose at the amalgamated odors of damp fur, perspiration, dried blood, and body odor; I don't believe I've smelled this horrid since I was a pup in diapers.

Doc checks my stitches, prescribes an antibiotic and something to help manage the pain, and rises to his feet. "You're going to need those dressings changed twice a day, especially that bite on your shoulder and the gashes on your back. Do you have any family nearby to help you?"

Shaking my head, I start to say, "No…" But I pause at the familiar patter of footsteps crossing the concrete floor beyond my door.

I hear several shouts, and suddenly a foolhardy faerie is trying to shove her way inside my rank lockdown cell, the location of which is a closely guarded secret. No one other than Jake's pack and a handful of vampires knows of its existence in the basement of the fire station.

Rob tries to block Sophie, who's shouting, "Let me through—I know Teddy's here, and he's hurt! But why is he staying in this dreary basement? Teddy likes blue skies and bright flowers and pretty sunsets. Are you trying to depress him or something?"

What is Sophie doing here?

How did she even find me?

And when did she learn so much about me? She's right of course... I adore all those things.

Hang on! The love of my life is ten feet away, pounding on my beta's chest; I glance down at myself, horrified. Yanking the thin blanket up to my chin, I hiss, "Don't let Sophie see me like this... or heaven forbid, smell me!"

But there's a loud scuffle as Rob yelps indignantly, "She just bit me!"

And then Sophie charges into the room, her face flushed from her spat with Rob, her hair a glorious tangle around her gorgeous face. Jake spreads out his arms to stop her and growls, "You shouldn't be here, Sophie! You're not pack!"

But Sophie tickles Jake's underarms, causing him to curl into himself with a surprised chuckle, and then she dodges around him to reach me.

I don't know whether to be delighted or dismayed Sophie has gone to the trouble of tracking me down. Either way, I clutch my blanket more tightly, mortified she's here to witness my utter degradation.

When our eyes meet—or partially meet, since one of my eyes is swollen shut, and the other is only half open—Sophie begins to wail, "Oh Teddy, oh my gosh! Oh my gosh!"

She neither gags at my stench nor retreats at my injuries. Dropping to the floor beside me, Sophie takes my battered face in her hands and whispers, "How can I help?"

I lick my split lip, which stings, unsure how to reply; there are so many possible responses. I close my one eye, which I realize is leaking; a tear trickles down the side of my face.

Sophie is here... Somehow, despite all the secrecy surrounding our pack... she found me. That has to mean she cares, at least a little.

Doc says gently, "Come along, my dear. I believe you may be able to assist Teddy later. But first, he needs some privacy so he can bathe and dress."

Doc helps Sophie to her feet; she allows him to guide her to the door, obviously in shock at my sorry state. The vampire calls back over his shoulder, "Teddy, I'll replace your bandages after you've washed up, and then you may go home."

After Doc escorts Sophie upstairs, Jake gives me a hand up. "Let's go, Barker. You need a shower... and then you need to talk to Sophie. We're not going through *this* again."

"Going through what?" I drape the blanket around my shoulders and wobble, but Jake steadies me. I'm lightheaded with lack of food, and there isn't a part of my body that doesn't hurt. Even the soles of my feet are scraped raw and painful. Jake leads me to the service elevator and punches a button to take us up to the men's locker room.

"Mate blight," grunts Jake. "Which was entirely preventable if you'd just told Sophie how you felt."

"Easy for you to say," I grumble, leaning against the wall of the lift for support. "You haven't met your fated mate yet."

Jake's head snaps up, as if he's trying to recall something just beyond the reach of memory, and his eyes grow misty. As the elevator door swooshes open, Jake shrugs. "That's true. But after watching how much you've suffered, I'm planning to tell my mate as soon as possible; there's no way I'm putting myself through that torment."

As we shuffle down the hall toward the men's room, I mumble, "Good plan, alpha; I'll be sure to remind you when the time comes."

CHAPTER 28
FAERIE NURSE

SOPHIE

Sunday, July 15

Doc guides me upstairs to an empty conference room where I collapse into a chair, lean my elbows on the long, oval table, and hiccup through my tears. Since Marv's visit yesterday, I've been so consumed with worry and guilt over Teddy that I've accomplished absolutely nothing. I put a sign on the shop at four this morning that reads, "Closed until Further Notice," because I couldn't possibly bake knowing Teddy was lying injured somewhere.

I look dreadful too. My eyes are swollen from crying, my hair's a tangled mop, and I'm wearing an old gray tee from my high school gym class that's a bit snug, but it's my last clean top.

Doc Demetrius steps out of the room long enough to murmur something to Elvira, and a few minutes later she's placed a box of tissues, a bottle of water, and a packet of crackers in front of me. I pass on the crackers but gulp down a third of the water bottle. Meanwhile Doc and I haven't said a word to each other, but I find his silent presence as soothing as Zosia's purrs; it must be something to do with his vampiric sensitivities. Cassia claims vampires make the best therapists, and she should know; she's been in therapy for a couple of years trying to manage her panic attacks.

"Oh Doc," I murmur, my voice thick with emotion. "Teddy looks awful—and I've only seen him from the chin up. How is he... really?"

Doc's upper fangs catch on his lip; I gather he wants to answer me honestly while also protecting Teddy's privacy. "Teddy was in a fight with another werewolf and based on his injuries, I'd say they were pretty evenly matched. He's been bitten, slashed, and bruised—but he will recover. "

"If only I'd told Jake about Rafe sooner, this wouldn't have happened," I sniffle, dabbing my eyes with a tissue.

"Oh, that fight would have happened sooner or later," says Doc.

"Because of *me*."

Doc pats my hand. "No, my dear, because of *them*. Apparently Teddy and Rafe fought each other once before, although neither knew the other's identity until now."

"What?" I'm struggling to process the fact Teddy and Rafe actually know each other. "But how... and when?"

Doc holds up his palm. "I gather it has something to do with Teddy's last pack. However, you'll need to get the particulars from Teddy; in fact, I believe it will be cathartic for him to talk about it with you. That young man is carrying around a great deal of pain... as well as unresolved feelings."

Scowling, I say, "I've tried to get him to talk about his old pack, but he clams up every time."

"And why do you think that is?" Doc tents his silver eyebrows.

"I'm not sure." I shrug, feeling somewhat miffed about Teddy's secrets all over again.

Doc removes his spectacles, cleans them with a cloth from his pocket, and replaces them on the bridge of his nose. "I suspect Teddy doesn't wish to be vulnerable around you. He wants you to look upon him favorably."

"But I do."

"Do you really?" asks Doc.

I've known Doc all my life and trust his discretion; he's also a very sympathetic listener. I decide to tell him about my fight with Teddy. How I wish I could utter an incantation and take back everything I said, but even my mother's most powerful spells can't change the past. Even worse, words spoken in anger seem to linger the longest.

When I'm finished telling Doc, he says, "Thank you for explaining; that gives me insight into Teddy's state of mind." He pauses and appears to be choosing his next words carefully. "What are your plans now for the bakery, and your... ah... friendship with Teddy?"

"I will apologize to Teddy and try to be a better..." I hesitate because I'm not sure how to categorize my relationship with Teddy. Is he a business associate, an employee, a friend, or something more? My heart thumps hard when I consider the possibility of Teddy being something more, but I dismiss it; how could that sweet, wounded man ever really forgive me after the way I behaved?

"I want to be a better friend," I say lamely.

"And the bakery?"

"I've closed it for now, and I'm returning Teddy's ownership shares; I've already ripped up the document." In a small voice I add, "It wasn't the same... working there all day... without him."

Doc smiles, as if he approves of my decision. "Earlier, you asked how you could help Teddy, and while he's too embarrassed to ask anything of you, he's in great need of assistance."

I sit up straighter. "What does he need?"

"A nurse—and I believe a faerie nurse such as your-self is exactly what Teddy needs most." Then Doc murmurs to himself. "Yes... that will do quite nicely indeed."

"Alright," I reply, unsure what's involved but more than willing to do whatever I can. "What sort of nursing is required? You know I'm a baker, not a healer, right?"

Doc chuckles. "You don't need formal training for what I have in mind. Besides, you have more healing skills where Teddy is concerned than you realize." Doc explains about Teddy's dressings that must be changed twice daily, half of which Teddy can't reach, and the extra protein he's going to need while he heals. Appar-ently I'll be feeding Teddy a lot of bone broth, eggs, and fish.

When Doc leaves to check Teddy once more before

releasing him, Elvira hands me a sheet of instructions about caring for him. Glancing down at the list, I realize this is a full-time job, at least for the next week or so.

I guess the bakery is going to remain closed for longer than I anticipated, because Teddy is coming home with me.

CHAPTER 29
MY FLORENCE NIGHTINGALE

TEDDY

Sunday, July 15

"I don't like that idea at all, Doc," growls Jake. "Sophie doesn't strike me as a good fit; she's no Florence Nightingale. And under the circumstances... wouldn't it be best if she and Teddy lived apart?"

"Let's ask the patient." Doc gives me a bright, toothy smile, his upper fangs mirroring the overhead lighting. "What do you say, Teddy?"

At first I was horrified at the idea of Sophie tending to my injuries... until I remembered her gentle touch when she bandaged me up last time... and her delectable, springtime scent... and her pouty, kissable lips, even when she's spouting nonsense at me.

"Doc knows best," I say, trying to be diplomatic. After all, Sophie is my alpha's bonus sister; he's extra sensitive where she is concerned... but then again so am I.

"Fine, Barker!" snaps Jake, his eyes twin slits. "But if

you can't control your wolf, I'll haul your butt out of that cottage faster than you can say 'Tinker Bell.' Am I making myself clear?"

"Yes, sir," I reply meekly, but I can't help the smile spreading across my face. "Ow," I mumble when my split lip starts bleeding again.

Jake arches one dark eyebrow at me but says nothing more. Ten minutes later, Rob is lowering me into the passenger seat of my old Caddy. I groan and grimace but manage not to yelp out loud; after Rob closes the door, he hands Sophie my car keys. "Good luck, and if he gets out of hand, bite him; it worked on me."

"Ha-ha, very funny." Sophie is wearing cutoff jean shorts and an old t-shirt that she's obviously outgrown, revealing more of her curves than my heart can handle at the moment.

Maybe Jake is right after all; being in such close proximity to my mate could be a bad idea—not because of my inner wolf, which is safely tucked inside until the next full moon—but because Sophie's nearness might just kill me with unrequited love.

Rob leans down to the open window as Sophie scurries around to the driver's side. "If you need any... er... manly assistance, just call."

"Manly assistance?" I ask. Between my lack of sleep and the painkiller Doc gave me, I'm pretty groggy.

Rob rolls his eyes. "Yeah, like getting in and out of the shower, wolf cub."

"Oh... got it. I'll let you know."

Rob pats the roof of the car and steps back as we pull away from the fire station. It's a hot, humid, summer day, and we drive with the windows down because the air conditioning in this ancient car can't blow hard enough to cool anything larger than a grasshopper.

An awkwardness descends between Sophie and me; at least we're only a few blocks from the cottage, but the traffic on Main Street is slow because of the Riddle Hill Summer Fest.

Wait a minute... Why is Sophie here and not at the bakery, handing out samples? When I ask her, she compresses her lips and keeps her eyes planted on the road. "I closed the bakery for now."

"But why? It's your dream... it's what you wanted..." My voice trails off.

Sophie waits until she pulls around a double-parked car before answering. "It's still a dream, but the bakery's not going anywhere. It can wait a couple weeks until you're feeling better."

"But you'll miss the height of the summer season... and all the tourists... I don't understand."

Sophie doesn't reply until she parks in the cottage's driveway. "It wasn't the same without you... working in the bakery, I mean."

I wish I wasn't so doped up, because I'm not sure I understand. Is Sophie saying what I think she's saying? Does she actually want to work with me again?

Then she heaves a huge sigh, her hands gripping the steering wheel. "I'm so sorry about our argument the other night, especially after you gave me such a wonderful surprise. I said some things I shouldn't have, and I was stupid to fire you; I hope you can forgive me."

When she glances at me with tears fringing her

lashes, I'm momentarily speechless. I sputter, trying to clear my throat, which has thickened all of a sudden. "Of course I forgive you, but our argument wasn't all your fault. The reason you were so upset in the first place was because I told you at the last minute I wouldn't be able to work this weekend."

Sophie sniffs. "Because of your werewolf condition, which I still don't get, nor do I understand why you were in that icky sick room at the fire station."

I rub my eyes; there's no way I'm telling Sophie about the whole fated mate thing until I'm feeling better... and I'm sure she's not being extra nice just because she's feeling guilty. "I promise to explain about my condition at the appropriate time, which isn't right now. It's... complicated... and it's worse at the full moon."

"But you will tell me at some point?" Sophie presses.

"Yes, I'll tell you... but you need to let *me* decide when the time is right."

"Alright," she sighs. "Let's go inside so I can fix us some lunch. Zosia will be ecstatic to see you; she's been very mopey lately."

As Sophie helps me climb out of the car, I bite back several groans but she notices. "Where does it hurt?" Sophie asks, placing her hand on my chest... *on my chest.*

I take several deep breaths to steady my pulse; my heart's thrumming faster than a jackhammer during road construction season. "Um... everywhere, I guess..."

Sophie's soft gray irises flare. "If I ever see Rafe again, I'll give him a tongue lashing he'll never forget. What a smarmy, handsy lowlife!"

I'm only half-listening as I gaze at Sophie's lovely

face; a fine sheen of perspiration glistens on her brow, giving her a dewy complexion. It takes several moments for me to process her last statement.

"Did Rafe get handsy with you?" I growl.

"I think we'd better get you into a chair; Doc says you could get dizzy while you're taking those painkillers." She tries draping my arm around her shoulders, but I refuse to budge.

"Sophie, tell me. Please... I want to know."

She shakes her head. "Why? So you can get in another fight with him?"

"If that's the only way to keep him away from you, then yes." My voice takes on a steely quality that probably surprises us both; I sound almost alpha-like in my fierceness.

Sophie's eyes lock onto mine. "I'll tell you about Rafe if you'll tell me about your old pack and how you know him."

My shoulders sag; it's bad enough Sophie has to see me like this, but what happened before was so much worse. On the other hand, if I want her to open up with me, then I need to do the same.

I nod my assent, and she helps me into the cottage. I lean a bit more heavily on Sophie than strictly necessary, dipping my nose close to her hair for one delicious whiff before she deposits me on the green chair. "I'll be in the kitchen making lunch," she calls over her shoulder.

"*Pah! Pah!*" screeches Zosia, who zooms out of my old bedroom and leaps into my lap. The only reason I'm not whimpering in pain is because Zosia weighs next to nothing, and she manages to miss the worst of my injuries.

"Hey there." I rub behind her ears. "I missed you too." Zosia purrs and *meeps* a few times, flailing all nine of her white tails and bonking me in the face. Chuckling, I rearrange the little fluffball, continuing to pet her until I doze off.

"Teddy, your lunch is ready." I hear Sophie's voice and struggle to open my eyes; whatever Doc gave me is pretty potent stuff. Then I feel her fingers gently tracing the gashes on my forearms, and I debate keeping my eyes closed so she doesn't stop. But my lips twitch, giving myself away.

"I saw that! Now you're just pretending to sleep."

I blink my eyes open, startled to see Sophie's face six inches from mine. Not sure if I'm dreaming, I blink a second time, but when I open them again Sophie has already shooed Zosia off my lap and is setting up a tray table in front of me piled high with scrambled eggs, fried ham, buttered toast, cherry jam, and orange juice. She joins me in the adjoining chair, dragging over another tray table.

Although I had some kibble and dried beef jerky during my confinement, and one of the firefighters gave me a turkey-and-cheese sandwich after my shower this morning, I'm still famished. After we've both eaten, Sophie brews us a pot of coffee, which I might have missed even more than a homecooked meal these past two days.

I wait until she's sitting down again, a mug in her hands. "Before I tell you about the night my alpha died, I want you to know I'm not the same scared kid I was then... I've learned to fight back... to defend those I care about."

A thin line forms on Sophie's brow. "I'm not here to judge you, Teddy, but to hear your story. I want to understand what happened, and why it still haunts you."

So I tell her... all of it: my shame, my fear, my anguish at losing Jarrod. Surprisingly, I'm not quite as emotional this time around; perhaps unloading it all on Jake and finding acceptance in his pack has helped to heal some of my rawness. When I'm finished, I say hoarsely, "If Miss Dragonfly hadn't found me and nursed me back to health, I don't think I would have survived the night."

Sophie was quiet throughout my story, occasional flickers of concern clouding her features. "I can't believe Rafe turned out to be the same werewolf you fought before. Don't you think it's a strange coincidence?"

"Perhaps it's not such a coincidence after all, when you really think about it. There are only so many supernatural villages and wolf packs. Rafe merely moved from one side of Lake Michigan to the other. I suspect he wore out his welcome in his home state and decided to relocate to Wisconsin."

Tilting my head to the side, I add, "Now it's your turn; I want to hear about you and Rafe."

And so she tells me about meeting him that first night I arrived in Riddle Hill, and her initial attraction to him; at that my hands curl into fists, which fortunately Sophie doesn't notice. But after she describes his behavior in the water with her, and later at the wedding shower, I can't help it. I pound my fists on the arms of the chair. "That weasel! Now I wish I'd done more than break his nose!"

"Are you trying to tell me Rafe looks worse than you do?"

When I nod, she chuckles. "I don't think we'll be hearing from that creep again."

"But what about your friend's wedding?"

Sophie shakes her head. "I called Pru last night to tell her I couldn't deal with Rafe at her wedding, and she told me not to worry. Rafe had already texted Vreeland to apologize and let him know he wouldn't be able to make it after all. I guess he's going out of town for a while. Problem solved."

Sophie beams at me like a young girl, and I don't have the heart to tell her Rafe will be back, when he's good and ready; he'll make me pay for breaking his nose.

After lunch, Sophie leaves to run some errands and go to the laundromat. I nap until dinnertime, which we eat on the tray tables again. "You need to drink every drop of that bone broth."

I shake my head, staring at the enormous plate of food: salmon with fresh lemon sauce, fried potatoes, fruit salad, and a steaming bowl of bone broth. "I may be a werewolf, but there's a limit to my appetite."

"Every drop, or I'll spoon feed you." Sophie crosses her arms.

"I'd like to see you try," I attempt a smirk, but my split lip is so sore all I can manage is a grimace.

Sophie sets aside her tray, perches on the arm of my chair, and picks up a spoon. I begin to perspire, beads of sweat dotting my brow. Mongrels and moonbeams! I'm not sure I'll be able to swallow anything with her luscious body leaning over me like this. I snatch the spoon from her outstretched hand. "I think I can manage."

"That's the spirit," she grins, sliding off my chair and returning to her meal.

After dinner, I climb to my feet and slowly stretch my limbs. "I guess I'd better change out my bandages."

"I went to your flat and packed a bag for you; Rob let me in." Sophie hovers behind me as I shuffle in my flipflops over to my former bedroom.

I push open the door, pausing on the threshold. Rather than the chaos I'm expecting, I'm surprised to find the room as orderly as I left it, the Feng Shui still intact. The only change I notice, and a very good one at that, is the mattress now rests on a simple, black bedframe; I'm relieved to be able to sleep on an actual bed rather than on the floor. "The bedframe finally arrived, I see."

"Yeah," says Sophie wryly. "If Leslie T. Barker had arrived when he was supposed to instead of several days early, he wouldn't have had to sleep on the floor."

"Leslie T. Barker was quite anxious for a fresh start... He still is."

Sophie looks up at me, her cheeks flushing pink. We stare at each other, not saying a word, until I wobble slightly.

Gah! This helplessness is crushing what's left of my male ego.

Sophie grips my arm. "I left a clean towel, bowl of water, and antibiotic ointment on the dresser, along with a fresh package of bandages. Why don't you change, and then call me when you need me to replace the dressings on your back."

"Er... what's the best way, do you think?" I ask, my throat going dry at the thought of Sophie seeing my gruesome injuries... and tending to them.

Sophie inclines her head at the bed. "I think it'll be easier if you're lying on your stomach with your shirt off. If you need help with the backs of your legs, maybe wear a pair of shorts."

"Got it," I croak through dry lips, waiting until Sophie closes the door behind her before sagging onto the bed.

Could this get any more awkward? What was Doc thinking when he suggested Sophie should be my nurse... and what was I thinking when I agreed?

Gritting my teeth, I manage to peel off my clothes and change into a pair of running shorts. Then I proceed to replace the bandages on my battered, bruised torso, arms, and the fronts of my legs; I'll need Sophie's help with the rest. I poke my head out of the bedroom to let her know I'm ready and then shuffle back to the bed, stretching out on my stomach.

"O-oh, Teddy!" cries Sophie with a soft whimper. "You're so... wounded."

I knew it; this was a horrible idea. I start to rise from the bed with a grunt. "You shouldn't have to deal with this, Sophie. Leave the dressings for now; you can take me to Doc's clinic tomorrow."

"No!" Sophie crosses the room and sorts out the supplies on top of the dresser. "I volunteered for this, and

I can do it." She adds more softly, "I just didn't realize how badly you were injured."

"If you're sure…"

"I'm sure." She pushes me gently back down onto the mattress and begins to remove the dressings, her cool touch soothing my inflamed skin.

Sometimes, as she's cleansing one of my gashes, I groan at the sharp sting, and then she rests her palm on my back, waiting until I murmur, "It's okay; keep going."

When Sophie reaches the deep bite on my shoulder and I shudder, she hisses with the fierceness of a Viking princess, "I *hate* Rafe!"

When she's finally finished, Sophie rises from the side of the bed, picks up the discarded bandages, towel, and bowl of water, and carries them out into the hall.

Then she whispers, "Sweet dreams, Teddy," as she pulls the door closed behind her.

CHAPTER 30
MY WOUNDED WEREWOLF

SOPHIE

Late, July 15

Until I met Teddy, the last time I wept this much was in high school, when Derek Taylor (Cassia's dumbo ex-husband) asked her to senior prom instead of me. *But now I'm tearing up all the time!* It's like there's this deep well of ragged emotions buried within me that Teddy's managed to tap... and voila... I'm a walking cloudburst.

And here I go again, sobbing as I wash out the water bowl, discard the soiled bandages and gauze, and change into my shorty pjs. When I finally stare at my swollen eyes in the bathroom mirror, I hiss, "Get a grip! Teddy doesn't need your guilt... he needs your spunk and your strength."

I tumble into bed, Zosia curling up at my feet, and stare up at the ceiling. Teddy's story about almost dying —at the hands of his disloyal beta and thuggish Rafe—is too harrowing for me to fully absorb. I've gained renewed admiration for Auntie Dragonfly; not only did she help Teddy heal from his physical wounds but from some of his emotional scars as well.

I lean over, blow my nose again on a tissue, close my eyes, and try to clear away the image of Teddy's battered body. I was so moved when I was changing his dressings that I brushed aside his golden strands of hair and contemplated kissing the back of his neck. But nurses don't go around kissing their patients, even if some patients could really use the extra comfort; I gave myself a good mental shake and returned to cleansing his cuts and bites.

I awaken sometime after midnight to whimpering; it's probably Zosia, who makes all kinds of little noises when she sleeps. I'm just drifting off again when I hear a loud crash and then shrieks, and they're coming from Teddy's bedroom. I have this sudden, irrational fear that Rafe has managed to break into his room to finish him off.

I hop out of bed and run down the short hallway, flinging open his door with such force it bounces off the wall. Teddy is thrashing around, his sheets all twisted up around him, shouting and flailing at the empty air. I rush over to his side, startled to find his hands have grown furry and his nails have elongated into sharp claws.

Not knowing what else to do, I throw my arms around him and murmur, "Hush now, you're safe." I glance around and can't find anything amiss; Zosia must have knocked something over to create that crashing noise.

"Sophie?" Teddy's one eye opens; the other is still too puffy. "What happened?"

"You were having a nightmare... and, um... your wolf is showing." I point to his hands.

"I'm so sorry," he gasps, full of remorse as he retracts his claws. "I shouldn't be losing control like this."

"It's not your fault," I tell him, my hands grasping the front of his tee, which he must have donned before going to bed. Teddy is such a modest man; it's got to be mortifying for him to allow anyone other than Doc to tend to his injuries. "This used to happen to Jake when he had bad dreams after his parents died."

"But Jake was a teen; I'm a grown man. My wolf should be better regulated." Teddy shakes his head. "This isn't going to work; I'm imposing too much on you. I should leave in the morning... I should..."

The rest of Teddy's words are muffled into silence when I hold his gorgeous, damaged face steady and cover his lips with mine. My heart slams against my ribs as a tidal wave of raw emotion floods my senses, firing up my insides with the heat of a supernova.

I guess I'm not a very good nurse—because once I start kissing Teddy, and he grips my hair with a soft groan, returning the kiss—well I don't stop; I keep kissing him, and he keeps kissing me back, a round robin of kisses and sighs and small moans. When we finally come up for air, I discover I'm lying next to him on the bed.

I'm really a terrible nurse, totally unprofessional.

But kissing Teddy is like nothing I've ever known; it's hope and longing mixed with grief and pain, all hot and cold and tingly at once. Every part of me aches with such yearning for this damaged werewolf that I'm like a prodigal daughter who finally, after many seasons and stories, returns home to welcoming arms.

I don't believe I will ever have my fill of Teddy and his warm lips and his strong embrace. This is momentous, but I can't ponder what it all means right now; after all, I'm still Teddy's nurse.

I pull back slightly, giving us both a bit more space on the pillow.

Teddy raises one bandaged hand to my cheek and rests it there. "Thank you."

"For what?" I murmur.

His breath is warm on my face. "For fulfilling one of my lifelong dreams."

"How could kissing me be a lifelong dream if we've known each other for less than a month?" I tease him.

"I've known about you in the abstract for a long, long time... but now you're really, truly here. And trust me, Sophie Spellman Brownlee in the flesh is better than any dream."

"I think those meds are affecting you more than you realize," I say lightly, despite my galloping pulse and hammering heart. I roll over and sit up, swinging my legs out of bed.

"Don't go, please..." Teddy starts to say and then abruptly catches himself.

"The nightmares?" I ask, still seated on the bed beside him.

He takes a juddering breath and nods.

"If you promise to behave like a gentleman, I'll stay—just for tonight."

"Of course I'll behave like a gentleman." Teddy's face breaks into a smile, but I quickly press my finger over the split in his lip.

"Shh... don't smile or your lip will start bleeding again."

He kisses my finger, which I pull away as I stand. Raising his head, he asks, "Hey, where are you going?"

I scoot around to the other side of the bed and climb in, snuggling up against his back. "Where you can't kiss me."

"Hmm..." his voice hitches. "This'll work."

I drape an arm over Teddy's side, which he tucks against his stomach. We lie there for a few minutes, the silence lengthening, until I ask, "If you didn't own part of the bakery, what would you be doing instead?"

Teddy wraps one of his bandaged hands around mine and toys with my fingers. "I no longer own part of the bakery, so the question is moot."

"Oh, but you do."

"I do what?" he says.

"You still own part of the bakery."

Teddy's hand stills. "Sophie, what did you do with that document I signed, giving you my shares of the Rhyme 'N Riddle Bakeshop?"

"I ripped it up."

"What?" He starts to push himself up, but then flops back down on the mattress with a grunt. "Why would you do that?"

"Because it's what Auntie Dragonfly wanted... and it's the least you deserve after all your hard work."

Teddy raises his shoulders and shifts around, jostling the mattress. "But you're the baker, not me—the shop should have been yours from the start!"

I place my palm flat against his chest, and he immediately stills; it's almost like I have a magic touch when it comes to calming Teddy. "You never answered my question. If you didn't work at the bakery, what would you really want to be doing?"

"I've always wanted to be a firefighter."

"You sound exactly like Jake." Chuckling, I ask, "So that's why you're taking those training classes? It's about more than being a volunteer at the department, isn't it?"

"Yeah. I want to prove myself as a volunteer firefighter so Jake will hire me on full time when there's an opening."

I'm quiet for a moment, and then I whisper, "If Jake doesn't hire you I'll tickle him into submission."

We both chuckle and then say goodnight; I lie there a long while, listening to Teddy's steady breathing. When I'm positive he's asleep, I gingerly push aside his blond hair and place a tender kiss on his neck.

He doesn't even stir.

CHAPTER 31
A TIME FOR HEALING

TEDDY

Monday, July 16

I open my eyes to find feathers in variegated shades of copper and verdigris draped across my torso, partially obscuring my already impaired vision. Feathers? I come fully awake, forcing down a startled cry when I realize where I am... and who is sheltering me under her wings.

Sophie is pressed against my back, her breath coming in soft, low puffs, her luscious scent a precious balm enveloping me. Then everything comes flooding back: my nightmare, Sophie clutching my shirt and then soothing me with a kiss, her lips drawing me in like a shipwrecked sailor to the promised land. I drowned in the feel of her mouth on mine, in the strength of her embrace, in the twin beating of our hearts; if I didn't need air to breathe, I never would've stopped kissing Sophie.

She wasn't granting me little pecks for comfort's

"

sake; oh no, her kisses sizzled with heat, sending shivers from the top of my spine all the way down to my toes. Despite all my insecurities when it comes to Sophie, I can't deny this revelation: she obviously feels the pull of our mate-bond too.

But does that mean she really, truly likes me… or is she attracted to me because of a connection we share that we have no control over?

I huff out a sigh, realizing I'm on my own here; I don't know of any other mate-bond between a werewolf and a faerie… it's uncharted territory. I need to tell Sophie and give her the opportunity to withdraw if she feels it's all too much. That last thought sends a spike of pain through my core, and I shudder, which disturbs the slumbering faerie next to me.

"Oh, I didn't realize I extended my wing feathers last night; it's not something I do often, only when I'm feel-ing…" Sophie hesitates before adding, "… entirely at peace."

Okay, I really need to have that chat with Sophie; I can only hope her sense of peace doesn't flee immedi-ately afterward. I run a hand through her feathers, and she laughs.

"That tickles!" Her wing brushes against my side and disappears as she retracts it, and then Sophie is up and moving toward the door. "I'm getting dressed and will be back shortly to change your bandages so you can get dressed. Sound good?"

"Sophie," I call after her. "We need to talk."

Sophie's entire posture droops, like a flower wilting for lack of rain. She pivots around and raises her hand in traffic-cop fashion. "Please don't say kissing me was a mistake, or it never would have happened if you hadn't been on painkillers, or I'm a terrible boss for falling in love with you." She suddenly stops speaking when she realizes what she just admitted.

"You... love me?" My voice cracks as I shakily push myself into a seated position. I try not to cry out in pain, but every muscle screams as I lean forward too quickly, and I yelp.

"Oh, Teddy, what are you doing? Are you trying to torment yourself? Or me?" Sophie scrambles over to the bed, helps me to sit up, and piles an extra pillow behind my back.

I grasp her hands and draw her down until she's sitting on the bed facing me, but she tries to pull away, clearly embarrassed by her admission. "Please don't leave," I urge her.

"When will I learn to keep my big mouth shut?" she whines, trying to twist out of my grip, but I tug her close, so close our faces are inches apart.

"I love you Sophie—I've loved you since the moment we met."

"That's impossible!" she sputters. "I was covered in specks of old wallpaper, dried glue, and construction dust, and I distinctly remember you wrinkling your nose at me."

"I was in love but didn't realize it right away," I explain, holding onto her wrists because she's still attempting to wriggle free.

"That makes no sense," she pouts.

"It does if you're a werewolf."

"Brr!" she mutters. "Always the same excuse. If you liked me so much from the beginning, then why did you move out so abruptly? I know I'm a terrible house-keeper... and that eel in the tub was kind of off-putting... but I must have done something to really offend you."

Hmm... I can see now that I hurt Sophie more than I realized by not disclosing the real reason. "It happened right after your grandmother clipped your wings, and you were sobbing so hard I took you in my arms. Do you remember?"

Sophie finally stops trying to twist out of my grip. "Yes... I felt safe and warm, and then..."

"And then you shoved me away and told me not to touch you again. Remember?"

Sophie says quietly, "I remember."

"Well, that's when I realized... when I *knew* beyond any doubt exactly what you meant to me." I pause and peer into her large gray eyes.

She catches her bottom lip between her teeth and asks in a small voice, "What do I mean to you?"

"Absolutely everything."

Sophie drops her gaze, a knot forming on her brow. "But then why did you move out?"

"I knew being around you day and night without being able to touch you was going to drive me mad with longing because—" I take a deep, fortifying breath and then release it "—because you are my mate."

Sophie springs off the bed so fast I can't catch her. "Whoa!" She's wearing pink-and-white shorty pajamas that are a major distraction to any serious conversation, especially now that she's put her hands on her curvy hips. "I'm not sure what *you* think happened last night... but we certainly didn't mate!"

I compress my lips together to keep from chuckling, but she notices and glowers at me. "You're my *fated mate*, Sophie... my match."

Sophie returns to the bed and plonks down beside me. "I thought that only happened between two werewolves."

"I guess there are exceptions, because you're absolutely, positively my mate." I pick up a lock of her chestnut hair and twist it between my fingers. "My 'mysterious' werewolf condition is really no mystery at all; it's tied to this mate-bond between us. If we're not together, it hurts so much I can't be around anyone— especially you—during the full moon. That's why I locked myself away in the basement for the weekend."

Sophie is completely still and silent, so I continue to ramble. "But... er... that doesn't mean *you* necessarily have to feel the same about *me*. I have no idea how it works for faeries. And I don't want you to feel obligated to... to..."

She puts a finger to my lips and whispers, "You don't want me to feel obligated to do this?" Then she wraps her arms around my neck and kisses me so sweetly and completely that I forget why I was worried about telling her the truth.

When we finally break apart, I lean my forehead against hers and murmur. "I think my next full moon will be far less painful."

She smiles. "Why is that?"

"Because I'll be obligated to do this..." I thread my

bandaged hands through her silken strands and claim her warm lips, kissing my faerie mate until she has no doubt about my true feelings.

Sophie finally pulls back and pats my cheek. "I've been very remiss; it's time I start behaving like a proper nurse."

"Aren't nurses supposed to help their patients heal?" When Sophie nods, I draw her beautiful face toward me for one more toe-curling kiss. "Then I pronounce you the best nurse in Wisconsin... perhaps in all of North America."

She snorts. "Now you're just being silly."

"I'm baring all my secrets here, so please keep up," I tell her playfully.

But then my tone switches from lighthearted to serious. "You healed my most painful wound of all, Sophie." I press her hand to my chest, directly over my pounding heart. "You mended the rift inside here, buried so deep within my core no surgeon's scalpel could ever reach it."

"Oh, Teddy," she sighs. "Thank you for loving me back."

I frown. "Loving you back? I loved you *first*."

"Not really," she says, hopping off the bed and out of reach. "One look at Leslie T. Barker, standing in my bakeshop in his blue, button-down shirt and pressed khakis, and I was a goner."

"Really?" I ask, wondering how I could have misread her so completely. "But you started talking about a prospective boyfriend the night we met."

"What else was I supposed to do when you started lecturing me about wills and forfeiture clauses? It was a defense mechanism." Sophie goes to the door and pretending to be a nurse, says in clipped tones, "I shall return in ten minutes to change your dressings, Mr. Barker."

Despite the discomfort each time my bandages are changed, I'm looking forward to Sophie's soothing touch on my skin.

Afterward I'll get dressed and begin making plans for our future, in between naps, meals, and meds. The ugly green armchair is actually quite comfortable for contemplation, especially with Zosia in my lap.

And I want to speak with Nash as soon as I'm able; I'd like his blessing before I propose to his daughter.

CHAPTER 32
HIGHS AND LOWS

SOPHIE

Monday, July 16

I'm soaring, my head in the clouds, my feet barely touching the floor as I quickly shower and dress. *Teddy loves me! The kindest, sweetest, handsomest man I've ever known loves grumpy old me!*

Grumpy old me...

Hmm, come to think of it, I *am* older than Teddy—by five whole years! I'll be twenty-nine soon, and Teddy just turned twenty-four. A stab of worry pierces my happiness-bubble; I sure hope his mate bond thingy is accurate and hasn't given him a false reading, because I'm mad about that boy.

It's still hard for me to cleanse Teddy's wounds without a tear trickling down my cheek, which I silently swipe away. Since he's on his stomach, he doesn't notice how much it hurts me to see what Rafe did to him. When I'm finished, I lean over, kiss his shoulder

252

below the bite mark, and then rise from the side of the bed.

"Hey," says Teddy with a smile. "No fair; I can't return the favor while I'm lying here face down."

"That's not a problem, Mr. Barker," I reply in my frostiest, fake-nurse tone. "I will collect from you later, once you're fully healed. But interest compounds daily. One unreturned kiss today means you owe me two tomorrow, and then four the next day... and well, you get the idea."

"I'm up to the challenge, Nurse Sophie," quips Teddy as he slowly, painfully rolls onto his side facing me, "but I may need some extra time to pay you back."

"In that case I fear you shall never be able to make full restitution, Mr. Barker," I sigh dramatically. "You will be in my debt forevermore."

"Then I will be your faithful servant, Nurse Sophie, and my payment shall be in kisses, hugs... and other pleasantries." Teddy tries to maintain a straight face, but I collapse into giggles, and soon we're both laughing.

I gather up the water bowl and old bandages, ready to step out of the room so Teddy can dress, when I pause; someone is pounding on the front door. I put everything back down on the bedside table, hurry out to the living room, and pull open the door.

"Marv!" The giant cop seems relieved to see me; he gives another reassuring nod at Teddy, who's hobbled out into the hallway after me, tugging down his tee. "What's wrong?" I ask, fear gripping my insides. "Has anyone been hurt?"

"No one's been injured... but someone has vandalized

your bakery. They spray-painted the front of the building and smashed one of the windows; there's glass everywhere."

I clutch my stomach, which is suddenly churning. "Do we have any idea who might have done it?"

Marv shakes his head. "It appeared to have happened early this morning; there were no witnesses, or at least none who've come forward. But I'll need you to unlock the shop so we can take a look around. I'd like to find whatever was tossed through the window."

Teddy drapes an arm around me, but I jump when he accidentally pinches my waist with his claws. "Ow! Your fingernails are kinda sharp."

"I'm sorry," says Teddy, immediately retracting his claws. "My inner wolf is reacting to the possibility this was Rafe's doing... It's the sort of spiteful, cowardly act he specializes in."

I turn to gaze up at Teddy's bruised face. "But Rafe told Vreeland he was going out of town."

"I wouldn't believe anything he says," mutters Teddy.

Scowling, Marv nods. "We've been trying to track down MacTire for the past few days, but he's disappeared without a trace after your fight. We'll keep looking for him, but in the meantime, be extra cautious until we can bring him in for questioning."

"Thanks, Marv," I say with a small shudder.

He nods. "I'll wait for you outside."

After Marv leaves, I turn to Teddy and whisper, "I'm scared."

Teddy wraps his muscular arms around me, drawing

me protectively against the solid wall of his chest. "I promise I won't let Rafe get close to you."

I pull back just far enough so I can peer into his swollen face. "It's not me I'm worried about—it's you!"

Teddy kisses my forehead. "I can take care of myself."

"Uh-huh. I can see how well that turned out!"

He folds me into his chest once more and rubs my back. "Let's not jump ahead of ourselves; perhaps it was rambunctious teens having a bit too much fun."

I don't reply, relishing the warmth of Teddy's arms. But deep down in the pit of my belly, I'm afraid Rafe could be hanging around, waiting to cause more trouble for Teddy and me.

Reluctantly, I step out of his embrace. "Marv's waiting; I'd better go. Don't forget to take your meds. I'll be back as soon as I can."

"Alright, but don't try cleaning up the bakery by yourself."

"I've got this, Mr. Clean." I raise one eyebrow. "And I promise, once you're up and around, you can re-sweep the floorboards to your heart's content."

That makes Teddy chortle. "Fine... just be careful."

"You're such a worrywart; this is Riddle Hill, the safest little supernatural town in the Midwest."

Teddy huffs out a sigh and then tucks a loose strand of my hair behind my ear. "Call me if you need anything."

"Of course," I reply, savoring his touch. We both know I'm not calling him; he needs time to heal, and I'm still his nurse.

As I walk down to the end of the driveway, I spot

yellow crime-scene tape fluttering in the summer breeze; Marv and his faerie partner, Sam, have cordoned off the front of the bakeshop. I take a deep breath, steeling myself to round the corner and face the damage.

I'm thankful I'm wearing my sturdy Converse sneakers, because something crunches underfoot; my picture window is nothing but a thousand tiny shards that sparkle like loose diamonds on the sidewalk. Gloom descends on me, and I don't want to see anymore, but Marv is calling my name. I slowly raise my gaze from the ground to the shop itself and let out a loud gasp. "Why?"

The vandals smeared red paint all over the front of my beautiful bakery, and from the looks of it, they sprayed the inside of the shop through the broken window. My white wrought iron tables—a gift from Teddy—are now speckled with red paint like so many drops of blood.

I gulp down the bile rising in my throat; I think Teddy may be right. This *feels* like something Rafe would do. Rubbing my arms, I shiver, chilled to my core despite the sunshine.

"I'm so sorry, honey," says my mother, who must have spotted me from the café's window across the street. This is her first day back at work after the flu, and the last thing I want is for Mom to be fretting over me. "Who would do such an awful thing?" She wraps her arm around my shoulders and gives a squeeze.

Marv says quietly, "We don't know yet, Miss Phoebe, but we'll chase down every fang, feather, and patch of fur until we find 'em."

My mother gives me another squeeze. "Your father

and I want to replace the window for you, so don't worry about that. Whatever else you need, just let us know. Nash can't leave the kitchen right now, but he's waving his spatula around and shouting faerie curses in Irish while he cooks."

That image causes my mouth to tip up at the corners. "Thanks, Mom." I wait for her to cross the street and reenter the café, relieved she's back where she belongs. Then I turn around to face my shattered bakeshop once more. Fishing inside my pocket, I withdraw the key and unlock the door.

"Wait here; we'll go in first to look around, not that I expect any surprises," says Marv. Sam and Marv stalk inside, creep around the room's perimeter, and open the doors to the bathroom and closet. While Marv inspects the kitchen, Sam pokes his head back outside and tells me I can enter.

My heart sinks as I gaze at the paint spattering my hardwood floors and marring Sophie's Greenest Green on my walls. "Whoever did this leaned through the broken window with his can of paint so he could cause as much damage as possible," says Sam, his brown eyes solemn. "This feels personal to me."

"Yeah, I agree," grunts Marv. He holds up a rock about the size of my fist in his gloved hand. "This rolled under one of the bakery cases. We'll dust it for fingerprints, but I'm not expecting we'll find anything useful."

Marv places the rock in an evidence bag, which Sam carries out to their squad car. "Jake doesn't know yet," says Marv. "He's on call at the fire station, so I haven't told him, but he's going to be spitting mad when he hears. We'll find whoever did this, Sophie; I promise."

I thank Marv and follow him out to the sidewalk; I don't have the heart to face the damage alone, but I also don't want to tell Teddy that all his hard work has been ruined. I'm about to lock up when a familiar, creaky voice calls out from behind me, "Hold up there, dearie. I brought some sponges that'll help you clean up this mess, but you need to use them right away."

"Granny?" I spin around. My grandmother is wearing baggy purple shorts, an orange-and-green plaid flannel shirt, and a blue ball cap; somehow the look works on her. She gives me one of the pails she's carrying, and I peer inside at an ordinary-looking sponge about the size of my hand.

"This can remove dried paint?" I'm incredulous.

"Shh," she puts a finger to her lips. "Not so loud; I see some non-supers heading this way."

Then it dawns on me; my faerie granny is giving me magic sponges! "O-oh... thanks, Gran!"

Granny reaches for the other sponge inside her pail. "Why don't you start cleaning the inside of the shop; I'll work out here. The magic's only good for a couple hours."

"But what'll you say if a non-super wants to know how a plain yellow sponge can remove dried paint?"

"I'll just tell 'em it's magic." Granny grins at me and winks.

Despite the heaviness twisting my gut, and my apprehension that Rafe isn't finished with Teddy and me yet, I burst out laughing.

Before we get started, I sweep up the broken glass on the sidewalk so Granny doesn't trip on it, and then I carry my pail into the shop. I've just placed the pail on the floor when my phone buzzes in my pocket; Teddy has managed to wait twenty-four minutes before texting me, which is better than I would've done if the roles were reversed. I underplay the damage, telling him it's going to take a couple of hours to clean up with my grandmother's help. He tells me he's going to make us lunch and signs off with a row of sparkly hearts.

I send Teddy a bunch of kissy faces and tuck away my phone.

Wait a minute; Teddy is going to attempt to do something in the kitchen other than clean it? That's awfully sweet, but I have a feeling I'll be running to Vlad's Victuals later for carryout.

I decide to start with the wall closest to the window and slowly swipe the yellow sponge across the spattered surface; when I pull the sponge away, not a single dab of red paint remains on the wall!

Granny's magic sponge is pure genius!

Two hours later, every speck of red paint is gone, and I feel as if I just relived my favorite childhood book, *The Cat in the Hat*. When I mention this to Granny, she chuckles. "Who do you think gave him the idea?"

Perhaps Granny was standing in the sun too long, because she's not making any sense. "Who do you mean," I ask, "the author or the cat?"

"The cat, of course."

What can I say to that?

Who knows if it's true, or if Granny is recalling some

other cat she conversed with; at her age, it's anyone's guess. I thank my grandmother, who lifts one skinny arm in a queenly wave and heads down Main Street toward her shop.

I can't leave yet, because I still need to finish sweeping the glass inside the bakery and wait for the gaping hole to be boarded up by my overprotective cousin; Jake texted me a little while ago when he heard what happened and told me he's picking up the plywood for my window.

I grab the broom and sweep up the shards, going over the floor twice; I debate sweeping it a third time, but Teddy will want to go over the entire floor again anyway, so I leave that job to my perfect, persnickety boyfriend.

Boyfriend... I'm dumping the pile of broken glass bits into a heavy-duty trash bag when I pause and straighten; I have an honest-to-goodness, totally amazing boyfriend!

Boyfriend... Handsome-as-a-Norse-god Teddy Barker loves *me*, cranky, careless, chaotic Sophie Spellman Brownlee!

I stop and pinch myself.

"What are you doing?" asks Jake, who's standing in the doorway.

"Um... just thinking."

"You were pinching your arm." Jake scowls at me, probably worried I'm losing it. He's brought his tool chest with him and sets it down on the floor.

"It's been a long morning."

Jake's frown lines deepen. "I'm so sorry Sophie; we'll find him, I promise."

"You think it was Rafe too?"

He nods. "Don't you? It sure doesn't appear to be a random act of vandalism."

I feel deflated all over again, which is depressing so soon after pinching myself with joy over Teddy. I huff out a sigh. "Unfortunately, I think you're right... which makes me really nervous, especially for Teddy given his history with Rafe."

Jake growls through gritted teeth, "I plan to track down that sorry excuse for a wolf before he causes any more trouble. The only good news here is that Teddy held his own against a larger, much more aggressive werewolf. Teddy is stronger than you may realize."

I hug myself and grin like a kid on her first day of summer break. "Oh, I know he's strong." And kind, gentle, loving, forgiving... but I don't say that to Jake, who's canted his head to the side.

Jake stares at me for a few beats and then says, "Teddy told you."

"About the mate bond thingy?"

When Jake nods, I say, "Yes, he told me quite a bit, actually." My cousin can tell by the happy grin plastered on my face that Teddy and I did more than talk about our mate bond.

"Ah yes, puppy love," grumbles Jake, but he's smiling.

"You should try it sometime; you might find you're a bit less growly."

Jake ignores that last remark and grunts, "Come give me a hand before you float away on Cupid's wings."

"You're such a grump." I punch his arm lightly.

"Takes one to know one," he quips, and we both chuckle. Then he adds softly, "I'm truly happy for you and Teddy."

"Thanks, Jake." A fleeting look of sadness clouds his eyes, and I realize how lonely he must be; it can't be easy being a werewolf alpha without a mate of his own. "She's out there."

"Who?" asks Jake.

"Your fated mate."

He shrugs. "Not everyone has one, you know."

We drop the topic and get to work nailing the plywood in place. I'm not a seer or anything... but I'm certain my lonesome cousin has a mate. I just hope for his sake she turns up soon.

CHAPTER 33
HONORABLE INTENTIONS

TEDDY

Later, July 16

"They taste better than they look." I assure Sophie, spooning the scrambled eggs onto her plate, alongside three strips of extra crispy bacon and a slice of scorched toast. I hobble over to the kitchen table with my own plate and sit down across from her. I'm still incredibly sore, but I have more energy today, which I attribute to my beautiful girlfriend, who heats my insides every time she gazes in my direction.

Right now Sophie is staring down at the eggs; she picks up her fork and pokes at them. "But they're *brown*."

"I know... just try them." I scoop up a forkful and pop them in my mouth. "M-mm. So good."

She takes a tentative bite and wrinkles her nose. "Did you scramble these eggs in bacon grease?"

I grin. "It's my one-pot cooking method, which

makes cleaning up so much easier." I nod at her plate. "What do you think?"

"Well... um... I think this was very thoughtful."

I start to laugh. "I guess brown eggs and black toast just aren't your thing, eh?"

Sophie's delectable lips curve upward. "Not really. Maybe we ought to stick to what we're good at. I can do all the baking and cooking, and you can do all the tidying and organizing—once you're feeling better, of course." She takes a few more bites of egg to placate me, crunches on a piece of bacon, and skips the toast entirely; I wind up finishing her breakfast on top of mine.

It's obvious to me Sophie is deeply disturbed by the vandalism at the bakery, because she keeps looking up at me and then away again, but she's refused to talk about it since returning to the cottage. I have a sneaking suspicion Sophie thinks she's protecting me, but I refuse to be coddled—and if anyone is going to be doing the protecting, it's going to be *me* watching over *her*.

"If you don't tell me about the bakery, I'm going to shuffle down to the end of the driveway and see it for myself."

Sophie pushes her plate away and hesitates, as if she's gathering her strength. Then she takes a steadying breath and describes the damage in detail. When she tells me the red paint spatter inside the bakery looked like dried blood, the backs of my hands grow furry, my fingernails lengthen into points, and my canines sharpen inside my mouth.

Sophie pauses; when she speaks again, her voice is an octave higher. "Your wolf is showing again."

"Sorry!" Inhaling sharply, I rein myself in, reversing the wolfishness. "I didn't mean to scare you."

"I'm not frightened of you... it's just I've begun to realize your werewolf shows up when you're more emotional... and I don't want this situation with Rafe to upset you or take away our happiness."

I reach across the table and wrap my hands around hers. "I won't let Rafe destroy our happiness... or come anywhere near you."

She glances down at our entwined hands, and when she looks back up, her eyes are glistening. "Just promise me you won't let him hurt you again," she whispers.

I bring her hands up to my lips and kiss her knuckles. The weight of her words sits on my chest; how can I promise what is out of my control? "I promise to keep him from hurting you any more than he already has."

Sophie scowls, snatching her hands from mine. "That's not what I want you to promise... and you know it!"

I want to lighten the mood and see her smiling again, so I say, "Tell me again about your grandmother's *Cat in the Hat* magic."

Sophie purses her lips. "I know what you're trying to do, but I can't be distracted that easily."

"Oh, I can think of much better ways of distracting you." I wink, but my puffy eye doesn't cooperate.

Sophie reaches across the table to run her fingers gently over my bruised face. "I can't bear to see you injured like this again."

I rise from my chair, tugging Sophie toward me. She resists, still unhappy I refuse to make promises I can't keep, but when I whisper, "Please come closer," she melts into my arms. We stand there a long time, Sophie nestled against my chest, holding each other. I love this woman with a fierceness that's painful... one more ache to add to all the rest.

I don't want to be parted from Sophie again, even to return to my studio flat, but I'm an old-fashioned werewolf; I will not live permanently with my mate until we're married. I want to propose to Sophie, but I'd prefer to have a job lined up first so I can contribute to our finances; it's going to take some time for a startup business, even for a bakery owned by someone as talented as Sophie, to begin turning a profit. On the other hand, I need her to know this "mate bond thingy" as she calls it means I'm not going any farther away than Rob's garage.

I glance down at my cuts and bruises. Even if I passed my initial exam at the fire station, I'm in no shape to participate in the physical training for another few weeks, putting me that much further behind on my goal to join the department. I sigh, nuzzling my face in Sophie's hair. When she finally steps out of my embrace, I feel a momentary pang of loss and quickly remind myself she's still here, standing right beside me.

She pauses, withdraws her phone from her back pocket, and gazes down at the display; the message must be a long one, because Sophie continues staring at it. My heart clenches as I consider the possibilities. "Is anything wrong?"

She glances up at me, slightly bemused. "Oh no... it's just a very long text from Cassia. My family is coming over tonight for dinner—all of them." She hands me her phone so I can read Cassia's message.

"Hey, Sophie, I'm so sorry about the bakery! I wanted to run over to help you with the cleanup, but we're crazy busy, and your dad's kitchen magic has gone kerflooey since he learned about the vandalism. The eggs are coming out green; the ham has yellow spots, and the butter is blue. The food tastes fine, and your mom says it's perfectly safe to eat, but she's been casting glamours all day to prevent the non-supers from freaking out.

"But it gets worse; Jake popped over to visit your dad in the kitchen... and the entire café heard your dad's colorful Irish when Jake told him you and Teddy had a mate bond. Uncle Nash likes Teddy, but he's not well-versed in werewolf bonds, and he's not happy Teddy is living with you while he heals.

"So heads up, cuz... your dad is making dinner for you and Teddy tonight, and he's coming over with your mom. Aunt Phoebe wants me and Olivia to come as buffers, and she invited Jake for the same reason. Granny got wind of the family dinner and has invited herself. Expect us at five o'clock."

"Should I be worried?" I hand Sophie her phone.

"I don't know what to think," she says. "My dad is normally super calm; I guess my mom's illness, the vandalism at the bakery, and learning about our mate bond has rattled him to the core. Other than his beard, my father's magic is always tightly regulated."

"What's up with his beard?"

"Dad's beard grows really, really fast; he has to trim it every morning. But when he's upset, it grows much faster. If he shows up tonight with a long beard, then he's very unhappy."

Rather than making me anxious, as Sophie probably expects, I smile at her. "This isn't funny!" she exclaims. "Don't you realize my dad's going to give you the third degree?"

"That's exactly what I'm hoping Nash does... it's time I tell him and the rest of your family how I feel about you."

"Oh... I see." Sophie seems surprised but pleased; she stands on her tiptoes and plants a feather-soft kiss on my lips. When I try to deepen the kiss she steps out of reach. "You need to take a nap, and I need to clear off the dining room table so we can eat there tonight."

"I can help," I offer, but Sophie notices me stifling a yawn.

She shakes her head. "You can go lie down; I've got this."

"But tidying and organizing are my super skills."

"No buts about it, Mr. Clean, you need your rest; besides, I have a plan."

Sophie's plan probably involves temporarily shifting everything from the dining table to the top of her bed, but I can see I won't win this argument. I shamble into my bedroom, shift Zosia over so there's room for me, and promptly doze off, dreaming of eggs the color of Sophie's Greenest Green.

When I waken I'm surprised to see it's past four; I slept the entire afternoon away. Slowly, painfully, I rise from bed and proceed to change into something more appropriate to greet Sophie's family than my gym shorts and tee. After fifteen minutes of fumbling I'm finally dressed in clean khaki slacks and a yellow short-sleeved shirt, and I've run a comb through my hair, detangling the worst of the knots.

Peering into the mirror, I frown; there's no way I can hide the gashes and purple bruises on my face and arms. Hopefully Nash doesn't see this as evidence of weakness and conclude I'm incapable of taking care of his daughter. I step out of my room in search of Sophie, but she's easy to find; she's in the bathroom with the door closed, belting out an old love ballad with all the gusto of a Broadway star.

Grinning at her off-key warbles, I cross the short hallway and push open the door to Sophie's bedroom. Sure enough, the contents of the dining room table are piled haphazardly on her bed and floor. Zosia has followed me and now stands on the threshold, probably considering her sleeping arrangements for the evening.

When she screeches, "*Wump!*" and scurries away, I chuckle and close Sophie's door. She set the table with mismatched plates and mugs in a rainbow of colors, and antique flatware that probably came from a garage sale; the overall effect is kitschy and cute. I gaze around the rest of the living-dining room combo and begin straightening up as best I can without straining my stitches.

The place is almost presentable when I'm finished, minus the stacks of boxes leaning against one wall that Sophie hasn't had the time to unpack; the number of boxes has declined dramatically since my arrival nearly a month ago, so she's making progress. As I pick up a pillow that Zosia must have knocked to the floor, I'm struck by a sudden inspiration and step outside.

A row of pink hydrangeas, orange daylilies, and yellow-and-white daisies gently sway on the other side of the driveway. Extending the claws on my right hand, I begin slicing through the flower stems until I've formed a bouquet. Returning inside, I search for a vase, trying to decide where Sophie would store one. On my third attempt, I discover a cut crystal urn in the bottom cupboard next to the stove (another of Sophie's hideaway spots), fill it with water, and place the flowers in the middle of the table.

Perfect; I'm nodding in satisfaction as a pair of slender arms reach around my waist, and the earthy scent of springtime—pulsing rainstorms and lush, green things—wafts up to my nose. "They're beautiful, Teddy. You have a knack for floral arrangements."

"Why do you sound so surprised?" I ask.

Sophie laughs. "Because you're a werewolf! Jake and Rob are more likely to step on a flower bed than notice it."

I spin her around until she's facing me; her gray eyes sparkle with humor and perhaps a touch of mischief. Her wavy brown locks are slightly damp, and she's wearing a blue-and-yellow print sundress that shows off her luscious curves; my breath catches in my throat. I'm leaning down for a kiss, drawn by those irresistible lips, when there's a firm knock on the front door.

Sophie blows me a kiss and whispers, "Showtime, wolf-boy. Behave yourself."

I smooth back my hair with a smirk and take some

stabilizing breaths as I attempt to get my skyrocketing pulse back under control. "I'll take a rain check on that kiss."

She winks, pulls open the door, and a chorus of voices greets us; the entire Spellman-Brownlee clan has arrived at the same time. While I expected Jake, as the werewolf alpha, mayor, and fire chief, to be prompt, I'm still surprised a group of faeries can manage to be on time for anything. Miss Dragonfly would have missed her own funeral arrangements if the undertaker and I hadn't coordinated everything.

As Nash steps through the door, I immediately check the length of his whiskers. Sweet moonglow, his thick brown beard is grazing his belt buckle!

Little Olivia dashes over to me and points at my bandaged arms. "How'd you get all those owies?"

"I had a little accident," I tell her.

"Do they hurt?" Her green eyes are serious as she gazes up at me.

"They did hurt, but they're better now."

"That's good." She slips her small hand into mine. "I'll hold your hand in case you're scared." An unexpected lump forms in my throat, and I have to swallow several times.

"Glad to see you're up and around," says Catbeam in her screechy voice; everyone else murmurs something similar.

My eyes meet Nash's, and instead of the fierce scowl I'm expecting, he gives me a slow head nod. "I understand you were looking out for Sophie when you were injured."

"Yes, sir."

Nash reaches out his hand and shakes my free one. "Thank you."

I nod, feeling suddenly embarrassed by all the attention. "I'd do anything for Sophie," I say softly.

Nash arches his dark brows. "Let's have dinner, and then we can have a chat."

"It's time to sit down," urges Olivia, who tugs me over to the table and points out the chair next to her.

After everyone is served, Sophie sits down across from me and proceeds to play footsie with me under the table. Is she *trying* to make me more nervous than I already am? I refuse to play along. She finally gives up and starts toying with her food, shooting me little glances from beneath her long fringe of lashes.

Now I'm wondering if I'm expected to say something to Sophie's assembled family. I tilt my head and mouth, "What?"

Sophie gives a side nod at the end of the table where Nash is sitting. "Beard!" she mouths back.

I raise my shoulders in a half-shrug. "So?"

Olivia asks, "What're you and Aunt Sophie whispering about?"

Ah, the innocence of children... and their ability to not miss a thing.

Sophie's eyes widen as if she has no idea what Olivia is talking about. "The weather," she replies stiffly. Cassia and Jake snigger at the same time, reminding me they had the same human mother.

After we've had our fill of beef and chicken tacos, fresh guacamole and homemade nacho chips, and refried beans, Phoebe passes around plates of Door County cherry pie with fresh whipped cream on top. I've just placed my fork down on my empty plate when Jake clears his throat.

I immediately still; this is my alpha, and although he is also Sophie's cousin, it's Jake's status as leader of my pack that gains my full attention. "I just want to say I'm relieved to see you're feeling better, Barker... er, Teddy... and I'm happy to report you received the highest score in your first firefighter's exam; I know you're going to miss a few classes, but given your test results, I have no problem keeping a spot open for you. If the rest of your training goes as well, you'll be on the volunteer roster by the end of October."

Sophie and Cassia applaud, and the rest of the table follows suit, even Olivia, who has no clue why she's clapping.

I'm thrilled and humbled at the same time; this is the second dream come true in as many days. How can a guy get so lucky? "That's great news, Jake... Thanks for letting me know."

I sense Nash's eyes on me so I swivel my head in his direction. Nash leans forward. "I understand Doc Demetrius asked Sophie to serve as your nurse while you're healing—" he waves his hand at Sophie but his gaze never leaves me "—which I find highly irregular. My daughter is a baker, not a nurse."

"Oh, Dad," mumbles Sophie. "It's no trouble at all, and—"

"That's beside the point," interrupts Nash, rubbing his beard, which has grown thicker and bushier since his arrival. I can't see the length since it's hidden by the table, but I wouldn't be surprised if it's now below his belt. "I don't understand much about werewolf mating bonds—" he shoots a glance at Olivia, who's stabbing one of the cherries from her pie "—but I don't like the idea of Sophie nursing you under the circumstances; seems irregular if you ask me."

Catbeam snorts. "Seems to me you're missing the point, Nash."

Sophie's father glances at his mother-in-law in surprise. "I'm not sure I'm following."

"If Teddy loves Sophie and vice versa, then it's the most natural thing in the world for her to help him while he's healing," explains Catbeam.

Nash pouts, considers, and then asks me point blank. "What are your intentions toward my daughter?"

Sophie rolls her eyes. "Daddy! You're embarrassing me; this isn't Victorian England!"

"I don't care what century it is; I'm your father, and I want Teddy to answer my question."

As Sophie folds her arms with a huff, all eyes turn to me, even Olivia's, who must realize something big is happening because she's stopped playing with her pie.

"My intentions are entirely honorable, sir," I say to Nash. "I love your daughter."

Then I turn my attention to Sophie, who's glanced up at those words. "I've been looking for you all my life, Sophie," I say quietly. "Only I didn't realize it was you I was seeking until I showed up at the bakery."

"Right after I broke the wall." She smiles.

I move our plates out of the way, reach across the

table, and grip her hands, which are trembling. "You fill me up, keep me sane, and hold me together when I'm flying apart. You're a symphony, a sonnet, a never-ending story that I will carry in my heart all my days. I want to marry you, if you'll have me... and if not, I will ask you every day until you take pity on me and finally relent."

Sophie's cheeks are damp, and she laughs softly. I hear sniffling noises; I think both Phoebe and Cassia are tearing up.

Why isn't Sophie saying anything?

"Please tell me the answer is yes," I whisper hoarsely, prickles of dread piercing my core. Have I misread Sophie's true feelings for me?

"Of course the answer is yes!" cries Sophie, who hurries around the table toward me, smiling through her tears. I slide my chair back so she can sit in my lap, wincing slightly at the gentle pressure on my injured thighs, but then her lips are on mine, and I'm lost in her kisses until Oliva asks, "Aunt Sophie, can I be a flower girl? Please?"

Sophie and I both chuckle, and my fiancée says, "Yes, Olivia."

"Yay!" shouts Olivia, adding, "And can I wear a pretty dress too?"

Cassia shushes her daughter. "Do you have a date in mind?"

"Don't you need a job before you start planning weddings and honeymoons?" grumps Nash.

"Oh, Nash, give it a rest," says Phoebe. "You were an unemployed chef when we got married."

"And you had to pawn your gold watch to pay for your wedding suit," quips Catbeam. "Good thing I knew the pawnbroker, a beady-eyed troll who demanded an incantation from me in exchange for your watch."

"And our honeymoon was a weekend in the Wisconsin Dells," says Phoebe. She reaches out for her husband's hand and curls her fingers over his meaty fist. "And it was quite lovely; I wouldn't have changed a thing."

Nash gives Phoebe a knowing smile, and then he lets out a low, growly breath. Looking at me, he grunts, "Are you really sure you want all this?"

"Absolutely positive."

Nash lets out a hearty belly laugh, his eyes crinkling in the corners like a jolly, brown-bearded Santa; when he's finished, he wipes his eyes. "Welcome to the family, Teddy."

CHAPTER 34
MATE BOND THINGY

Evening, July 16

Teddy's marriage proposal far surpassed anything my younger self could have imagined when I was a lovesick teen crushing over one boy after another. His words literally stole my breath away; I've never felt so cherished in all my life. Even if I live to be as old and wrinkly as Granny Catbeam, I'll never forget how my wounded werewolf poured out his heart and soul in front of my entire family.

I was so caught up in the moment that I neglected to give him my answer straightaway; Teddy's brow furrowed, his posture stiffening as he waited for my reply. How could he have any doubts about my feelings for him?

Then I was crying and laughing as I told him *yes!* I scrambled around the table and carefully climbed into Teddy's lap, ensuring I kissed away any concerns on his

277

part. I was oblivious to the fact everyone was watching our drama play out until Olivia's sweet voice grounded me once more.

When I reluctantly pulled back from Teddy's warm lips, I held his face in my hands, watching as the golden flecks of his inner wolf flared across his deep blue irises. His werewolf eyes locked onto mine, his gaze burning into my soul and heating my blood until my face reddened, and my heart lit on fire. In the span of a breath we were tethered, our mate bond sealed.

I am his... and he is mine. Teddy will protect me with his life, and I will do the same.

After my family leaves, with many hugs, congratulations, and a few pats on the back that cause Teddy to grimace in pain, we're finally alone. He takes my hand and leads me to the sagging brown sofa, where I nestle against his chest, thankful for my great-aunt Dragonfly, who managed to play matchmaker from beyond the grave.

Faerie aunties truly are a force to be reckoned with.

Teddy plays with a lock of my hair. "While you were in the kitchen washing up the dishes with your mom and Cassia, Nash offered me some shifts at the restaurant for the rest of the season."

I chuckle. "Cassia and Mom probably need the extra help, given all the new customers you've attracted to the café."

"What new customers?" he asks.

"Did you forget all those women giggling and batting their eyelashes at you?"

Teddy smirks. "Do I detect a hint of jealousy?"

"Not at all. I merely want to fly into a murderous rage every time one of them flirts with you."

We both laugh, and then Teddy cups my cheek with his injured hand. "You, and only you, are my mate, my hope, and my future. Don't you realize there will *never* be anyone else but you?"

My heart drums harder than the surf pounding the shore during a tempest; how do I even respond to such a romantic declaration, except to say *yes, yes, a thousand times yes*. As it turns out, Teddy doesn't expect me to say anything at all. He brushes his lips against mine, and then he kisses me, slowly and tenderly, until we're both breathless.

EACH DAY TEDDY heals a bit more; by the end of the week his pain is mostly gone, and he no longer needs my help changing his dressings. Even though I'm happy to have him stay in the cottage a little longer, Teddy insists on returning to his flat, probably because he wants to prove to my father he's a man of his word—which makes me swoon for him even more.

By the end of the second week following his fight with Rafe, Teddy is back at work, splitting his time between shifts at the café and working as my kitchen helper at the bakery. The plate glass window has been replaced, and we're ramping up to reopen this weekend. I'm teaching Teddy how to check my pastries and cookies for doneness, pulling them from the oven before they burn. His favorite job is taste-testing everything I bake; so far he hasn't found a dessert yet he doesn't love.

But there's one topic we both avoid. I can tell Teddy is still uneasy about Rafe; sometimes his sea-blue eyes narrow and lose their focus, as if he's trying to sense his whereabouts. Even Jake, with all his resources, has no idea where Rafe has gone. Meanwhile, I refuse to let my own concerns spoil what Teddy and I are building together. I'm finally in love with the right man, and I won't let a creep like Rafaellus MacTire come between us.

CHAPTER 35
A GRAND RE-OPENING

SOPHIE

Saturday, July 28

The morning of the bakery's grand re-opening is cloudy and cool, a welcome relief from the oppressive heat of the past few days. I've been baking since two, so nervous I couldn't sleep more than a few hours. I hear the purr of Teddy's old Caddy pulling into the driveway and fling open the back door to greet him.

"You look as luscious as a vanilla-custard half puff pastry," growls Teddy, giving my ear a playful nip. "Or is it a full puff pastry?" Shrugging, he plants kisses all along my jawline. "You look scrumptious either way."

I flutter my hands and sigh dramatically. "Be still my beating heart! All this talk of sweetmeats has me swooning."

Teddy pulls off my headwrap, entangling his hands in my hair. "If you really want to swoon darling, allow me..." he whispers.

"Teddy... er..." I start to say, but then he claims my lips, and I'm lost.

My fiancé's kisses turn my knees to three-berry jelly; I have cling to his neck to keep from toppling over onto my kitchen floor. When he eventually stops kissing me senseless, his sensitive nose is raised in the air. "Do you smell something burning?"

"Oh no!" I yelp. "My cookie bars!" I pull open the oven door just as the smoke detector starts blaring. Two full pans of my glorious Riddler's Magic Bars are scorched beyond saving. I should be upset about two hours of ruined work, especially since I have no kitchen magic thanks to my clipped wings, but after my sad and lonely grand opening two weeks ago, I'm not going to let a few burned cookies get me down.

"I'm sorry, Sophie," says Teddy after he silences the smoke detector. "I guess I'm not very good for your productivity."

I give him a wry smile. "How about a new rule: no more kissing when there's something in the oven. Deal?"

He grins. "Deal."

When the doors open at seven, Teddy and I are wearing black aprons with Rhyme 'N Riddle stitched in green across the breast pocket. I snap photos of my gallant werewolf as he helps customers, his brilliant smile earning grins from even the crankiest faeries. The pink scar above Teddy's eye gives him a slightly rakish look; when Doc Demetrius suggested plastic surgery, I shook my head and told Teddy I loved his pirate-captain good looks, which earned a shy smile in Doc's office and heart-stopping kisses later.

I think every single person I know in Riddle Hill—which is almost everyone—comes through our doors at some point to offer congratulations and make a purchase. Five customers placed special orders for birthday cakes and even one wedding cake, which is pretty exciting. In a weird way, Rafe's vandalism actually helped drum up extra support for our shop. And word has spread about the handsome werewolf who's part owner of the bakery; a lot of the ladies have come to flirt with Teddy.

What's that old expression? Something about learning to grin and bear it? I haven't mastered that trick yet, especially around flighty young faeries who have no compunction about fluttering their eyelashes at my fiancé. Sometimes Teddy has to wrap an arm around my waist to keep me from growling at them.

After her shift, Cassia stops in with Olivia, who rushes over to Teddy. "Hi, Mr. Uncle Teddy," she says brightly.

"There's no need to call me Mister," Teddy chuckles, "since I'm joining your family." He nods at the desserts on display. "You can have anything you'd like, so long as your mom says it's okay."

Olivia hops around and cries, "Anything?"

"*One* of anything," clarifies Cassia.

Olivia wanders over to the glass case to examine the selection, pacing back and forth to make sure she doesn't miss a single option. Finally, she points at a giant oatmeal-chocolate-chip cookie.

"Let's ask Uncle Teddy to wrap it up," says Cassia. "You can have that cookie *after* dinner."

"Okay, Mommy." Olivia skips to the window to watch the cars go by on Main Street.

"Are you really sure you want a December wedding at Mooncrest Inn?" asks Cassia, who's both my maid of honor and my wedding planner.

My face falls; I've always dreamt of getting married during my favorite time of the year. I know I'll be super busy with the bakery in December (at least I hope so), but there's something about the crisp winter air, crunch of snow underfoot, and extra holiday cheer that makes my heart sing. And I adore Mooncrest Inn, the only five-star resort for supernaturals in Wisconsin; it's my first choice for a wedding venue, and my second, and my third. "I guess Mooncrest Inn books up pretty far in advance."

"I'm fine with anything so long as it's this year!" exclaims Teddy, planting a kiss on my headwrap. "The day after tomorrow works for me."

I give his muscular bicep a playful slap. "That's not romantic."

"Oh, sweetheart," Teddy growls low in my ear. "I'll make sure it's *very* romantic."

I suppress a giggle. "I'm serious, Teddy. I really want to be married at Mooncrest Inn, and I adore the Christmas season. But I suppose we could do it in November, if there's availability."

"Well, I just want to be sure you're still interested in December," says Cassia, her green eyes sparkling with excitement. "Because there was a cancelation at Mooncrest Inn in December!"

"That's amazing!" I squeal, waiting for Cassia to tell me the date I'll become Mrs. Leslie Theodore Barker.

She pauses for dramatic effect. "How does December 22nd sound?"

"It sounds perfect!" Teddy and I say together, and then I'm flinging my arms around his neck, and he's lifting me off my feet. Cassia chuckles at our antics as Olivia jumps up and down, clapping her hands.

I might have clipped wings, a new business to launch, and nagging worries about villainous Rafe, but I doubt you could find a happier kitchen faerie anywhere.

CHAPTER 36

BEADY-EYED TROLL

TEDDY

Wednesday, August 15

"Are you sure this is the right address?" I glance over at Catbeam Spellman, who's furiously chewing on her bottom lip. She's dressed like a mad magician, in purple coattails, baggy red pantaloons, orange shirt with a ruffled front, and a green top hat she's holding in her lap. Apparently Catbeam has been hired to entertain eighteen second graders this afternoon at a birthday party.

We're parked in a small clearing inside the dense forest that forms the southern boundary of Riddle Hill, staring at a dingy, one-room hut. The woods are so thick and close here that tree branches scraped against the sides of Miss Dragonfly's Cadillac as I drove down the private road; I'll have to buff out those scratches later with a polishing cloth and plenty of elbow grease.

"Of course I'm sure," Catbeam grumps. "But before

we enter, there are a few rules you need to know when dealing with trolls."

"O-okay."

She holds up her fist, counting off the rules on her fingers.

"One. Never, ever accept their initial offer, or their second or third. Trolls love to haggle.

"Two. Trolls will always try to entice you with sparkly trinkets, which they sell at exorbitant prices. Don't fall for it. The good stuff is always out back or down below."

"But that's a one-room cabin," I point out.

Catbeam waves away my objection with a spotty, wrinkled hand. "The quality merch could be in that shed back there behind the bungalow, which is protected with so many charms no one is breaking into it. Or the beady-eyed troll could be hiding the good stuff underneath a cabinet or beneath a loose floorboard."

Catbeam gives me a curt nod and continues. "Three. Even if you find the perfect ring for Sophie, you need to walk away."

"What?" I cry. "That's the whole purpose of this trip! I want to surprise Sophie with an engagement ring for her birthday, and you told me the only place to go for unique, high quality jewelry at reasonable prices is Talo's Pawnshop."

"I know what I said, sonny, and that's true. However, the only way to get what you want at a price we both can afford is if you follow those three simple rules."

"What do you mean, at a price we *both* can afford? *I'll* be buying my fiancée's ring."

Catbeam glances upward as if seeking inspiration from the old Caddy's velour-upholstered ceiling. "Talo doesn't deal in something as mundane as currency."

"Then why are we here? I'm a werewolf; I can't offer this troll any magic tricks... er, no offense."

"None taken." Catbeam nods.

"All I have to offer him is a razor-thin wallet and my werewolf strength."

"And your superior sense of smell and your pleasant customer-service demeanor."

"Why would a troll need any of that?" I'm becoming increasingly suspicious of my future grandmother-in-law.

"Talo doesn't need any of those attributes, but I do."

Giving Catbeam a sidelong glance, I remind myself of the very first rule Miss Dragonfly taught me about bargaining with faeries; don't even try, because you'll never win.

Huffing out a long sigh, I say, "What do you want from me, Miss Catbeam?"

Catbeam gives me a broad grin. "First of all, call me Granny. Secondly, I merely need a strong werewolf like you to help me organize Catbeam's Comics 'N Games; you know, sort through boxes, move some shelves around, restack the merch, and general cleaning. And if a customer comes in while you're at it, I'd expect you to help them find what they're looking for."

"What about my superior sense of smell; where does that come in?"

"Ah, well." Catbeam grimaces. "A two-headed rat has taken up residence in the woods behind my shop; he sneaks inside whenever it rains, and I need your nose to help me sniff out his hidey-hole."

"What are you going to do with him when you find him?" I'm not a fan of rats, but I don't want to help Catbeam track down and decapitate any creature, however many heads it has.

"I'm going to trap him and sell him to the faerie circus; two-headed rats are extremely rare," says Catbeam. I didn't even know there was such a thing as a faerie circus, but I let that slide.

"I'm already working at the café and the bakery," I remind her. "Plus I mow Rob's lawn and clip his hedges once a week. And I'm still taking classes at night for the firefighter's certification exam. I don't have much spare time."

"I just need four hours a week from you until the job is done."

Hmm... if Catbeam is even half as disorganized as my lovely bride-to-be, I fear the job will never be done. Recalling Miss Dragonfly's warning about making deals with faeries, I realize I'm stuck between a boulder and a tree bole; I need Catbeam's help if I'm going to find the perfect ring for Sophie. "I'll donate four hours of my time every week for the next twelve consecutive weeks, at which point we will declare the job is done. In exchange, you will barter with the troll to purchase Sophie's engagement ring. No ring, no deal."

Catbeam tents her silver eyebrows at me. "I can see my sister taught you well. Fine," she huffs, "four hours weekly for twelve weeks."

"For the next twelve *consecutive* weeks," I remind her.

She shrugs. "As you wish."

"Let's shake on it, shall we?" I extend my hand to her, which makes the transaction binding on both sides.

Catbeam shakes my hand with a small scowl. "Wow. Dragonfly really overshared, didn't she?"

I smile. "Miss Dragonfly took pity on a naïve, half-dead werewolf. I can never repay her for all her kindnesses to me."

"Well you could always repay her kindnesses by helping her kid sister."

"Uh-huh," I murmur, and we both chortle as we exit the car.

Catbeam pops her ridiculous green top hat on top of her wiry gray curls and leads the way through a weedy non-path to the front door, which cracks open as we approach.

"Catty," rumbles a low, hoarse voice, "yer lookin' lovely as usual."

"Talo," murmurs Catbeam, "don't think you can sweettalk me into one of your stingy deals."

Hinges squeal as the door swings open, revealing a stocky, silver-haired troll with black eyes, pointy ears each sprouting a tuft of hair, an oversized nose, and a pale gray-blue complexion. "Ach, ye can't mean it, Catty. Ye know I'd never steer ye wrong."

Catbeam cackles and sways her skinny hips as she enters the shop. Sweet moonglow, I think she's flirting with the beady-eyed troll! "What about that pair of earrings you sold me in '69? They were brass, Talo, not gold. They turned my earlobes *green*."

"'Twas a terrible mistake, and I've made it up to ye

ever since, since ye never cease to remind me of those earrings."

Catbeam sniffs. "You'd best not be trying any of your tiresome troll tricks today; this is my granddaughter's fiancé, and he would like to look at some rings. But I should warn you, next to my grandson Jake, he's the most fearsome werewolf in Door County."

A low gargle of surprise escapes from my throat, and Catbeam gives my arm a warning pinch. I straighten my spine and stare at the troll, who squints up at me. "Well now, I'm sure we'll get along just fine, Mister... er, what's yer name?"

"Mr. L.T. Barker," supplies Catbeam quickly; there's probably a rule about not giving a troll your full name, which she neglected to tell me.

"How can I help you, Mr. Barker?" asks the troll, welcoming us into a tiny, cramped shop with exposed wood walls and shelves upon shelves of shiny, sparkly objects—jewelry, pen knives, compasses, small clocks, handheld mirrors, tea cups, candlesticks, paperweights, marbles, and so forth.

"I'm looking for a unique engagement ring for a beautiful faerie whose favorite color is green."

"And this is for Catty's granddaughter?" Talo scratches one of his hairy ears. "Is she the baker or the wedding planner?"

"The baker," I reply.

Talo approaches the wall of shelves containing mostly jewelry and begins to pick pieces off the shelf. When he turns back to me, he's holding a square, velvet-lined tray containing six gold rings that glimmer in the shop's dim overhead light; hmm... that fact alone tells me these rings are enchanted to look nicer than they are.

Granny Catbeam crosses her arms. "Nope. Just put them right back on the shelf, Talo."

"But—"

"We're not interested."

With a heavy sigh, Talo replaces his first set of rings and proceeds to make another selection, but Catbeam rejects them too, and the set after that. Talo finally shifts his bare feet on the wooden floorboards. "Please wait here while I step outside to gather the finest collection of rings ye will find anywhere in the known world."

Catbeam crosses her arms. "Don't keep us waiting too long. We haven't got all day."

When the troll exits through a small, narrow opening in the rear of his shop, I turn to Sophie's grandmother and hiss, "This feels like a waste of time."

"Have a little patience. That was all preamble... now we'll start getting to the good stuff."

"And when I find the perfect ring for Sophie, you still want me to walk away?" I ask.

"Of course!" replies Catbeam with all the confidence of a chess player plotting her next five moves.

Talo makes several more trips out back, each time returning with a ring or three in his tray; the jewelry is getting more upscale, and so is my anxiety. For one thing, no prices are posted, so even if I wanted to pay in US dollars rather than in faerie bargains, I can't. And Catbeam is pursing her lips a bit more with each new ring Talo presents, as if she, too, is trying to gauge the cost.

Finally, Talo presents me with a single golden ring inside a black velvet box. "My *pièce de résistance*," he says with a surprisingly good French accent. Delicate curlicues encircle the band, forming a basket of feathered wings on top. The wings encase a two-carat solitaire emerald, which is surrounded by a circlet of tiny, sparkling diamonds.

It's superb, and I have no doubt Sophie would love it. Talo is staring at my face, which I guess is super transparent, because he's smiling broadly and probably already doubling whatever price he had in mind. Catbeam pinches me again, and I cough. "If that's your *pièce de résistance*," I tell him. "Then I'm afraid I must be going. It simply won't do."

I turn on my heels and march toward the door, hoping the troll doesn't ban us from ever setting foot in his nonsensical shop again. But Catbeam's scratchy voice calls after me. "Are you absolutely certain there isn't *anything* here that would please Sophie? Perhaps that rose gold band Talo showed us earlier? That was rather pretty."

That's my cue to turn back reluctantly and take another pass through a couple of the earlier choices. Talo and Catbeam begin haggling over the rose gold ring I'm not even interested in, until Catbeam huffs in disgust at the price and hustles me outside.

"Now what?" I find these faerie-troll negotiation tactics thoroughly draining, but Catbeam is practically bouncing on her toes.

"Now it's time for us to go. We'll come back of

course, once Talo comes to his senses about his asking price."

"Seriously?" I grumble. "Sophie's birthday is the day after tomorrow! And frankly, I'd rather get my butt kicked by my entire pack then go through that stress-inducing shopping experience again."

Catbeam chuckles as I accelerate down the not-a-driveway, tree branches thwacking against the sides of the car. "You want the gold ring with the emerald, right?"

"It's perfect." I nod. "You don't think anyone else is going to snap it up while we're dilly-dallying, do you?"

"Of course not; Talo wants another incantation, and since I'm the second-most powerful faerie in Wisconsin, he wants one of mine."

"What if the most powerful faerie in Wisconsin shows up?"

Catbeam grins. "Phoebe isn't in the market for jewelry, sonny. You'll be giving Sophie that ring for her birthday or my name isn't Catbeam Gladiolus Magnificat Spellman."

I have to bite my bottom lip to keep from laughing out loud at her ridiculous faerie name.

CHAPTER 37

PERFECT AND EXQUISITE

TEDDY

Friday, August 17

I'm Sophie's date for Pru and Vreeland's wedding, and tonight is the rehearsal dinner. I've met the vampire couple twice now, and I really like them. I can see Vreeland and myself becoming friends, something I never would've expected before moving to a supernatural village where werewolves and vampires freely intermingle.

Although I'm not part of the bridal party, I plan to drive Sophie to the chapel for the rehearsal and later to the dinner afterward. I'm not letting her out of my sight for two reasons; today is her birthday, and I'm still uneasy about Rafe. Despite the fact no one has heard from him since the vandalism episode, I don't think Rafe has suddenly grown a conscience.

I'm planning a proper birthday celebration for Sophie on Sunday, but I want to give her the ring before we leave. I keep patting my jacket pocket to make sure the little black box is still tucked inside; after dealing with Catbeam and Talo's nutso negotiations—we had to return to his shop two more times to secure the deal—I'm anxious to see the ring on Sophie's finger.

I'm sitting on the brown sofa beside Zosia, giving the white fuzzball a belly rub, when Sophie's bedroom door opens. Rising nervously from the couch, my fingers graze the box in my pocket as I wait for her to enter the living room. But when she does, I simply stand there and forget to breathe.

Sophie is wearing a short, sparkly, copper-colored dress that hugs her figure in all the right places. Her hair is down, which is rare these days given the long hours she spends baking, and her gorgeous chestnut waves cascade over shoulders and down her back. Her pillowy lips are a glossy shade of deep coral, and her gray eyes twinkle as I stare at her; I'm awestruck.

At some point I manage to croak, "Wow!"

"What's the matter, wolf-boy... fox got your tongue?"

"I'm okay now," I murmur, grinning. "I just forgot to breathe for a minute back there."

Sophie chuckles as she breezes past me to the door. "I guess we better get going; as the maid of honor I need to be on time."

"Wait... please. I have your birthday gift."

Sophie turns around, her brow puckered. "But we're celebrating on Sunday."

"This is burning a hole in my pocket," I say, withdrawing the velvet box from my jacket and handing it to her. "And today is your birthday, and well, I want you to have this now."

Sophie stares up at me and then down at the box in her hand, which I notice is quivering slightly. "Go on and open it," I say, suddenly unsure of myself. "And if you don't like it... we can..."

"Oh, Teddy!" Sophie squeals as she opens the box. "This is exquisite... it's absolutely perfect!"

"Exquisite and perfect are words I reserve only for you," I rasp low in my throat.

Sophie starts fanning her face with her free hand, her eyes glistening. "Oh no—I think I'm going to cry! Now I'm really going to be late."

"Please don't cry." Taking her perfect, exquisite face in my hands, I plant a butter-soft kiss on her lush lips, careful not to muss her hair.

Sophie smiles, but a single tear manages to escape, which I quickly swipe with my thumb. Then I release her and nod at the box in her hand. "Would you like me to slip that on for you?"

"Yes, please," she whispers.

I remove the band from the box and place it on her finger. Sophie holds up her left hand, waggling the emerald ring, which winks and sparkles. "It's beautiful, a perfect fit."

"Do you really like the ring?" I'm still insecure when it comes to Sophie, probably because I need her so much more than she needs me. She has the power to complete me in ways I never believed possible.

"I love it," she says. "And I love *you* more."

"Well if you're really sure..."

"About you or the ring?" Sophie teases, taking my hand and leading me out to the car.

I pause, my hand on the car door. "Both."

Sophie's eyes lock on mine. "I've never been surer of anything in my life." And then she adds with a mischievous grin, "Wolf-boy."

Snorting at her silly nickname for me, I close her car door and step around to the driver's side. As I'm starting the old Caddy, Sophie holds up her hand again to gaze at her ring. "Where did you find this?"

"It's kind of a long story."

"Tell me on the way to the chapel."

"Alright." I give her a sly wink. "This story begins, as all the best stories do, with a faerie bargain, a beady-eyed troll, and a wolf-boy in love with a faerie princess..."

Sophie's brilliant giggles fill the car. "Not Granny Catbeam and Talo the pawnbroker!"

"The very same."

"Now I know you love me," she quips.

"My dearest Sophie." I pick up her left hand and plant tender kisses along the inside of her wrist and all the way up to her elbow, smiling as she trembles at my touch. "I'm yours for as long as life endures."

CHAPTER 38

BROKEN WINGS

SOPHIE

SATURDAY, AUGUST 18

After Teddy dropped me off at Spectra's Salon this morning to meet Pru and the other bridesmaids for our hair and makeup appointments, he promised me one more birthday surprise... but what could possibly top my gorgeous wolf-boy fiancé and his lovely emerald ring?

I'm holding Pru's bouquet and mine as she and Vreeland exchange their vows inside Mooncrest Chapel, a beautiful, historic old building with lots of polished wood and stained glass. My mind keeps wandering as I envision Teddy and myself where Vreeland and Pru are now standing in front of the altar—our happily ever after is four months away!

I keep scanning the pews, trying to spot Teddy, but I don't see any strapping Scandinavian types with flowing, shoulder-length locks. Where *is* that man? As my eyes rove over the crowd for the third time, I notice a dashing guy in a black suit with collar-length blond hair smirking back at me.

I scowl at him; who does that werewolf think he is, flirting with a soon-to-be-married woman? Then his handsome face breaks into a broad grin, and my eyes pop so wide Pru's mother gives me a concerned look from the front pew; I think she's worried I'm about to have a fainting spell like a noblewoman from one of those Regency novels.

I nod reassuringly at Mrs. Albright, who returns her gaze to Pru and Vreeland. Then I smile at Teddy, who looks so handsome and confident with his shorter hair that I could actually swoon for him right here in front of everyone, but I quickly get a grip. I'd never want to create a scene on Pru's wedding day by fainting because my fiancé is even more drop-dead gorgeous now than he was this morning.

I have no doubt his supermodel hairstyle is Spectra's handiwork, and I sigh. I've finally started getting used to all the ladies fawning over Teddy in his former, long-haired glory; now there'll be another round of flirtatious giggling everywhere we go.

It's not easy being engaged to a man as hot as Leslie Theodore Barker.

~

"WELL, WHAT DO YOU THINK?" he asks me after the rest of the guests depart for cocktails and appetizers in the main building next door. We're still in the chapel waiting for Julien Drakus to finish taking photos of the bridal party;

Pru is so sweet she wants Teddy in a few of the pictures with me.

"While I'll miss toying with your long hair, I really like your new look," I say, brushing a wavy lock from his forehead. "But why the change?"

"I liked my long hair too, but it's hot in the summer, and it requires a lot more maintenance, especially if you're working around food all day." Teddy's warm, steady gaze turns serious. "And it felt like a part of me I was ready to leave behind, now that I'll be marrying my evermore mate in a few months—"

"Your *evermore mate*?"

Teddy chuckles. "I think it's more poetic than fated mate, don't you?"

"Whether it's the hand of fate that brought us together or Miss Dragonfly's ingenious matchmaking, I love the idea of being your evermore mate," I whisper.

Teddy wraps his arms around my waist, draws me closer, and kisses the top of my head. "Me too."

Julien waves us over, and we pose for another round of photographs before Cassia releases everyone except for the bride and groom. As Julien snaps more photos of the couple, Teddy and I head to the inn for appetizers, entering the lounge area with its massive Victorian-style mahogany bar, reputedly a gift from Queen Victoria. Granny Catbeam claims the bar was crafted by a pair of wood nymphs from Normal, Illinois, which as it turns out isn't such a normal place after all; apparently it's a favorite hangout for nymphs and dryads pretending to be college students.

As I predicted, Teddy is flocked by every woman in

the lobby, both waitstaff and guests. He's always polite, smiles sweetly, and answers their questions in his low, raspy voice that still makes my insides quiver. But instead of getting upset, I find myself chuckling as Teddy gently tries to disentangle himself from two fiftyish vampire ladies who are draped all over him.

It's not that I'm no longer jealous, but I'm more confident these days about Teddy's feelings for me. As I'm sipping from my glass of craft root beer, which I never drank until I started dating Teddy, I can't help grinning at my handsome, helpless fiancé.

Cassia comes alongside me and whispers, "Don't you think you ought to go rescue your man? Poor Teddy looks like he might drown soon in all that female attention."

I set down my mug on a small, high-topped table and feign a dramatic sigh. "I suppose you're right."

I saunter over to the women, sidestep around the bleach-blonde vampire staring adoringly up at Teddy, and throw my arms around his neck. Then I kiss my werewolf fiancé so thoroughly every female in the room between nineteen and ninety realizes this particular Nordic god is most definitely mine.

The next few hours fly by in typical wedding reception fashion—a three-course dinner, dancing to a live band, and too many speeches—until Teddy and I finally slip away from the inn's ballroom and wander outside. We head toward the broad front lawn that gently slopes down toward the road and the glimmering bay beyond, the water reflecting the glow of the crescent moon above.

I lean my hand on Teddy's shoulder for support and bend over to remove my heels. "Oh, that feels good," I murmur, wriggling my toes in the cool, slightly damp grass.

"I saw the other bridesmaids wearing flipflops; what happened to yours?"

"I gave mine to Pru's mother when one of her straps broke."

Teddy chuckles softly. "My kindhearted faerie."

"Shh," I tell him with a laugh, "don't tell anyone. Let's not ruin my reputation as your grouchy fiancée; it's the only way I'll be able to keep all the ladies at bay."

Teddy wordlessly reaches behind my head and starts pulling out my hairpins, flinging them all over the lawn.

"What are you doing, you crazy werewolf?"

"Freeing your luscious locks so I can do this," Teddy murmurs, entangling both his hands in my hair and claiming my mouth. Teddy's kisses are simultaneously sweet and sizzling, heating my core and sending warm tingles all the way to my fingers and toes. My heart soars, ten-thousand wing feathers fluttering inside my chest, and I have to grasp Teddy's lapels so I don't melt into a swoony puddle on the grass.

When he finally releases my lips, he pulls me against his chest, and I can feel the rapid thrumming of his heart. "I've wanted to do that all night long," he whispers.

"I'm glad you waited until after the photos," I reply, smiling. "Spectra would be horrified to see what my hair looks like now."

Teddy grins and takes my hand, guiding me back up the lawn toward the inn, where the reception must be nearly over. I stifle a yawn; tomorrow is Sunday, a busy day for our bakery. It's time to say goodnight to my vampire friends and head home.

As we approach the inn's circular gravel driveway, Teddy pauses and stares down at my bare feet. "Why don't I head inside and see if I can scrounge up a spare pair of flip-flops for you. Either that, or I can carry you across the gravel, up the steps, and into the inn; that would be much more fun." His white teeth flash as he gives me a mischievous grin.

"Let's hold off on any dramatic damsel-in-distress antics, wolf-boy. I'll wait here while you go ask Cassia for a pair of flip-flops; I'm sure she has spares tucked somewhere."

"As you wish, my beautiful faerie boss." Teddy gives me a quick peck on the lips and turns to leave. As he starts across the driveway, I notice movement around the side of the inn, probably another couple who stepped outside for fresh air and a cuddle under the stars.

Then my heart stutters and skips a few beats.

No, it's not another couple at all.

It's *him*, dressed all in black.

His face is paler than moonlight and oddly shaped; it takes me a moment to realize Rafe has partially shifted, his nose and mouth lengthened into a muzzle, his furred hands tipped with sharp claws.

Rafe bares his canines and charges toward Teddy, who hasn't picked up Rafe's scent in the still night air; my fiancé is whistling softly, unaware of the danger. I shriek Teddy's name, and he turns, but I know it's too late. My gorgeous werewolf is going to be wounded once more, torn and slashed by stupid, smirking, jealous Rafe.

And I won't let that happen to him again.

With a loud cry, I transform into my faerie form, my wings swooshing open through the slits in my gown. It only takes several flaps of my powerful wings to propel me into the air toward Teddy. I land in front of him, twisting my body to wrap my arms and wings around him protectively, and I wait for the impact as Rafe hurtles toward us.

Rafe's claws tear into me, crushing feathers and breaking bones as my wings are ripped apart. Now I'm screaming and sliding slowly down, down, down, as Teddy howls my name and catches me before my head hits the gravel drive. There's a flutter of activity above me; I glimpse Rafe's shocked face, and then he's gone, running away.

Agonizing pain courses through my back and wings; blood pools inside my dress and trickles to the ground. My breath is coming in short gasps as Teddy leans over me, weeping and crying, "Oh, Sophie, hang on darling, don't leave me... please don't... don't..." His voice cracks, his tears falling into my face and hair.

I want to reassure Teddy, tell him I'm not leaving him, but the excruciating pain is more than I can handle. My head is so woozy... and my eyelids are... too... heavy...

CHAPTER 39
BROKEN HEARTS

Saturday, August 18

"Sophie! Sophie!" I'm half mad with grief, screaming her name as I cradle her crumpled form in my arms. Someone must hear my cries, because suddenly I'm surrounded by people from the inn; an older man with pointy ears and a trim gray beard takes over, calling an ambulance.

One of the staff drapes a blanket over Sophie, who's unconscious, her wings dangling at wrong angles from her back. I periodically check her pulse, panicking at the irregular heartbeat. I don't know the first thing about faerie wings, but even I can see they've been shredded by Rafe's claws.

At some point Cassia joins me on the driveway, weeping quietly over her cousin. I'm so afraid of losing Sophie that the paramedics have to pry her out of my arms when they arrive. They let me ride along in the

306

ambulance with her, probably because they can see I'm in no condition to drive myself to the hospital. As we're leaving, I ask Cassia to call the rest of the family and meet us there.

When we arrive, Sophie is whisked away into the emergency room, and Marv shows up to take the police report on the incident. I'm so upset I'm dry heaving, and Marv drags me outside so I can get some fresh air. He waits until I regain a modicum of self-control, and then he asks, "What the blazes happened?"

"Rafe happened," I spit out. "He came out of nowhere, partially shifted, obviously bent on attacking me, but I didn't catch his scent until it was too late. Sophie must have spotted him because she screamed my name. As I was turning around, she flew into me and draped her wings around me." I have to stop speaking to catch my breath again. "Sophie took the blows intended for me. Now she's lying in there with bloody, torn-up wings, and I'm out here without even a scratch."

I run my hands through my hair, pacing around the parking lot. "I want to howl and whine and break some-thing, but nothing I do is going to heal Sophie and lessen her agony." I look at Marv. "What can I do? Tell me what to do."

Marv speaks in a quiet, authoritative tone that helps to soothe some of my frenzied desperation. "You can tell me everything you remember about Rafe, what he was wearing, how fast he was moving. You said he'd partially shifted; I need a complete description. Give me all the details you can recall."

Slowly, haltingly, I tell Marv everything I can remember, and then I stumble back inside the hospital. Sophie's parents and Granny Catbeam arrive shortly afterward, followed by Jake and Cassia. I tell them what happened, breaking down only once, when I describe how Sophie came between Rafe and me.

"It should have been *me* protecting her, not the other way around," I mutter, rubbing my eyes with the heels of my hands. "I'm so sorry."

Granny places a hand on my shoulder and squeezes. "Sophie is a brave faerie who loves you deeply; she never would've stood by and allowed you to be injured if she could do something about it."

It's been several hours since the ambulance arrived with Sophie, and we're still waiting for news of her condition. A team of surgeons is working on her, resetting her wing bones and stitching up the damaged muscles and sinews in her back. Phoebe says the most time-consuming part will be repairing her wings, given the number of tiny bones that were crushed in the attack.

I'm broken inside, terrified Sophie will never fully recover. I can't make eye contact with her family, too ashamed of my failure to keep her safe. I couldn't save Jarrod from the beating that killed him, and I couldn't save Sophie from having her wings ripped apart by Rafe.

Someone, Cassia I think, tries to hand me a cup of water but I shake my head; my stomach is so knotted up I can't keep anything down, not even water. I'm sitting on one of the plastic chairs in the hospital's secluded waiting room for supernaturals, leaning forward with my elbows on my knees and my head in my hands.

Sophie's family are murmuring softly among themselves, their wings partially unfurled against their backs.

My head's still in my hands when I hear the chair creaking next to me as a large, warm body takes the seat. It's my alpha; I'd know his scent anywhere.

"Teddy," says Jake quietly, "look at me."

I take a shuddering breath and obey, gazing at him through watery eyes. Like me, he's remained in his man-form even though we both might feel better if we shift. But it's easier to communicate with Sophie's family and doctors this way.

Jake murmurs, "You've got to keep it together. Sophie is going to need a lot of rehabilitation, and we're all counting on you to help."

I nod, so full of bleak remorse and crushing sadness I'm unable to speak. We sit like that, side-by-side in silent solidarity, waiting for news of Sophie.

Finally, a female faerie with black hair and burgundy wing feathers enters the room and asks for the Spellman-Brownlee family. We immediately surround the doctor, who gives us a brief, compassionate nod. "The initial surgery went as well as we could have expected. However, Sophie's wings were badly damaged; we're not sure they'll ever be fully functional again."

Phoebe cries, "Oh my poor girl," and buries her face in Nash's chest.

My stomach twists, my hands curling into fists at my sides, but my aggressive stance is useless now; Rafe is long gone.

Nash asks the doctor whether Sophie can have visitors, and she shakes her head. "Sophie is in the ICU. Once she's moved to a room, likely tomorrow afternoon, you'll be able to visit."

"I need to see my mate," I growl low in my throat, my inner wolf struggling to remain in check; there's no point antagonizing the medical staff.

The doctor narrows her eyes at me. "Is Sophie your fated mate?"

"Yes, ma'am," I grunt, and the rest of the family nods in agreement.

"Very well," she replies, obviously aware of the intense, highly charged bond between werewolves and their mates. "You may see her for five minutes, and then you will need to wait along with the rest of the family until we move Sophie."

"Thank you." My tone is clipped, but it's the best I can do as I barely hold myself together.

"We'll wait here for you," says Nash, his deep throat raspy with emotion. "Come tell us how she is."

The faerie doctor hands me off to a vampire nurse with an unfortunate overbite, her long, pointy fangs protruding over her bottom lip. She guides me to Sophie's bed inside the well-lit ICU, which contains twenty beds, half of which are occupied. Machines whir and beep, and some of the patients moan; I avert my gaze to allow them their privacy.

Sophie is lying on her stomach on a bed in the corner, her wings stretched out on either side of her, bound in so much white gauze not a single feather peeks through. Each wing is resting in a sling that is suspended from a pulley above the bed. Her face is turned toward me, her eyes closed. I can hear her breathing softly, and a guttural noise sounds deep in my throat, my wolf whining for my mate.

The vampire reminds me I have five minutes, after which she'll escort me back to the waiting room. I thank her and drag a chair over to the side of the bed so I can watch Sophie as she slumbers. A loose chunk of chestnut hair has tumbled onto her brow, which I gently brush back. Her hand is curled into a loose fist on the bed near her cheek; I wrap my fingers around hers, relishing their warmth.

And then I spend the next four-and-a-half minutes telling Sophie all the ways I love her. I think the corner of her mouth twitches upward once, but I can't be sure.

After I reassure her family that Sophie is sleeping peacefully, everyone heads home except Jake. "Why don't you crash at my place tonight?"

I shake my head. "Thanks for the offer, but I'll need to look after Zosia while Sophie is in the hospital."

"I forgot all about Zosia," admits Jake. He claps a hand on my shoulder. "Alright, let me know if you need anything."

"Actually, I could use a lift back to Mooncrest Inn—I rode in the ambulance with Sophie."

A short while later I'm saying goodbye to my alpha and standing beside my car. Before I climb inside, I walk over to the gravel driveway where Rafe attacked us. One of the inn's staff has already raked fresh gravel over the blood stains and picked up the loose feathers.

If only Sophie's wings could be mended so easily. I drop to my knees in the spot where she fell, place my hand on the gravel, and whisper a prayer for my faerie sweetheart.

I want to see Sophie giggling brightly again, swaying her hips as she sings off-key, scowling when someone (usually me) annoys her, unfurling her wings when we're alone, and bending over her recipe books, anxious to try something new.

I want my evermore mate to be fully healed.

I want Sophie to be radiantly herself again; I've never wanted anything more in all my life.

Rising, I gaze up at the night sky and howl out my heartache.

CHAPTER 40
GRADUATION

SOPHIE

Wednesday, October 10

I smooth back Teddy's hair, which has been tousled by the stiff October breeze sweeping off the bay. A thunderstorm is heading our way, and Jake is keeping one eye on the sky as he welcomes the guests. Everyone associated with the fire department—full-time firefighters, volunteers, and family members—are seated on metal folding chairs in Riddle Hill Park, an expanse of green lawn overlooking the water.

"It's time." I smile at Teddy. "The others are already up there with Jake. He's about to start his speech; I know all the signs."

Chuckling, he brushes his lips over mine. "Thank you."

"For what?"

"For not leaving me," Teddy whispers before walking up to join the other graduates.

I frown at his departing back, not sure what he means by that last remark. Why would he even suggest such a thing? I adore that wolf-boy more with each passing day, not less.

Teddy has been my steady rock since the attack by Rafe, who's managed to disappear again without a trace, making it impossible to press charges against him. Meanwhile, Jake has provided Rafe's physical description to all wolf packs and supernatural police forces throughout the Midwest; if Rafe is in the vicinity, we'll know about it. And if he comes near us again, we'll slap him with a supernatural restraining order, which has a lot more teeth than the non-super version.

But honestly, I try not to think about Rafe at all. I caught a glimpse of his face when he realized he'd hurt me instead of Teddy, and I saw the horror and remorse in his eyes. Perhaps he learned his lesson, but Teddy doesn't think so.

Despite all the pain—and the rehab I'm still undergoing to slowly rebuild my wing strength—I have no regrets about stepping in front of Teddy and taking the blows meant for him. And even though Teddy made me promise I'd never do anything so foolish again, I'd still do it if it meant sparing him.

When you truly love someone, don't you want to bear their hurts and burdens?

Teddy takes his place between Rory, a nice werewolf I went to high school with, and Maisie, who runs Howling Shores Pub along with Wes, her mate. Maisie has been helping me understand werewolf behavior and what it means to be bonded with one. She's sweet and smart and bursts out laughing every time I ask her about my mate bond thingy with Teddy.

Jake welcomes everyone and gives a short speech about the important role firefighters play in our community, wrapping up with a few reminders about upcoming events, including the Firemen's Ball in December, which is the department's largest fundraiser of the year.

The ball occurs the weekend before my wedding, which is coming so fast I'm almost afraid to blink because before you know it, I'll be walking down the aisle! Not that I'm complaining—far from it.

I want to treasure each moment between now and then, until Cassia reminds me how much we still need to do for my wedding. At least I don't have to worry about the honeymoon, because Teddy is planning everything; we're going to Costa Rica right after Christmas.

My head positively spins every time Cassia takes me through one of her endless checklists. Even so, I still love her to pieces; she and Olivia have visited me regularly since I came home from the hospital, cheering me up and reminding me to do all my PT exercises, which Cassia knows I'd fluff off if I could.

And then there's Granny Catbeam, the one person I never expected to move in and assist me with certain daily tasks that I won't let Teddy do until we're married. She took over Teddy's room for six weeks, helping me bathe, changing my dressings, and hovering like a mother hen. Granny and Mom even helped Teddy keep the bakery running on the weekends; they baked small batches of our favorite desserts that Teddy sold on Saturdays and Sundays. I'm finally able to return to work, but

I'm not putting in fourteen-hour days, at least not until the holidays, when Riddle Hill swells with tourists again.

There's one change at the bakery I'm not overjoyed about, but I'm learning to live with the new ancestor portrait hanging in a prime spot on the lefthand wall. I could tell Teddy really wanted Miss Dragonfly's ghostly presence inside our shop, and since we have her to thank for the inheritance and for bringing us together, how could I say no?

Sometimes Auntie Dragonfly wakes up long enough to remember something ridiculous that Granny Catbeam did eighty years ago and scolds her like she's still a teenager. Granny chews her bottom lip and stalks out of the shop with a loud huff, and Teddy and I have to stifle our giggles.

After the ceremony Teddy returns to my side and hands me his diploma, which is signed by Jake as the fire chief and bears the town's golden seal. If you have super-natural eyesight and can read the tiny typeface printed inside the seal, you'd see this: Village of Riddle Hill, Keeping Supernaturals Safe Since Salem.

At the very bottom of the certificate, printed in even smaller font, is the town's mission statement: Riddle Hill is an inclusive community. All with wings, scales, fangs, fur, fins, talons, and tails are welcome here.

My handsome fiancé is beaming as I smile up at him. "I'm so proud of you, Mr. Head-of-the-Class."

"Hmm," he smirks. "I kind of miss you calling me Mr. Clean."

I snort out a laugh and then wince slightly at the pinch in my back.

"Are you alright?" Teddy grips my arm, his hand suddenly covered in blond fur.

"Relax, wolf-boy," I tell him, tapping the back of his hand, which becomes less hairy as he gets his inner werewolf back in line. "It was just a muscle twinge thingy."

"A muscle twinge thingy?" he cocks his head to the side. "Can you be more specific?"

"I think that's an apt description of a passing, temporary ache in my back, the result of an injury and subsequent surgery."

Teddy rolls his eyes. "You're impossible."

I grin at him. "But you love me anyway."

The gold around his blue irises flares brighter. "For as long as life endures."

I wrap my arms around my gorgeous, hunky werewolf and stand on my tiptoes to plant a firm kiss on his warm lips. A few, fat raindrops pelt my shoulders, and I break away with a contented sigh.

As Teddy hurries me to his old Caddy, I twine our fingers together and repeat softly in his ear, "For as long as life endures."

EPILOGUE – BEAUTIFUL SCARS

TEDDY

Wednesday, December 26

"What are you doing? You already carried me across the threshold back home." Sophie's giggles ring out, filling me with such abundant joy I want to hold her a little longer in my arms, just to hear her laugh again. I fling open the door to our Costa Rican condo and parade Sophie through our rooms as she snorts with laughter.

"I'm sorry, but I just don't think this place will do," I say, feigning a serious tone.

"What's wrong with it?" Sophie gazes around, still cradled against my chest.

"For one thing the furniture alignment is all wrong."

She tries to humor me, compressing her lips to look as concerned as I'm pretending to be. "The Feng Shui thingy isn't working, huh?"

Now I'm trying hard not to chuckle. "It's not working

at all," I say sternly. "Even worse, there are dust bunnies in the closets... and... and those towels."

A small frown line forms on Sophie's brow. "What's wrong with the towels?"

"They match." I pretend to shudder.

That's when Sophie realizes I'm joking; there isn't a single matching set of towels in our cottage. "Put me down, wolf-boy," she chortles. "You had me going there for a minute."

I place her gently on her feet and kiss the top of her head, grateful she's mostly recovered from her injuries. While her wing feathers will take another year or so to fully grow back, the delicate bones and sinews have mended. Sophie still grimaces from the occasional cramp in her back muscles, generally when she's skipped her physical therapy regimen. Then she'll grunt in disgust at her "lazy self" and redouble her exercise routine.

I pull open the condo's rear door and peek outside. "Did you see we have our own hot tub? And the beach is practically in our backyard. Goodbye snow and clouds, hello sea and sunshine! Let's get into our swimsuits and grab some rays."

After changing, we gather up our assorted beach paraphernalia—sunglasses, paperback novels, water bottles, towels, and sunscreen—and head toward the cabana where we rent a pair of beach chairs and a very large umbrella. Sophie looks absolutely adorable in her brightly colored caftan, wide-brimmed hat, and large, tinted shades.

I dump our stuff on one of the recliner-style chairs, anxious to dive into the turquoise waters, and hold up the sunscreen. "Do you need me to put some on your back and shoulders?"

Sophie shakes her head. "Um... no thanks. I put some on before I got into my suit."

"Okay. Can you do my back?" I hand her the bottle, and Sophie rubs the lotion into my back, gently massaging the muscles. "That feels so-o good."

I feel her fingers tracing over the scars on my back, many from my recent bout with Rafe, but some from earlier fights. By the time we reach our twenties, all werewolves have a few scars, mostly from friendly tussles that became too animated, occasionally from more serious battles.

I turn around and take Sophie's hands in mine. "Ready for a swim?"

She shakes her head and steps back, withdrawing her hands. "Why don't you go on ahead. I'm a little chilly."

"You're chilly? It's eighty-two degrees. You're not getting sick, are you?" I narrow my eyes, wishing hers weren't hidden behind her dark shades.

"No, I'm fine, really..." Sophie turns away, hurries over to the chair, and plunks herself down. "I'll watch you swim."

"Alright." Shrugging, I toss my sunglasses on the other chair and start trudging across the sandy beach toward the water.

Something's definitely wrong, but I'm not sure what. Sophie was all smiles from the time we left home, drove to O'Hare Airport, boarded the plane for Costa Rica, deplaned and went through customs, rented a car, and arrived here… the entire time, really… until I suggested going for a swim.

I stop suddenly, recalling her fingers trailing across my scars. She can't be… she's not… I re-trace my steps back to the large blue-and-white striped umbrella and Sophie. She's still wearing her caftan, despite the fact tiny beads of perspiration are dotting her brow.

I fold my arms and stare down at her.

"What's wrong?" she asks.

"That's what I'd like to know."

"What do you mean?"

I motion for her to scooch over. Sophie swivels her hips, swinging her legs over to the side, and I sit beside her on the long recliner. "May I?" I point to her sunglasses. When she nods, I remove them and drop them into her bag. She quirks her brow, shooting me a puzzled gaze.

Then I pick up Sophie's left hand, admire the sparkly emerald ring that I purchased with a faerie bargain, and kiss her knuckles. "Tell me the real reason you're still wearing your cover-up despite the heat."

She tries tugging her hand away but I grip it tighter. Her lower lip trembles slightly as she stares down at our entwined hands. "I don't want anyone else to see them," she whispers so softly I lean closer to hear her. "They're so ragged and ugly."

"But I have scars too," I say gently. "Are mine ugly?"

Her head snaps up. "Of course not! Your scars are part of who you are. But it's different for a faerie… especially a female faerie. We're not accustomed to actual fighting; our battles generally involve words, recipes, spells, and occasionally, a round of hair pulling."

"Now *that* I'd like to see," I tell her, bumping her shoulder.

She snorts but glances away again. I tilt her face toward me. "Tell me again how you got those scars."

She blinks her eyes closed and sighs. "You know how; I came between you and Rafe."

"Because?" I prompt her.

"Because I couldn't bear the thought of him hurting you again."

"Exactly."

"But that doesn't change the fact my scars are hideous," Sophie whispers. "I'm afraid of people staring at them."

"Let them stare," I rumble protectively. "Your scars are beautiful, sweetheart. Whenever I see them, I remember what you did for me."

Then I tip up her chin, sealing her warm lips with mine, savoring her springtime scent, reveling in the fact she's right here beside me, safe in my arms. "Your scars remind me how much you love me; a werewolf female would proudly show off the scars she earned protecting her mate."

Sophie pulls back to give me an assessing gaze. "Is that really true?"

"Of course it's true; just ask Maisie."

Sophie inhales deeply, removes her big, floppy hat, and pulls us both to our feet. Then she whips off her caftan, tosses it at my chest, and shouts, "Last one in the water has to change Zosia's litter box for the next month!" She races past me with a wicked grin, her legs pumping hard as she dashes toward the water.

"Hey." I wrinkle my nose. "No fair!"

No one else is staring at Sophie's scarred back except me. As my eyes roam over every white, jagged line scoring her smooth skin, a low growl escapes from my throat. The memory of catching Sophie in my arms that night, her wings torn asunder, still haunts me and probably always will.

I quickly swipe at my damp cheek and force a grin when Sophie glances back at me, her smile victorious as she splashes first into the water.

Then I jog toward my brave, beautiful wife, cherishing her enticing curves, her bright peel of laughter, her chestnut hair tumbling over her shoulders. And with a loud whoop, I sweep my glorious evermore mate into my outstretched arms.

SOPHIE'S SPECIAL RECIPE

RIDDLER'S MAGIC BARS

Despite the fact Teddy's searing kisses made me burn several batches, these are wolf-boy's favorite cookies. I might be a magicless kitchen faerie at the moment, but I promise you're going to believe in magic when you taste these yummy treats.

Cookie Bar ingredients and instructions:

¾ cup butter

¾ cup brown sugar

¼ cup white sugar

2 teaspoons vanilla

1 egg

1 egg yolk

1 ½ cups flour

1 teaspoon baking powder

½ teaspoon salt

6 ounces (or more if you like) chocolate chips

GREASE AN 8-INCH SQUARE PAN. Using a mixer, cream butter for 1 to 2 minutes. Add in both sugars and combine. Add vanilla. Add egg and egg yolk, beating until combined. Sift dry ingredients together, and then add to the creamed butter mixture. Mix thoroughly and then add chocolate chips. Pour into the prepared pan and smooth. Bake at 350 degrees for 30 minutes, or until set. When partially cool, cut into bars and remove from pan. Place on cooling rack. Makes 16 servings.

Serve with your favorite beverage (coffee, tea, milk, or Teddy's favorite, root beer). Save at least one cookie bar for Granny Catbeam... otherwise she may clip *your* wings!

Thanks so much for reading *Rhyme, Riddle, and Romance*! I hope you enjoyed this clean and cozy paranormal romance about Sophie, the kitchen faerie with a big heart but poor judgment, and Teddy, the young, somewhat broken werewolf in need of a fresh start. Please consider taking a moment and leaving a review, even a sentence or two. Reader reviews help other readers discover new books—and they are vitally important for indie authors like me.

I've wanted to write about Sophie and Teddy's romance ever since I published *Half a Faerie*, where you can read about their wedding from Cassia's and Will's perspectives. It was fun, and a bit challenging as an author, to write about Sophie and Teddy after publishing the other books in the series, especially since I needed to introduce villainous Rafe, who appears next in *Half a Faerie* and then again in *Return to Mooncrest Inn*, where he fights Jake Spellman in a final showdown that you won't want to miss.

Producing a book is a collaborative process, and this one is no exception. Many people helped to shape this story, including my husband Steve, who read and commented on early drafts; my daughter Caitlin, who provided invaluable marketing advice; my daughter-in-law Lexi, who crocheted the cutest gargoyles; my son Doug, who always encouraged me; and my sister-in-law Beth, who created the recipe for Riddler's Magic Bars. Martha Reineke of MK Editing provided insightful writing and editorial feedback, Diogo Leite of Book Design Company designed the gorgeous cover and character art, and my ARC team of readers and reviewers have been wonderfully supportive. I adore you all—thank you!

Lastly and most importantly, I give thanks to my Heavenly Father, the Author of the greatest story ever told. All other love stories pale in comparison to His.

Toni Cabell

John 1:1

BOOKS BY TONI CABELL

If you're looking for sweet, slow-burn romance with swoony kisses, second chances, and funny, heartwarming characters, don't miss the complete **Faeries of Door County** series. Winner of Best Paranormal Romance, each novel is a standalone story set in the same cozy small town:

- *Rhyme, Riddle, and Romance*
- *Half a Faerie*
- *Return to Mooncrest Inn*

A fast-paced adventure full of magic, romance, humor, sword fighting, dangerous creatures, and the power of light versus darkness, **Serving Magic** is a YA Epic Fantasy series with Steampunk and Regency vibes. Winner of The Wishing Shelf Book Awards and recognized by Indies Today as a Top 5 YA Fantasy series by an indie author:

- *Lady Apprentice, Book 1*
- *Lady Mage, Book 2*
- *Lady Liege, Book 3*
- *Lady Spy, Book 4*
- *Lady Reaper, Book 5*

In the arid hills of Toresz, there's one thing more dangerous than divining for water... falling in love with the enemy. **Water Witch** is YA Romantasy duology packed with action, danger, intrigue, royal politics, and romance. Winner of The Wishing Shelf Book Awards:

- *The Lightness of Water, Book 1*
- *The Way of Water, Book 2*

Find all Toni's available books and upcoming new releases on tonicabell.com and Amazon. All her novels are also available in audiobook format on Audible and Apple Books.

About the Author

Toni Cabell is a closed-door fantasy romance author whose books reflect her Christian values, which means you'll find no swearing, no excess violence, and no spice. Here's what you *will* find...

- Clean fantasy | magical worlds
- Wholesome romance | just kisses
- Deep friendships | quirky families
- Sassy and strong gals | swoony and protective guys
- (YA books) Swords and battles | no gory descriptions

Her novels have won Silver and Bronze Medals in The Wishing Shelf Book Awards, two Gold Medals in the Global Book Awards, multiple B.R.A.G. Medallions, and awards for writing Clean YA Fantasy from Incipere Awards.

Toni lives with her handsome husband in a small village along the shores of Lake Michigan, where she's able to walk to the bookstore, library, coffee shop, and bakery (although not always in that order). She's happy to report her adult children reside nearby and provide her with a steady supply of affection, amusement, and just the right smattering of chaos.

Toni loves to stay in touch with her readers. Please sign up for her newsletter at tonicabell.com, where you can download two free novellas:

Toni posts regularly about her indie author journey, life lessons, what inspires her, and her books on Instagram and Facebook. Also consider joining her Reader Group on Facebook, @onceuponaswoon, where she hangs out with some of her closed-door author friends and readers like you.

www.ingramcontent.com/pod-product-compliance
Lightning Source LLC
Chambersburg PA
CBHW020242010826
48973CB00006B/1620